AN UNUSUAL WAGER

The Mismatched Lovers
Book Four

Fil Reid

ARE YOU SIGNED UP FOR DRAGONBLADE'S BLOG?

You'll get the latest news and information on exclusive giveaways, exclusive excerpts, coming releases, sales, free books, cover reveals and more.

Check out our complete list of authors, too!

No spam, no junk. That's a promise!

Sign Up Here

www.dragonbladepublishing.com

Dearest Reader;

Thank you for your support of a small press. At Dragonblade Publishing, we strive to bring you the highest quality Historical Romance from some of the best authors in the business. Without your support, there is no 'us', so we sincerely hope you adore these stories and find some new favorite authors along the way.

Happy Reading!

CEO, Dragonblade Publishing

Additional Dragonblade books by Author Fil Reid

The Mismatched Lovers Series
A Sham Engagement (Book 1)
A Hint of Scandal (Book 2)
A Duchess of Mystery (Book 3)
An Unusual Wager (Book 4)

The Cornish Ladies Series
The Cornish Mermaid (Book 1)
The Cornish Bride (Book 2)
The Cornish Inheritance (Book 3)
The Cornish Widow (Book 4)

Guinevere Series
The Dragon Ring (Book 1)
The Bear's Heart (Book 2)
The Sword (Book 3)
Warrior Queen (Book 4)
The Quest for Excalibur (Book 5)
The Road to Avalon (Book 6)

The Lyon's Den Series
The Cornish Lyon

CHAPTER ONE

THE HEAD OF Jonathan Wintringham, 6th Earl of Dunster, was likely to explode if he moved. Alas, for him, this was not an unusual occurrence. Nor was waking up in his bed still in last night's clothes and with his boots on. Nor, for that matter, would it have been a surprise had he found himself in someone else's bed. Although, on this occasion, a cursory glance around the room with barely open eyes proved to him that he was, at least, at home and in his bedroom rather than passed out on the floor of his study, something that had happened to him more than once.

Anything to avoid the dreams.

He closed his eyes again because that single glance had only served to worsen his pounding headache. And this, in turn, heralded the nasty sensation that he might be about to cast up his accounts, something which his valet, Arnold, would strongly disapprove of. He must have imbibed considerably more than usual last night, and, unsurprisingly, he could remember nothing about it, nor, mercifully, if his sleep had been bothered by the bad dreams that so frequently haunted him.

He had a vague memory, the dredging up of which only served to worsen his headache, of leaving White's in the early hours of the morning arm in arm with his great friend Walter Farrington. Hadn't they been heading in the direction of some gambling den or another? Whatever had occurred after that, however, receded into blank oblivion. He couldn't even recall arriving at the den, nor which one it had been.

He tried swallowing, but his mouth felt as though he'd been licking up the sawdust at the Exeter 'Change. Possibly in the monkey's cages. Before they'd been cleaned out. His tongue was thick and appeared to be glued to the roof of his mouth, and his eyes hurt so much they might at any minute fall right out of his head. Which was why he was refraining from opening them again. Too much light meant too much pain. The not unfamiliar thought that it might be preferable to be dead arose.

Best to lie still and hope for a miracle that might end his suffering, unlikely as that probably was. So far, his life had been singularly devoid of miracles and more a series of disastrously bad judgments. He pushed the dark thoughts out of his head with an effort that only redoubled the throbbing.

At least the bed was comfortable, and his own. He reached out a wary hand to grope the other side of it. And at least he was alone. The few nights he'd made the mistake of bringing home a woman after a night's heavy drinking had led to mornings of deep regret and vows never to do such a thing again. He was an exponent of keeping his amorous encounters to the property of the lady of the moment, not inviting them home with him.

Jonathan, who at thirty-two had been Earl of Dunster for just over half his life, had, as he himself freely acknowledged, a bit of a reputation. From time to time, although he didn't like to admit it even to himself, it became a reputation that hung around his neck like a lumpen lead weight as he sought to live up to it.

Not for nothing was he known to his friends and enemies alike as the Black Earl, a nickname he'd acquired shortly after he'd inherited his father's title. This was not, as one might have expected, due to his jet-black hair, strong black brows, and eyes that could also have been taken for black, but rather to what all who knew him well liked to refer to as his black heart. Being known as the possessor of this black heart was something Jonathan had himself gone out of the way to cultivate. To the extent that he'd started a few rumors that he'd sold his soul to the devil. People loved to believe rubbish like that.

For Jonathan had been a boy, then later a man, who did everything hard. He drank hard, even at school, he played sports hard, he gambled hard, he drove his horses hard, and he womanized hard—this last being something he'd begun even before he inherited the title from his late and not-lamented father. The ladies he'd benefitted with his presence could indeed all vouch for his hardness.

So, in truth, last night had been no different to most other nights spent in Town with his like-minded and admiring friends, some of whom he could have disparaged as sycophants. In order to maintain his reputation, he often woke, as he had this morning, with no recollection of what he'd been up to the night before, and this almost never bothered him. Although there had been the occasion when he discovered he'd climbed the tower of St Bride's Church in Fleet Street while in a state of deep intoxication. Possibly that very intoxication had been the reason why he hadn't fallen to his death. Drunks always seemed to have a sense of self preservation, and he was no different. Not that he would have ever referred to himself as a drunk. Nothing so base as that.

His mother would probably have been horrified by his lifestyle, not that he cared. And besides which, hadn't his father been exactly the same, and yet she'd still loved him above all else. Including her only child.

However, as she hadn't left the Dower House at Luxborough since his father's unexpected and never-mentioned demise, she wasn't about to find out. And his aged grandmother, bless her confused soul, would not have understood unless in one of her rare moments of clarity. Kitty, on the other hand… No. Best little Kitty didn't hear rumors of any of his excesses. Kitty had to be protected at all costs from everything.

The door opened and someone entered the room on not-quite-silent feet. Recognizing his valet, Arnold, by his cautious step, Jonathan kept his eyes closed and cleared his throat. "Don't draw the curtains." His voice emerged as little more than a rasping croak.

"My lord," Arnold said, from somewhere near the window, definite reproof in his voice and definitely ignoring his master's instruction not to draw the curtains. "I feel I must inform you that it is gone eleven o'clock in the morning and you have a visitor awaiting you downstairs. Mr. Trubshawe has put her in the blue parlor."

Jonathan kept his eyes firmly shut against the painful daylight. Why was Arnold shouting? And he should know by now that eleven o'clock in the morning was not the time to be waking his master. He tried licking his lips. "A visitor?" That was better—a bit less of a croak this time. Sometimes he wondered if his man took perverse pleasure in discomfiting him. Only his unparalleled valeting skills had prevented Jonathan from giving him his marching orders on more than one occasion. He had an uneasy feeling Arnold was fully aware of this and played on it shamelessly.

"Yes, my lord. Mr. Trubshawe said she is most insistent on seeing you this morning and has been waiting for some time already. And that she implied she had an important appointment with you." Arnold possessed the uncanny skill of imbuing most of what he said with disapproval, even when it was anything but.

"She?" Jonathan opened one eye with caution and regretted it as daylight battered at his aching eyeball. "A lady?" He cast his mind back, such as it was at this time of the day and with so terrible a hangover, over the ladies he'd most recently been associated with. There was quite a long list. "Did she give her name?"

"No, my lord. Mr. Trubshawe said she did not. Apparently, she claimed you would know who she was."

It could be Lady Delamere, his most recent conquest and with whom he'd been carrying on a most enjoyable relationship while her elderly husband resided at their country estate nursing his gout. And his piles, if his wife was to be believed. His interest was piqued, despite the crashing headache, as it always was by mention of a woman. "Did you see her? What did she look like?"

Arnold, who was next best thing to a Puritan, cleared his throat and harumphed, a clear signal that he felt more than his usual disapproval. "I did see her, as it happens, as I was in the front hallway when she arrived. As to her looks, I would say she is young, my lord, and not well-dressed. A little shabby in appearance, if I might be so bold as to say. But a lady. Nothing common about her whatsoever."

Arnold was well aware that his master's tastes didn't always run to members of the ton.

Jonathan frowned, which hurt his head some more. Couldn't be Lady Delamere then. She was always attired in the height of fashion and no one could have called her shabby. She also wouldn't go out calling this early in the morning. She'd still be asleep, just as he should be. Plus, no one could have called her young for the last twenty years.

"Young?" He forced his other eye open and regarded Arnold myopically, the feeling that his eyes were about to pop out of his head returning with a vengeance. Could that happen with a headache? The sort of headache you got when you'd imbibed several bottles of fine claret, half a bottle of port, and more than a few brandies, which was his normal fare and which he now concluded he must have exceeded.

"Yes, my lord." Arnold was picking up Jonathan's discarded coat and cravat from where he'd thrown them in a crumpled heap on the floor not so very long ago. "Would you like me to ask her to leave, my lord?"

"Is she pretty?" Jonathan asked. He was not a man to turn away a pretty girl, nor the opportunity to become much better acquainted with one. Not even when he was feeling as crapulous as he was this morning.

"Passably so, my lord. Does your lordship wish me to have the maids fill you a bath before you go down?"

"Then I'll see her," Jonathan pronounced. "No bath. Not yet, anyway. I might have one later. Help me up. I find myself a little under the weather."

DOWNSTAIRS IN HIS Lordship's blue parlor, Miss Verity Farrington was standing in front of the empty fireplace and studying the portrait which hung above it. This excellent piece of art showed an imposing man of middle age with a fine head of hair already streaked with silver. He sat in a high-backed chair in front of a window, and the artist had captured the light on his face with consummate skill. She studied this face in curiosity. He might once have been called a handsome man, but age had rendered his features hard and cold with an unrelenting line to his set mouth. Cruel, even, for want of a better word. Not the face of a man it would be easy to like.

She shivered. Hopefully this was not the man to whom her father had dispatched her this morning. It would be an underestimation to say how disturbing that would be, and probably frightening. However, she would cope with it if she had to. She was well used to coping with anything life threw at her and had no illusions concerning her own strengths.

Determined not to be intimidated by a mere portrait, she turned away from it and studied the rest of the opulent room. The walls were indeed a deep blue, being covered in exquisite silk wallpaper that must have cost a lot of money. She'd learned from Papa to assess the wealth of a man by many giveaways: his clothing, the jewels his wife wore, his horses, his carriages, his house, and his house's decorations and furniture. And this house could not hide the wealth of its owner.

In her travels, she'd seen the inside of a great number of fine town houses in cities such as Paris, Florence, Vienna and Rome, and recognized this as one of the most impressive. Long windows opened onto a well-laid-out garden of surprising proportions for London, with a broad terrace and steps down into a verdant area already thick with summer flowers. A little sigh escaped her lips. A garden, with all its connotations of permanence and slow fruition, represented the stability she'd not known for years. A garden to walk in and inhale the many scents that must be hanging in the air. Maybe she would be able to do so occasionally if this encounter went well.

She turned away from that enticing vista and surveyed the rest of the room, anxious to learn clues about the man Papa had sent her to call upon. More portraits hung on the other walls. This was a family fond of images of themselves. Opposite the fireplace another large painting showed a beautiful, dark-haired young woman dressed as a shepherdess, a style that had once been made popular by a certain French queen. She sat on the ground beneath the spreading branches of an oak tree, a little boy of about four or five standing by her side.

In the distance, water glimmered and, beyond that, the shadowy form of an enormous house appeared almost ghostlike. The woman was dark in appearance, with abundant curls hanging down her back. She didn't look English at all. Perhaps Spanish? The little boy, a sweet expression on his chubby, baby face, matched her, his hair the blue-black of a magpie's wing. An interesting picture.

Verity had seen a lot of good paintings in a variety of houses on her travels across Europe with Papa. As Mama had been of Breton origin, both she and Papa had been able to pass themselves off as French with ease, and thus had gone for the most part unmolested in a Europe that had been war-torn. She'd seen Venice and Florence, lived in Rome for a few years, been to Spain and Austria and Switzerland and more lately France itself. Although she and Papa had not been back to Brittany, Mama's home country, since her mother had died there. Never to Brittany. Papa had flatly refused.

It had only been her father's ill health that had brought them back to England a few short weeks ago. And since then, things had not gone well for them.

She abandoned the painting of the intriguing woman and the raven-haired little boy and returned to the window. She'd visited the Palace of Versailles and walked in the Jardin du Luxembourg in Paris, as well as the rose gardens at Malmaison, so she knew a well laid out garden when she saw one, and recognised the hand of a woman on this one, but most likely some time ago as the garden was mature. Possibly a French woman. Interesting.

Was there a woman here still, or did this earl she was seeking live here in this huge house alone? That he was unmarried, she was certain, for even in the circles she and Papa moved in, she'd heard of the Black Earl. And Papa would not have sent her here at all had he been happily married. That he was a gambler and rake went without asking, or Papa would never have crossed paths with him. Perhaps, knowing his reputation, there was a mistress in residence who liked to walk in that beautiful garden she was already envying? A large part of her hoped this might be true, with what she had to do today in mind.

She'd walked around here from the lodgings she and Papa were sharing first thing this morning, not having wanted to delay things. If she'd thought about it any longer, she might have refused to go, and that would have been a mistake with terrible consequences. For Papa and possibly for herself as well. Almost certainly for herself if she stopped to think about it, as her fate was so closely tied to Papa's.

And now she'd been waiting here in this beautiful, overblown parlor, that she was beginning to despise for its decadence, for almost two hours. What time did earls get up? Surely before half past eleven? The steady ticking of the clock on the mantlepiece had kept her apprised of the time. As a habitual early riser herself, she couldn't understand why anyone would want to waste half the day lying in bed. Although, of course, that was what Papa did most of the time, and more so now he was so unwell.

The stiff-backed valet with the snooty expression had come to see her over an hour ago now and informed her that His Lordship was indisposed but that he would inform him of her arrival. As indisposed as Papa was this morning, no doubt, or she wouldn't be here. She'd left her father snoring in his bed, the stench of alcohol on him strong enough to make her lightheaded. She knew better than to disturb him on the morning after a bout of gambling and heavy drinking.

She frowned. If His Lordship was anything like Papa, then when she finally met him, he, too, was unlikely to be in a good mood. Papa was anything but his best on the morning after a long gambling and drinking session.

Pursing her lips in resignation, she turned back to study the richly upholstered, and not very inviting, seating and chose a demure pink velvet chair to settle on. She'd tried each seat in turn during her vigil, and this was the only one she'd not perched on so far. She smoothed her skirts down, regretting the fact that she had no smarter clothing to have worn. In this lush room her gown looked even more faded than it had done when she'd set out, and she was acutely aware of the hopefully invisible darning she'd done on the right elbow of her navy-blue spencer. Glancing down at her feet, it dawned on her that her boots, too, gave away her impecunious state, so she tucked them under the hem of her gown and got on with what she was good at doing. Waiting.

The ticking of the clock on the mantlepiece filled the room. Being at the back of the house, no street noises could venture inside to disturb the peace. Only it was not peace. Not for her anyway. She felt anything but peaceful and, within the confines of her stays, her poor heart pattered in anxiety. She was like a duck, outwardly serene as she glided over the water, but with her feet paddling like mad out of sight.

She bit her lip. Should she stay any longer? She could leave right now, and he would never know who had called on him this morning. Only if she did, what would happen to Papa, who didn't have the money to settle his debts to this obnoxious, spoilt, and entitled member of the aristocracy? She hadn't spent her formative years in France without gaining a healthy dislike of the aristos. And this particular one had the power to send poor Papa to prison—to the Marshalsea or the Fleet, or even Newgate, and she wouldn't be able to get him out because she would never be able to find the money to repay the debts he owed. That she would be alone in the world didn't matter. What mattered was Papa.

The door opened.

Her head swung round.

A man stood in the doorway.

Their eyes met.

He was tall and slim, his wide, muscular shoulders clearly visible as he was not wearing a coat of any sort, only an unbuttoned brocade waistcoat over a loose white shirt. Dark, wavy hair in such a state that it gave him the look of someone who had just got out of bed, which she assumed he probably had, curled about a face so handsome it almost took her breath away. Black eyebrows winged across his forehead over a strong, aquiline nose. Beneath the nose curved a mouth that could have been as cruel as the one belonging to the man in the portrait, who must surely be his father. However, at this precise moment, it hung slightly open as though in shock.

Perhaps he'd been expecting her to look different.

He came in and closed the door behind himself and bowed. "Dunster at your service, madam. I do not have the pleasure of your name." His voice was deep, but his tone a little curt as though having been disturbed before midday had annoyed him.

Let him be annoyed. His annoyance could not compare to hers.

She rose to her feet, forgetful of the need to hide her shabby boots. "Verity Farrington, my lord." And she curtseyed, acutely aware of the uncomfortable sensation prickling over her that he knew what she looked like naked. Heat rushed to her cheeks. This was not going to be easy, especially as he didn't appear to have recognised her name. Could he have forgotten last night? Might she have the chance, even now, to escape? But only if he'd also forgotten how much Papa owed him. And that would be unlikely.

He took another step towards her, puzzlement now mixed

with something akin to acquisitiveness. "Please, be seated." His brow had furrowed slightly, but he'd remembered his manners. His face had the same sort of gray tinge to it Papa's had when he had a terrible hangover. That might be in her favor.

Obediently, she did as she was asked, remembering to hide her boots beneath her skirts again. However, she was not feeling in the least bit obedient.

He moved to the fireplace and rested a negligent hand on the mantlepiece near the clock. Did he need its support to remain upright? Possibly. He had long, elegant fingers, on one of which a heavy gold ring glittered.

He managed the slightest of smiles, his brow puckering as though doing so had given him pain. Definitely a hangover. Verity could spot one a mile off. She'd seen enough in her time. "And what might I be able to do for you… Miss Farrington?" He raised those black brows in a question, which only served to render him more handsome. And, from the wince he gave, give him more pain. She couldn't help but think that a good thing. He deserved some pain as he'd caused Papa so much of it.

However, she must not become distracted. This whole affair called for concentration and resolution, and determination on her part. She sat up as straight as possible and drew in a fortifying breath. "I have come to settle my father's debt to you, my lord."

His dark eyes remained disconcertingly blank as though this meant nothing to him. Once again, she found herself wondering if he could have forgotten. A sense of indignation that he could have cast from his mind so fateful a wager rose in Verity's breast. That he would have forgotten it had never occurred to her until now. If she'd guessed, she most certainly would not have come. But she was here now, so she had to continue.

He frowned. "Your father's debt? He owes me money? Who is he? Do I know him?"

Ignoring what many others might see as an insult, she swallowed. "My father's name is Anthony Farrington." How difficult it was to keep her voice steady. "Last night he lost heavily to you at cards. I do not know what game you were playing as I was not present, but…at the end, he found he had only one thing left to stake, and as gambling is in his very blood, and without a doubt he was in his cups, he staked it. And he lost. I am here to settle his debt." She bit her lip again.

"You come bringing me money?" his lordship asked, eyeing her shabby attire up and down as though, rightly, he suspected she had none. There was a cruel and calculating curl to his lip that robbed him of his good looks and rendered him frightening. But she would not be cowed.

She shook her head. "No. My father lost the last of our money at the card table, as you must know." He must have been very drunk not to remember this. More drunk than Papa, probably, which was saying something. She began to wish Papa had not remembered as well. "As I have said, he found he had only one thing left to stake." She paused, sat up a bit straighter and looked him boldly in the eye. "Me."

"You?" His dark eyes widened and his voice rose in incredulity. "Your father staked his daughter in a bet?"

This was more difficult than she'd expected. Vexed by his tone, she scowled at him. "Yes. He staked me, and he lost. I have come here to surrender myself to you and save my father from incarceration in the debtors' prison."

He was staring at her in what had to be amazement. Or plain shock. "Are you are telling me that I have won you at cards?"

She nodded. "Yes, my lord, you have."

CHAPTER TWO

JONATHAN STARED AT the young lady seated on what had, an aeon ago, been his mother's favorite chair. The chair where he remembered her with her sewing in her hands when, as a small child, he'd been brought in by his nurse, pink and clean from the bath, to be kissed and patted on the head before bedtime. The chair she'd occupied when he'd thought she loved him. How he'd looked forward to that moment all day long when he could bask for a moment in that longed-for approval. Although sometimes, but not often, it had been marred by the brooding presence of his father.

A chair of significance, and now, it seemed, it held a conundrum.

"Are you sure?" he asked, eyeing her up and down in appraisal. Not quite the sort of woman he was used to associating with, although he had to allow that if she hadn't been wearing such a shabby gown and spencer and that unfashionable bonnet, she would have been quite beautiful. She had the loveliest blue eyes and beneath the terrible bonnet, hair of a rich auburn just asking for a man to run his fingers through it. It wasn't like him to miss an opportunity where a beautiful young lady was concerned, but she had caught him unawares and really not in any fit state for receiving a guest.

She nodded, her lips pressed together to make them thin. "I am quite sure, my lord. In fact, I could not be more sure." He saw her swallow as though nervous. Then she cleared her throat, her expression becoming resolute. "He informed me of this on his return last night, or perhaps I should say this morning, from whatever den of iniquity he'd chosen this time for the making of his fortune."

Her brow furrowed in a frown as though she strongly disapproved of both her father and the man she saw before her. "Where he was unfortunate to encounter you, my lord, and through his own foolhardiness fell into your debt." Her pale brow furrowed further, and her tone implied that this was not an uncommon occurrence. And that she was not amused by it. Nor, most likely, by having been gambled away by her profligate parent.

What sort of a father gambled away his child? A girl as pretty as this one? Try as he might, Jonathan could not bring to mind anyone he'd been playing cards with on the previous night, nor the fact that he'd been playing cards at all. Nor where he'd been to do so. Everything was a total blank from leaving White's to waking up this morning.

He considered his words with more care than he was wont to do, but at the same time part of him was weighing up the obvious benefits of having won a young lady in a bet. Even with a pounding head, he was not blind to what this could lead to. "I'm afraid I must admit that I have no recollection whatsoever of last night. I am ashamed to say that I must have had too much to drink." He bestowed an apologetic smile on her, although in truth he wasn't ashamed at all. Winning a young lady in a wager was not something he'd ever done before, and the novelty of it appealed to his adventurous nature. His friends would no doubt approve. "What exactly did he tell you? Pray elucidate."

She clasped her hands together as though this question was hard to answer. How very pretty she looked in her agitation. He was liking this more and more. "My father returned to our lodgings in the early hours of the morning, as is his custom when he is out gambling, and woke me with the noise he was making falling over everything." She squared her shoulders. "You say you had too much to drink. Well, he is an old man and not large, and he cannot hold his liquor as well as someone like you."

She gave a little shrug and wrinkled her delightful nose. "He was, I have to admit, reeling drunk. But not so drunk as to forget to inform me that I now belong to you, to do with as you wish…" She set her jaw. "I am sure you could find employment for me. I am more than capable with my reckoning, and if you have no use for me in your offices, then I am also considered an excellent cleaner so would make an acceptable housemaid."

Did she really think that? A girl as beautiful as she was and she wanted actual employment as a servant? She thought a man with his reputation would set her to work in his kitchen, perhaps? He almost laughed, but her earnest expression stopped him. The laugh died in his throat.

She raised those wide blue eyes, eyes he could have quite happily drowned in, and was gazing up at him with more than a hint of a challenge.

Many thoughts tumbled through Jonathan's still drink-addled brain, not least the things he would like to do with such a potentially beautiful young lady who'd just dropped into his lap like a gift from the gods. However, his headache had got worse and his stomach was making complaining noises. One thing he felt sure of though, was that she was not lying. What reason would she have for doing so? For she did not look all that happy about the arrangement her father had made. Not happy at all, in fact.

What to do?

Of course, the first thought that came to him was that he could make her his mistress. Her plain gown hinted at a luscious body hidden beneath that he would very much like to explore. She had the air about her of being untouched, so seducing her would be fun, and even if her father had used her before to pay his debts, no doubt he could, with his skills, awaken passions she might not know she possessed. It wouldn't be too hard to persuade her to want him, and to perhaps keep her for a while. After all, he was the Black Earl.

Some money spent on clothes, and she would be so much improved he could take her out on his arm in society. To the theatre, to Almack's or to Vauxhall or Ranelagh Gardens. The last two being better, in his opinion, than Almack's. The thought that Lady Delamere would be green with envy was an attractive one. Lately she'd begun to be more demanding, as though she felt she had rights of possession over him. It would be fun to teach her a lesson and parade this young woman before her in the glory of her youth.

He looked Miss Farrington up and down more closely, assessing her possibilities. A trim figure with the suggestion of small, pert breasts beneath her shabby spencer. Long legs, slender arms and small feet, which she'd been assiduously trying to conceal from him beneath her gown, no doubt due to the parlous state of her boots. A heart-shaped face boasting full, kissable lips, a delicate nose, and those mesmerizing eyes. She'd make a good mistress, and she seemed convinced she'd have to do as he wished, so it wouldn't be hard to persuade her. Even if she had implied she was willing to work as a servant, being a mistress would surely be a more attractive proposition than drudgery. He was well aware of his own attractions, and, being an earl and before that the only son of an earl, was well used to getting his own way since an early age.

But then something dawned upon him, creeping its way in through the clouds in his still fuzzy, aching brain.

Her name.

Farrington.

It had to be a coincidence; her having the same name as his friends Walter and Robert. Lots of people must be called Farrington. Lots of people in London and even more in the provinces. Hundreds, if not thousands. But he'd better make sure. It wouldn't do at all to make a mistress out of some distant relation of Walter, his best friend. Walter might call him out for it if he got to know, which he certainly would. Impossible to keep one's mistress a secret for long in London. Most of the ton must already know of his relationship with Lady Delamere. A relationship he was planning on ending even as he considered Miss Farrington's alluring body.

He ran his fingers through his hair in some consternation. Better check. "You say your name is Farrington?"

She nodded, watching him a little warily, like a deer in front of a hunter, which only made her more desirable. Despite the still pounding headache, parts of him were beginning to stir. The parts of him that always stirred when in the presence of a beautiful woman. He fought to regain control of himself, but, once a hunter, always a hunter. Perhaps it was an apt description for someone in constant pursuit of the opposite sex. Confidence that he would find it easy to persuade her to like him, and to have his way with her, grew.

However, first back to the possible problem in hand. Then the seduction afterwards. That would get rid of his headache in the nicest possible way.

He narrowed his eyes. "Might you, perhaps, be related in any way to Viscount Somerton?" An off chance, surely? Walter's elderly father never came up to Town, and he and Walter enjoyed a difficult relationship. Jonathan had a vague idea Walter had more family elsewhere, but could not be certain of his information. It was not a subject he and Walter had ever discussed.

She kept her gaze fixed on his face, those gorgeous blue eyes wide with innocence. Or were they? "Lord Somerton is my uncle."

"Good God." He couldn't help the expletive. His grandmother would have reproved him for taking the Lord's name in vain and, if she could have reached, she would have boxed his ears even now. Had she been having one of her spells of clarity, that was.

"No, he is my uncle, not God." Was that a twinkle of

amusement in her eyes? Was she laughing at the discomfiture he'd been unable to hide?

He gathered his thoughts. If only he hadn't had quite so much to drink, for that was surely making his understanding of the situation more difficult. This interview was not heading in the direction he would have liked. He swallowed. Thoughts of seduction had vanished, as had the effect they'd been having on certain parts of his anatomy. "So, Somerton's offspring are your cousins?" He couldn't hide the slight rise in his voice and knew she'd noticed.

She nodded. "They are, although I have not seen them since I was a child, as my father is estranged from his brother." She paused. "And we have been away on the Continent for most of my life. At least, since my grandmother died when I was nine years old." Her eyes clouded with something that might have been old grief. "She brought me up until then, you see, as my mother and father were…abroad. We lived in the Dower House at Somerton. I only really had anything to do with my cousin Robert, as the others were much older than me. Walter was always away at school, and Emily left home to be married when I was just a small child. I have not seen any of them since my father came to take me away with him."

This was worse than he'd expected. How had he not known Walter had an uncle? Although, if he was honest, hadn't Walter mentioned the man a long time ago when they'd both been boys? From what he now recalled, a bit of a black sheep uncle, but an uncle, nevertheless. And a cousin. A very beautiful cousin. Or she would be if someone took her in hand and spent some money on her. Why had Walter never mentioned her? Not that it would have changed anything about last night, and whatever had happened in that black void of his blank memory. But it would have been interesting to have been told that Walter's uncle had been off, gallivanting about Europe on a prolonged gambling spree. With a daughter. The daughter who was now sitting in his mother's chair and looking at him expectantly.

"Ah," he said, for want of anything else to say.

"Are you acquainted with my uncle and cousins?" she asked, her tone conversational.

He nodded. "Walter and I have known one another since our days at Eton." Walter, the like-minded friend with whom he'd unleashed himself on London at the age of eighteen with the sole intention of enjoyment. And eradicating those bloody bad dreams.

Wait. Walter had been there last night, hadn't he? A vague memory of his friend at his side while he'd been playing cards now surfaced. How had he not thought to warn his best friend that the man he was gambling with was his long-lost uncle? How had Walter not warned him to refuse the wager of a young lady, his actual long-lost cousin, to settle a bet? Had Walter been even more drunk than he himself had been? Or, did he not even know the man at the table had been his uncle? He was going to have to have words with Walter. Strong words.

He returned his gaze to Miss Farrington's undeniably pleasing visage, his attitude to her somewhat changed. "So, now that you are here, what am I supposed to do with you? Employ you as a servant? I think not."

The fact that Walter was now involved, albeit unintentionally, bothered him. He couldn't take this beauty as his mistress, much as he liked the idea. He couldn't repudiate her because presumably Walter had witnessed the whole exchange. And, although he'd not realized that the man offering his daughter to the Black Earl was none other than his own long-lost uncle, he'd very soon be apprised of the fact. And when he did know, he'd expect Jonathan to do the honorable thing. He'd be deeply offended if Jonathan cast his cousin aside—just as offended as if he'd taken her into his bed. Which if he hadn't realized who she was, he would most certainly have tried to do.

He abandoned the mantlepiece and threw himself down in another seat, leaning forward and putting his head in his hands. It felt as though it might fall off if he weren't careful.

"Are you unwell, my lord?" A gentle voice interrupted his dilemma.

"A little."

"Water," she said. "You are suffering from lack of water. Shall I send for a servant to fetch you some?"

She might well be right. His mouth had gone dry again and his head throbbed, only now this was partly due to the problem her arrival had created. Although it was a bit unfair to accuse her of creating it when it had clearly been his own fault for accepting a young lady in payment of a debt. He must have been addled, or he would at the very least have made sure she was pretty before he'd done so. Only luck had provided him with a girl of such beauty. Not that he could now avail himself of her obedience. He nodded, wondering how many people knew about this unfortunate wager. And how long would it take for the story of it to circulate around Town. This could turn out to be more than awkward.

Water was sent for. When it came, she insisted he drink several glasses.

"You will feel better soon. I know this cure works well for a sore head, as I've made my father drink water on numerous occasions, even though he doesn't like to. Have some more."

"Water is not my usual choice," he muttered as she handed him a fourth glass. The jug was now nearly empty, yet for some reason he found it hard to refuse her. She had a capable air about her reminiscent of his own nurse when he'd been a small child. He had a feeling he was face to face with a lady of some determination.

Her eyes glittered with amusement. "I can see that." Now she was definitely laughing at him.

"I'm sorry," he said, straightening up. "As I remember nothing from last night, this news has come as something of a shock to me. As has your relationship to my friend Walter." He licked his lips, worrying again about how many witnesses there'd been to this wager. Not that it would have mattered had she not been his best friend's cousin. If only he could remember.

She smiled. "I must own that I too am somewhat surprised that you are a friend of a relation of mine. Not that he would be aware of my existence, I imagine." She frowned. "I suppose my papa was too drunk to realize the identity of your friend." She sighed. "He so often is." A hint of resigned sadness showed in those blue eyes and her shoulders, so determined until now, sagged.

Jonathan was just considering that the best solution here might be to acquit her father of all his debts, as he could well afford to, and send her back to him forthwith before anyone found out what he'd agreed to, when the parlor door swung open and Trubshawe, his long-serving butler entered. He cleared his throat as though about to make an important announcement. "Mr. Farrington, my lord."

Oh no. Not now.

Walter Farrington, much to his country-loving father's disgust, was a darling of the ton, and dressed to match. From the top of his exquisitely coiffed Grecian hairstyle, via the high points of his collar and the embroidery on his waistcoat, down to his highly polished top boots, everything about him spoke of sophistication and his fondness for his own appearance. Jonathan was one of the few who knew that beneath that foppish façade lurked a man after his own heart. A womanizer, yes, but also someone who could strip to his breeches and slog it out in a bare-knuckle fight if he had to…and win. Although in truth, he much preferred peaceful negotiation.

On a gust of perfume, Walter entered the parlor, swordstick in one hand and quizzing glass in the other, and halted on the threshold, his gaze moving from his friend's horrified face to the vision of loveliness who was staring at him in open, avid curiosity.

No trace of recognition showed in his eyes as he stared at Miss Farrington, thank goodness. Although that ignorance was not going to last long.

CHAPTER THREE

WALTER'S NAME AND identity had not been lost on Verity. From her position on the pink chair, she took in this paragon of manly perfection with more than a touch of surprise. As a child, she'd once or twice glimpsed her exalted, much older cousin when he'd called to visit Grandmama at the Dower House, and as far as she could remember he'd never looked like this. Of course, back then he'd only been a schoolboy, although to her he'd seemed a man grown.

She had the vaguest recollection of once or twice peering at him between the banisters on the Dower House's landing. She'd been too small to look over the top of them. Below her she'd glimpsed the brother Robert, who'd been considered too ill to go away to school, as had been so often mentioned, but only the top of his dark head. All she'd been able to see had been a young man in a smart but staid suit standing in the hallway outside Grandmama's parlor.

As for what he was like, all she'd had to go on had been Robert's view of his exalted and much-admired older brother. Robert, to the small Verity's disgust, had wanted to emulate Walter in every way, from his choice of clothes to his cricketing success at Eton, that he was most annoyed he'd never be able to repeat. To the extent that Verity had made the decision not to like Walter at all, if she were to ever meet him face to face. Up until now, though, she'd never had the chance.

And to her surprise she found he looked like a dandy and a fop, and not a young man who'd been a rowing blue and his school's top batsman. She took a moment to wonder if Robert would have ended up the same if he'd been allowed to follow in his brother's footsteps. It would be fun to meet her childhood friend again.

However, as a young woman who had traversed the length and breadth of Europe with her papa, she was not unused to seeing young gentlemen who looked like this. He, however, had clearly never seen a young lady such as herself, because he was staring quite rudely at her. She sat up a bit straighter and allowed herself the slightest of admonishing frowns in the hopes he would remember his manners.

He didn't. "Well, stap me," he exclaimed, his brown eyes running up and down her in a most uncomfortable manner, especially when one considered he was her cousin. "Is this her? You've done well out of that bargain, Jonnie my boy. A little in need of smartening up, but what a beauty. Did the old fellow send her round last night?" He bestowed a lascivious wink on his friend, who had the grace to redden.

For an uncomfortable moment, Verity found herself at a loss for words, and, as she gathered her thoughts, Lord Dunster got in before her.

"Walter," he began, a distinct air of discomfort in his tone. "Pray allow me to introduce you to Miss Verity Farrington."

The newcomer seemed to freeze for a moment as this pronouncement sank in, his eyes losing their expression of lascivious delight and taking on one of deep, disbelieving shock followed by acute embarrassment. His mouth opened and closed as he presumably sought, as she was doing, for words.

"Your cousin," Lord Dunster said, hammering the revelation home with a strong hint of irony this time.

Verity decided it might be wise to stay silent and see what happened.

Walter finally found his voice, which seemed a trifle high this time. "My cousin?" His Adam's apple bobbed. "Here? In your parlor?" He made it sound as though he'd surprised them in Lord Dunster's bedroom. "With you? The Black Earl?" A frown settled on his brows which might have been due more to confusion than anger. "How? Why?" His voice rose again, as if in pleading. "She ain't the girl…from last night…is she? She can't be."

Silence on her part was definitely the best decision. It was quite fascinating observing the discomfiture of these two taken aback swells. Almost as much fun as fleecing them of their blunt might have been if she'd met them under different circumstances. If ever two gentlemen deserved to be swindled, it was these two, who clearly had thought, up until now, that was, that winning a girl at a game of cards was a good thing. Until they discovered one of them was related to her.

Lord Dunster's frown matched Walter's. "She is indeed the young lady from last night. And I would myself like to know the answers to those very questions." He shot a glance at Verity, who returned his look with equanimity. This was really turning out to be quite amusing, if only she didn't still have that sensation of imminent doom hanging over her.

Walter's eyes widened. "You think I know?" His voice now rose to a most unmasculine squeak, very much at odds with his powerful and exquisite appearance.

Lord Dunster nodded. "I most certainly do. How is it that last night I was able to sit down to play cards with a gentleman, in your presence I might add, whom you did not recognize as your own uncle?" He gave an exasperated shake of his head. "Was there no hint of family resemblance to your own father—his brother?"

Walter's mouth opened and closed a few times and his eyes slid back and forth between Verity and his friend, possibly in search of a rescue that was not coming. "You mean the old fellow you fleeced was…*is* my Uncle Anthony? The one we're none of us supposed to talk about?" His eyes returned to Verity's face, but now they held a hint of fear as he stared at her as though she'd just sprouted an extra head. "Uncle Anthony who ran off to the Continent with a French hussy?"

As the import of how insulting his last words were sank in his cheeks blossomed with hot color. More opening and closing of his mouth. He must be searching for a way to extricate himself from this large hole he was busy digging. "I-I mean a French *lady*." His brows knit as he came to the obvious conclusion that this was also not a terribly polite description of Verity's mama, but, as he so obviously couldn't recall her name, what else could he have done? Verity felt a pang of sympathy for him.

"That is indeed the gentleman to whom I am referring," Lord Dunster said, enunciating each word with alarming clarity. If Verity had been Walter, she would have been shaking in her shoes. As it was, she was quite enjoying this. Her unusual upbringing had prepared her for most eventualities, although this was rather an unexpected one.

Walter, to her surprise, seemed to suddenly discover a second wind. "You mean you have compromised my cousin?" he exclaimed, doing his best to sound affronted but only coming over, in her opinion and probably also in Lord Dunster's, as something of an idiot. How had she never discovered Robert's older brother was so afflicted? Robert, her childhood playmate until she was nine and he thirteen, had always been quite sensible, and from what he'd told her of his brother, she'd assumed Walter was too. How wrong could one be.

Lord Dunster uttered a low growl which was really quite attractive. "Miss Farrington has not been compromised," he managed between what must have been gritted teeth.

How delightful to have so disconcerted both these gentlemen. She began to feel her morning had purpose. More purpose than she'd thought it would, at any rate.

Walter was gaining righteous impetus. "Well, she's here, ain't she? In your house. In your parlor. Alone with you until I arrived. After you won her in a game of cards, which ain't at all respectable for a girl. If that ain't compromising her, I don't know what is.

Has she been here all night?" He hesitated. "Did you...?" His voice trailed off, no doubt in response to his friend's furious glower.

Lord Dunster shook his head with vehemence. "I can assure you she has not been here all night. She has not been compromised, and I have not taken advantage of her in any way. She arrived a short time ago to surrender herself in payment for her father's debt."

Time to interrupt. "Actually," Verity said with aplomb, "I've been here now for just over three hours. I walked around here first thing this morning, but His Lordship wasn't up. I had to wait for him to rise."

Walter huffed but was not about to be quelled. "Three hours? Unchaperoned? In the house of the worst rake in London? She's as good as compromised, you know, because everyone present last night witnessed you accept her from her father in lieu of money. In payment for her father's debt." He shook his head in what looked like despair. "Gad, what sort of man surrenders his daughter to a rake like you without a second thought?" Another shake of his head. "And what's more, everyone saw her father write out that promissory note gifting her to you."

Verity's ears pricked. There'd been a promissory note? Papa had not informed her of that indelicate occurrence. Somehow it made everything much more formal. She glanced at Lord Dunster who was standing very still now beside the fireplace, as though turned to stone, in fact.

"There was a promissory note?" For once his voice held a hint of anxiety in with the iciness. He clearly knew nothing of this, or had lost it.

"I'll say there was," Walter retorted, more confident still. "You got two of the fellows to witness it so you could keep the old codger to his side of the bargain. In fact, they volunteered. Thought it was very funny. You said you didn't want him legging it overnight without handing over the girl." He reddened further. "The young lady, I should say. Teesdale and Broughton witnessed it for you. They thought it a grand joke that you'd won yourself a…" His voice trailed off and his face took on an even deeper shade of red.

What had he been going to say? Some impolite reference to a woman a man had no intention of marrying, no doubt, but on using for his own gratification. Even if what she'd intended to offer had been her skills with a balance book, or at worst with a needle or as a cleaner. The most polite term Verity could think of was "mistress," but there were a lot worse available. Indeed, she'd arrived this morning braced, if all else failed, to face just such an eventuality if it meant saving Papa, horrible as it would have been to her.

As Verity had no idea who Teesdale and Broughton were, this bit of Walter's diatribe meant nothing to her, but it seemed it had a strong effect upon Lord Dunster. His face, already a rather pasty shade of gray, paled still further. He leaned as though in need of support upon the mantelpiece and his broad shoulders sagged. "Not Teesdale."

Walter nodded. "Yes. Teesdale." He paused, then added as an afterthought, "He was quite gleeful about it."

"So, it'll be all around Town by now," Dunster said. "Everyone will know."

Walter gave a shrug. "I fear you're correct. Maybe just those who are up and about which won't be many, as yet. But you know how gossip flies around Town. This isn't going away, Jonnie. And now I find that the lady in question is not some nobody but my own fair cousin." His earlier display of nerves had vanished and with it had come a more than passing resemblance to how Verity could recall Robert looking.

It was time she interrupted again, so she fixed Lord Dunster with an enquiring gaze. "So, what is it you wish me to do, my lord, now you know the extent of your commitment? Shall I assist your estate manager in his office, or ready myself to clean the kitchen?" She smiled sweetly. "I am yours to do with as you wish." Let him dare. She was on firmer ground than that which she'd arrived on. Walter could be her knight in shining armor, and she was free to say what she wanted now.

Lord Dunster gave an exasperated shake of his head. No doubt it needed clearing. If she hadn't so despised men who drank too much, Papa included, she might have felt sorry for him. But as with Papa, it was a self-inflicted wound, and to be despised.

Walter, however, seemed to have no such problem clearing his head. "There's nothing for it," he declared, with some degree of smug satisfaction. "You'll have to marry the girl. I mean the young lady. I mean Cousin Verity. It's the only way out of this. Everyone will know who she is by this evening, thanks to Teesdale, and I won't have my family's good name besmirched." A rather wicked grin sneaked over his visage. "Who would have thought it, the Black Earl driven to earth by a slip of a girl." He turned and beamed at Verity. "Congratulations, Cousin Verity, on imminently becoming a countess."

Verity stared at the two young men. Did they think they could decide for her in this matter? Had neither of them thought to ask her if she was in agreement? She was about to object to this when it occurred to her that it might be quite amusing to allow the pompous Lord Dunster, who so obviously thought so much of himself, to think he had been snared by a nobody. For that was what the look on his face was telling her. Let him stew a while before she decided to set him free.

JONATHAN'S HEADACHE HAD somehow grown worse than before, if that were humanly possible. It was not even midday, he'd not had any breakfast, he had a hangover of epic proportions, and somehow, he had just become engaged to be married. How had that happened? Yesterday he'd been just a plain and simple rake, out for his own enjoyment to live up to his reputation above all else, and today? He was a man staring down the barrel of a gun that would send him up the aisle whether he liked it or not. A gun in the hands of his best friend.

Bugger it, but he could think of no way out of this. If he refused, Walter would be obliged to call him out, and one of them might end up dead. He had no qualms about his own possible death as that might put a final end to his bad dreams, but he didn't want to be responsible for the death of his best friend. And on top of that, everyone would know why Walter had called him out and he'd become a pariah of the ton rather than the much-feted partner of so many lovely ladies who all seemed to find him devastatingly attractive. As they should. Because he was.

He'd have to marry this shabby, but unfortunately well-connected, girl, instead of making her his mistress, which might have been a lot more fun. Indubitably would have been, in fact.

He took another long look at her, assessing her this time not as a prospective mistress, but as a prospective wife. Two quite different things.

Beauty in a wife was not the most important thing, although it could be considered a bonus. After all, his own father had chosen to marry a beauty, and look how that had ended. Having a beautiful, loving wife had not caused his father to abandon a life of utter self-centered debauchery. A life he himself had expended a lot of energy in emulating. The ability to produce an heir, on the other hand, was important, as well as hailing from a good family, which this girl did, or he wouldn't even be considering marriage. Although from a rather dubious younger brother's line. A good thing he didn't require a bride to bring a dowry with her, as it was clear this one would not be doing that.

He considered her body again, this time as though choosing a mare to breed from. She was not a thin little wisp of a thing, but a young woman whose threadbare gown inadequately concealed pleasing curves. Curves his grandmother would have referred to as 'child-bearing hips.' Well, that was one good thing. And so far as he could see, she seemed robust and sensible. No point marrying a woman given to megrims and always taking to her bed. Healthy skin, bright eyes—so blue he nearly got himself distracted—thick hair of an attractive hue, and reasonably tall. A strong young woman. And the niece of a viscount. Ideal wife material, really. Or was he just trying to convince himself of this because he could see no way out of it?

She frowned. "Might I enquire whether you like what you see, my lord?" Her tone bordered on sarcastic.

Feisty too. Bedding her for a while and creating an heir would not be a chore. Already the bits of his anatomy that had been previously engaged in surveying her reactivated themselves. Yes, taking her to bed would be fun. He bestowed his best seductive smile on her. "I would be a fool not to."

It appeared to have no effect. Not something he was used to.

"Then that's settled," Walter said, interrupting. "For the sake of propriety, she's coming home with me this morning, and I'll be in touch with you when I've arranged a Common License and an appointment at the nearest church. She can't possibly stay here with you until that comes through. It just won't do." He frowned. "Even if you did win her over a hand of cards." Was he enjoying his friend's discomfort?

She turned her beautiful eyes upon her cousin. "Dear Cousin Walter, I have no objection to remaining here until the ceremony can be arranged. I am sure I'm quite safe with Lord Dunster…now he knows who I am."

Was she laughing at him again? Jonathan could feel his life spiralling around him in a most alarming fashion. He was no longer in control, and he didn't like it one bit.

Walter certainly wasn't laughing. His exquisite brows furrowed in anxiety. "Oh no, no, no. Not at all the done thing, Cousin Verity. I insist on you accompanying me back to Somerton House where my mater is in residence." He harumphed in what might have been satisfaction. "She will bestow a pleasing air of respectability upon this marriage. Have no fear. Staying here with Jonnie wouldn't be at all appropriate, you must know. Not at all. No, not at all." He gave a weak smile to Jonathan. "I believe my young cousin has lived extensively abroad, Jonnie, so she won't be familiar with our customs here. You must forgive her ignorance."

Ignorance? She was indeed laughing at him. Now he was certain. Not only had he been bullied into marriage, but the cause of it all was laughing at his discomfort. Not, of course, that he was likely to admit that the true cause was probably himself and his propensity to drink and gamble at the same time. Even if he knew it. Easier to blame her and her father and Walter. If Walter hadn't turned up when he had he could have sent her packing with her father's debts written off. Damn Walter for being so inopportune in his arrival.

"In fact," Walter said with determination, oblivious to his friend's ruminations, "I think I shall take her home now, before this becomes more serious and anyone discovers she's been here for so long this morning. People will say anything could have happened in the three hours she could have been alone with you, and I don't wish to give them ammunition. I shall put about a rumor that you are engaged to be married to my cousin through a long-standing arrangement. That will lend much-needed propriety to this…er…arrangement." He ran a hand through his perfect coiffure, thereby making it stand up on end in an alarming fashion that might well have horrified his valet. "I hope."

He held out his arm to Miss Farrington. "Come, my dear Cousin. My mater will be delighted to welcome you into our home, I'm sure. Uncle Anthony's long-lost daughter." He didn't look totally convinced of this, and Jonathan found himself wondering what Uncle Anthony had done that had led to such a long estrangement. No doubt, if he married Miss Farrington, he would eventually find out. If she even knew herself.

With a look Jonathan couldn't read, Miss Farrington rose to her feet and tucked her hand into Walter's proffered arm. She curtsied. "Until we meet again, my lord."

And they were gone.

When the door had closed behind them, Jonathan, whose legs had taken on a decided weakness, sat down in the seat Miss Farrington had just vacated and put his head into his hands. The headache had not abated one whit. If anything, it had grown worse. Reaching up, he rang the bell, and Trubshawe arrived, valiantly attempting to disguise an open interest in what had gone on between the three of them behind closed doors.

"Water," Jonathan said, remembering Miss Farrington's advice. "No, make that coffee. Strong and black. A large pot. Lots of sugar. Now." He'd have ordered food, only he didn't think his now churning stomach could have coped.

Trubshawe departed. Being a butler, he would never share his gossip with the other servants but keep it to himself to savor. He was probably doing a fair bit of savoring right now. Especially if he'd had his ear to the door, which Jonathan would not have put past him.

The coffee came and Trubshawe departed. Jonathan poured himself a cup, downed it, and poured a second. The coffee tasted bitter and burnt and contributed nothing to settling his stomach. Maybe water might have been a better idea. It grated on him that she was probably correct in this matter.

What he needed was to think clearly and what he wasn't doing was just that. His head felt thick with the remains of last night's overly liberal alcohol intake, the headache, and what had just happened to him in so short a space of time.

This was ridiculous. How could a young lady have called on him like this and ended up with him having to marry her? He was only thirty-two, for goodness' sake. Too young to marry yet. He'd had no intention of doing so until he was at least forty, if then. It was so much more fun having mistresses he could just cast aside when they became boring or demanding. He'd had so many of them he'd lost count.

But…he couldn't deny that Miss Farrington was a pretty little thing and he'd relish taking her to bed. Beautiful, even, and probably more so when naked. And it might be fun for a while, and if it wasn't, he could send her off down to Luxborough, his country estate, so long as she was along the way to producing the required heir. He'd hardly have to see her after that, save to plant another child, and could get on with what he'd been doing since he'd left Eton. Namely womanizing, gambling, and in general having fun and shutting up those unquiet souls that visited his dreams. A wife would be detrimental to all that. A wife would not be fun.

Yes, he'd get her with child, and dispatch her off out of the way as soon as he grew bored with her. An excellent idea. Even Walter wouldn't be able to fault that.

CHAPTER FOUR

"ANTHONY'S LITTLE GIRL? Good heavens. I can hardly believe my eyes. The last time I saw you, you can't have been more than eight years old, playing so happily with Robert at the Dower House." Josephine, Viscountess Somerton, extended a plump hand to take Verity's, her eyes brimming with girlish excitement. "I thought never to see you again, my dear. In fact, I suppose, if I considered it, I imagined you married to some foreign gentleman, an Italian count was my fancy, and bringing up a family in one of the capitals of Europe. Lost forever to we Farringtons. I must own that this is a quite wonderful surprise!"

A small, compact woman, a little reminiscent of a well-fed sparrow, Lady Somerton was probably in her late fifties. Her hair, which must once have been as brown as her older son's, had gone completely gray, but she had his soft brown eyes, or rather, he had inherited hers. And now she was smiling in genuine welcome for her prodigal niece.

Verity heaved an inward sigh of relief. On the journey in the hackney coach Walter had summoned to take her to her aunt's house in Fitzroy Square worry had nagged at her, despite her newly rediscovered cousin's confidence that his aunt would welcome her with open arms. What if her aunt wanted nothing to do with her? After all, her father had been, in his own words, the pariah of his family, and surely they would all view her in the same way. Even if Walter were to vouch for her, as he assured her he would.

But her worries had been unfounded and pushed her anxiety to one side. She would think about it later. Instead, she swept an elegant curtsey to the woman who was her aunt, Papa's much-disliked older brother's wife. "Delighted to make your acquaintance, Lady Somerton." At least she'd met enough members of the European nobility to know how to behave when she met an English viscountess.

The fact that she had an aunt still hadn't quite sunk in. Of course, she'd known this family existed, mainly from Papa's rants about them when in his cups, although that had not given her a good impression of them. His descriptions, though, had been somewhat assuaged by her own vague memories of her happy childhood in the Dower House. She still cherished fond memories of playing with the sickly Robert, and of distant views of his family at the big house. However, all of that had receded during her travels with Papa, and, over the years, they'd become little more than dimly recalled fairy tales. And now here she was, holding her aunt's hand, soft and warm in her own and being regarded with such compassion and joy it brought tears stinging to her eyes.

She bit her lip to prevent those tears from falling.

Lady Somerton, her face suffused with pleasure, tugged Verity gently towards a large and opulently embroidered settee. "Do sit down, my dear, and tell me all about yourself. It is a rare delight to welcome a long-lost relative back into the fold. I confess myself overcome with happiness to be able to do so. And let us not be formal with one another. You must call me Aunt Josephine, and I shall call you Verity. Such a lovely name, I've always thought. You are my only niece, after all, and we must continue on first-name terms."

Verity, a little overcome by such an effusive welcome, sat beside her aunt, who did not relinquish the hold she had on her hand.

Walter began to sidle towards the door, as if intending to

effect an escape, a furtive expression on his face.

He was to be out of luck. His mother spotted him and wagged a warning finger. "Nonsense, Walter. I won't have you leaving so soon after your arrival. Sit down. I insist. I see so very little of you as it is. You are not to go sneaking off now you've brought me your little cousin. I said sit." That last command held pure steel. Despite her dainty appearance and soft brown eyes, a core of determination ran through Verity's aunt, and she seemed to know her son all too well.

Walter perched on the edge of a chair, looking sheepish and awkward and plainly wishing to be anywhere but here.

"Now," his mother said, in tones that brooked no refusal. "Tell me how you came upon little Verity. I want to know everything."

Walter, now resembling a schoolboy dragged before the headmaster, shot Verity an appealing glance. He didn't seem to possess any improvisation skills to speak of, and the truth might be a little too much for his mother.

Feeling sorry for him, Verity came to his rescue. "Cousin Walter came upon me by chance with my papa, whom he recognized." Mostly true, apart from the second bit, as if Walter had done so last night, she wouldn't be sitting here. Despite having helped her father in his double dealing, she was an honest girl at heart, and the last thing she wanted to do was to be forced to lie to her aunt from the moment she met her.

She smiled at Walter in the hopes of reassuring him. He was not, however, a good fellow conspirator, so she soldiered on alone. "He very kindly suggested that I might like to reacquaint myself with the members of my family I have not seen for so many years." She swallowed, hating the lie she was about to tell. "My papa has business matters that need attending to, so I have come alone to pay my respects. My papa sends his apologies."

If he was even awake yet, he most certainly would not have done this. He'd never had anything good to say about his brother and his wife, nor his mother, the grandmother who had brought

Verity up until she was nine. She'd often wondered why he'd not at least been grateful for that, as Grandmama had done him the favor of caring for his only child for nine long years. But he never had, and he clearly resented them all. A mystery.

Aunt Josephine's expression betrayed the fact that she probably hadn't believed that last bit, but it was the sort of polite half-truth that was acceptable in society. Whatever she thought privately, she smiled sweetly. "How very kind of your papa. And I'm grateful to him for it gives me more time to spend with my only niece."

"She needs a place to stay," Walter put in, a little gruffly. "I said she could stay here as you'd be quite the perfect chaperone. She don't have one, you see, and it ain't right for a young lady like her to be gadding about Town by herself. Hope you don't object, Mater." He paused, looking hunted. "She's engaged to be married, by the way." This came across as something of an afterthought.

His mother's eyebrows rose, as well they might. "She is? How delightful. Then of course she shall stay here with me, and I will be more than happy to be her chaperone. It's so long now since your sister married, and her girls are as yet far too young to need my help." She fixed Walter with an enquiring expression. "Tell me, Walter, to whom is she engaged?"

Verity, settling into this, and not in the least resenting being discussed without being asked for any input, regarded Walter in expectation. As he'd chosen to jump in with both feet, she was content to let him sort this out.

"Um, er, to Jonnie Dunster."

An awkward silence filled the drawing room. Walter fidgeted on his seat looking as though he'd like to bolt. Verity waited for her aunt's reaction to this news.

Aunt Josephine broke the silence. "To Dunster?" Her voice rose. "Are you certain you have that right? You can't have misheard?" She looked at Verity. "You are engaged to the Earl of Dunster, child? Is that true?"

Well, not quite true. There'd been no actual proposal, as he'd not gone down on one knee and asked for her hand. In fact, the more she thought about it, the more she found it ridiculous, and the more she didn't think she truly could be engaged. Not formally, at any rate. But for now, it might be best to say yes. She sat up a bit straighter. "Yes, it is quite true." She managed a smile. "We have been promised to one another for a…while. And I am here in London for the marriage." None of which was a lie, if you counted less than an hour as "a while," and could get away with saying the marriage would be in London, which she was sure it would be. But she didn't like where this was leading. She more than ever didn't want to begin her new relationship with her aunt on a lie.

On top of that, all of this was what Walter and his precious Lord Dunster had decided, so she could hardly say anything different. Well, what Walter had decided. Lord Dunster had been looking a bit stunned, if she was honest, when they'd left, much as she herself was. Serve him right for gambling with an old drunk like Papa. One of the high points of her morning so far had been leaving him looking as though someone had poleaxed him.

"Absolutely," Walter said. "Engaged since they were children." Which most definitely *was* a lie.

His mother raised an eloquent eyebrow. "Really?"

She didn't sound at all as though she believed this.

"Not quite since they were children," Walter amended, sounding panicky. "Bit of an exaggeration on my part. But a long time, anyway. A very long time." He really was a terrible liar.

His mother sighed and turned to Verity. "That all sounds very nice, I'm sure. But my son takes me for an idiot all too often, and I think I would rather have the truth, as an idiot I am not. If you two don't mind."

Heat swarmed up Verity's cheeks. "It's part of the truth," she said, determinedly looking her aunt in the eye. "I am indeed engaged to be married to Lord Dunster and the wedding will be here in London, once Walter has arranged it for us, as he has so kindly offered to do."

Aunt Josephine's eyes widened. "Walter is setting himself up to organize weddings for his friends now, is he?" She couldn't hide her obvious astonishment. "I had no idea he possessed such hidden talents."

"Um, sort of," Walter mumbled. "Jonnie's, at any rate. Said I would. As a favor, don't you know. To help and all that."

"A favor?" repeated his mother, sounding more than ever shocked. However, Verity had not missed the twinkle of amusement in her eyes. She was enjoying this.

Walter really was the worst conspirator out, even though he'd so boldly seized the initiative at Lord Dunster's house. Perhaps his present confusion was due to a healthy fear of his mother.

Verity sighed, wishing her cheeks felt less fiery. It was going to be up to her to confess, as confession was what was called for here. She'd always thought honesty was the best policy. Not a lesson her father had taught her, but one she'd learned for herself. She had to be honest here, even if after she'd learned the truth, Aunt Josephine refused to have anything to do with her and threw her out onto the street. She'd just have to return to Papa's lodging house and see if he'd come to his senses yet. And to avoid this marriage and his debt, they'd have to flee. Back to France, most likely. Somehow, in the last few hours, she'd come to two conclusions: firstly, that gentlemen like Lord Dunster deserved to lose their money at the hands of people like Papa; and secondly, that he was not really a gentleman at all.

"I'm sorry, Aunt Josephine. I have to tell you the truth. The full truth, not just the little part of it that Walter and Lord Dunster would like you to know."

Aunt Josephine returned her gaze to Verity, her expression expectant, but still not disapproving. "Please do so, Verity. I am sure if my son's previous adventures are anything to go by, it's going to be a fascinating tale."

Walter took on an offended expression but, probably wisely,

remained silent.

Where to start? The beginning felt a long way distant now, even if it was only last night. Although perhaps she needed to go back further than that to explain her situation now. She took a deep breath. "After grandmama died and my papa collected me from the Dower House, he and my mother took me to France to visit her parents in Brittany. I think Papa intended them to have the next upbringing of me, so he and Mama could keep on doing what they'd always done. Roaming around Europe from one gambling den to the next. But my mother was taken ill while we were there and died."

The mother who'd shown scant interest in her child even then. "Papa decided he needed me to take Mama's place in some of his, er, ventures…so he took me with him after Mama's death." No need to mention how she'd been forced to learn the tricks he and Mama had used to swindle gullible rich people out of their money. That was a part of her life she wanted no one to know about. How embarrassing would it be if Aunt Josephine and Walter found out what she'd been part of.

"You poor motherless child," Aunt Josephine said, patting the hand she still held, her voice full of sympathy. "Adrift in an alien world."

"Not so very alien," Verity admitted. "I soon learned to speak fluent French, and Papa taught me Italian and German as well, and a little Spanish. I can hold my own in Russian, too. Children adapt well to new things, I can assure you."

"You speak all those languages?" Walter put in, sounding suitably impressed. "Stap me, but I have trouble with English sometimes."

His mother shot him a hard stare. "As I am fully aware."
He shut up.

"So how did you end up here in London, and how long have you been here" Aunt Josephine asked. "You are indeed with your father, I assume? That much was true, I think."

Verity nodded. "I am with him. Or, I should say, I was with

him until last night. I confess that the tale of our meeting with Walter was only partially true. I apologize for that."

Aunt Josephine frowned, but didn't withdraw her hand. Sympathy still exuded from her. "What is the truth then?" Her voice was gentle. "You will find me a good listener and I do not shock easily. Not after having brought up a son like Walter."

Walter gave a huff of annoyance which was quelled by a look from his mother.

Verity swallowed. "You probably already know that my papa is a gambler. What you may not know is that he is also a…drinker." The guilt at revealing this about Papa bit into her heart. But it needed saying, or the story would mean nothing. "We have spent the last thirteen years traveling in Europe, moving from one gambling table to the next in constant search of the fortune Papa was convinced he could win with his next hand." Or cheat his way to. "Suffice it to say that he never has made his fortune, and when he has won, he's gambled it away at the next table or in the next city." She swallowed. "But he's an old man now, and has been unwell for some time. He wanted to return to England, but it was not with any intention of finding a marriage for me."

"Then how is it you find yourself engaged to Lord Dunster?"

This would be telling her aunt exactly how bad her father had become. How low he had sunk. Could she do it? Yes. She had to. After lying to her, she owed her aunt the truth, or she would not be able to hold her head up high again, nor stay with her. Ever.

She pressed on, despite her reservations. "Last night my father was gambling, as usual. And drinking. Lately he's been doing more of that than before, and with it, his losses have grown. He found himself at the table with Lord Dunster."

"And me," Walter put in. "Only I didn't know it was Uncle Anthony. He don't look anything like Pater."

Aunt Josephine squeezed her hand gently, ignoring her son. "What happened, child?"

The sensation that the last thing her aunt intended was to

hurt her prompted Verity to press on. "He lost. As is usual for him nowadays. He returned home to our lodgings in the early hours of the morning and informed me that he had used me to pay off his debt to Lord Dunster. Before falling asleep he instructed me to present myself at His Lordship's house first thing in the morning. As payment." She swallowed, more than aware of how terrible this sounded and cringing inside that her aunt should know she'd been willing to do so. Although she had, until she came face to face with Lord Dunster, been cherishing hopes of him valuing her accountancy or housekeeping skills.

Aunt Josephine put her free hand to her mouth. "Good heavens, child. Did you actually do that? Please tell me you didn't."

Verity frowned. "I did. For if I had not, Papa would surely have been sent to debtors' prison by Lord Dunster. And I would have had to go with him, or failing that, be left destitute and on the streets. I thought about it for a while and decided my papa's freedom was something I would sacrifice anything for. I had no option but to do as he commanded me." She paused, feeling a softening of the blow was required. "I went to offer myself as a servant, you understand."

"Walter!" his mother exclaimed. "And you were party to this?" Her tone was admonitory in the extreme as she glared at her son, her hold on Verity's hand tightening.

Walter's face blanched. "No, I wasn't. I just told you I hadn't recognized Uncle Anthony, didn't I? I had no idea the girl he was gambling was my cousin. No idea at all."

Aunt Josephine glowered at him. "Never mind that. But you did know your friend was accepting a human being, a young woman, in return for a debt." Her voice continued to rise with each sentence she uttered. "How could you? Have I not brought you up to know right from wrong? You've been too often in that dreadful man's company. Don't think I don't know his nickname. The Black Earl. How suitable a soubriquet that is. The man is the devil personified. If this gets out, Verity will be ruined. Ruined. Your cousin. Your long-lost cousin. The little girl Robert played with." She shook her head in despair and clasped her other hand over Verity's as well. "You poor child."

At least she didn't seem to be blaming Verity for any of this. Which in Verity's head had been a distinct possibility.

Walter did his goldfish impersonation. "I-I wasn't a party to it…I don't think…" But he was on uncertain ground here, as he'd obviously been present when this gambling payment had been suggested. Nothing could extricate him from that.

"Did you not think to stop him? To prevent this travesty?"

Walter straightened his shoulders. "I did the next best thing, Mater. As luck would have it, I called on Jonnie this morning and found my cousin in his parlor. Can't remember why I called, now, but I did. And he told me straight away who Verity was. Came straight out with it. Wasn't hiding it. So I said the only thing for it was that he had to marry her, because that rat Teesdale and old Broughton had witnessed it, and it was going to be the talk of Town very shortly, and what with her being my cousin, I wouldn't stand for it if he didn't marry her straight off. Put my foot down. Told him what's what. Would've called him out if he hadn't agreed, even if it had meant he killed me." He paused. "So that's why we're here. Couldn't leave her at his house, now could I?" He sounded quite proud of himself.

His mother heaved a deep sigh. "No, I suppose you could not. We will discuss your ridiculous inclination to call your friend out later." She turned to Verity, her eyes full of compassion. "And now, poor child, you find yourself engaged to the worst rake in London, if not in all of Great Britain, and must marry him to save your reputation."

Verity nodded. "Lord Dunster agreed, which I was glad about. I would not want to see Walter engage in a duel on my account. And Walter has very kindly said he will organize everything. Lord Dunster was a…little under the weather this morning, so perhaps organizing a wedding is beyond him at the moment. Although, I am not at all sure I truly wish to marry him. Or anyone, for that matter."

Her aunt tutted. "Nonsense, child. You have made yourself a very good match out of what could have been a terrible situation. And as for Lord Dunster being under the weather… well, I should think he was. Foxed, no doubt. The man has a reputation as a heavy drinker, and for many other things as well. Let us hope we can put his acceptance of you in payment of a debt down to an excess of drink. However, its consequences must be faced. You were very brave, child, to do as your father instructed and attempt to sacrifice yourself to save him from the debtors' prison, although I fear he is not worth it."

Verity bristled at this insult to Papa. "I must inform you that I love my father very much. He may be a gambler, and fond of his drink, but he has looked after me well these past thirteen years." If you counted living a hand-to-mouth existence between gambling tables and often running from authority as him looking after her. Possibly her aunt would not. But she did love Papa, or she would not have obeyed his command to give herself to Lord Dunster.

"Come here, child," Aunt Josephine said, holding out her arms, her gentle eyes glittering with unshed tears. "Let me welcome you properly back into your family. I intend to keep you safe with me until we can sort everything out properly." And she put her arms around Verity and hugged her close.

This came as something of a surprise to Verity, as no one had ever hugged her like that before. Not even Grandmama, whom she'd loved dearly and who she was sure had loved her back. And definitely not her mother in the short time she'd known her, a woman who'd shown little interest in her only child. After a moment's awkwardness, she put her own hands onto her aunt's back and held her to her. How fragrant she was, and how soft. Being hugged like this was most pleasant, and for a moment, she felt the unusual urge to burst into tears. Something she'd not done for a very long time. How was it that someone who was just being kind to her could make her feel so emotional? Papa would have frowned on such a show of feelings.

"I say," Walter said, sounding smug. "I knew you'd both get along." Which probably was a lie.

After a long minute, Aunt Josephine released her, a smile curving her lips. "I have made up my mind. We must make the best of a bad situation, my dear. You will marry your earl, despite his dreadful reputation, and become a countess, and you will do so from this house. I will personally supervise Walter's efforts to organize this wedding, as he has proved himself an incompetent far too many times and I do *not* wish anything to go wrong. And I will enjoy myself in taking you to my dressmakers and equipping you with a trousseau to match your new station in life." She held up an admonishing hand. "No. Do not argue with me. I have made up my mind and nothing you can say will change it." Her smile widened to one of supreme satisfaction. "You have captured for yourself one of the most desirable bachelors of the ton, my dear. A man it was thought no woman could lure up the aisle. I offer you my congratulations. And I welcome you into our family. Your family from now on."

What was there Verity could say to that?

Not a lot.

She began to think things were running away from her at an unstoppable rate.

CHAPTER FIVE

Aunt Josephine took charge of everything with alarming speed. Walter might have been relieved to have the burden of arranging a wedding removed from his grasp, but Verity was not. Her newly discovered aunt was a veritable force of nature. She might be small and soft in appearance, but it became obvious within a very short space of time that she was as determined as it was possible to be and not about to take no for an answer from anyone. Especially not from the niece she had just taken under her wing.

Having shooed Walter out of the parlor to go back to Lord Dunster's house and inform him that his mother had taken over the wedding arrangements, she turned her attention to what she called "matters in hand." Verity could only sit in stunned silence and observe in mounting trepidation the alarming efficiency of her aunt.

"Firstly, we must inform your papa of your safety and your changed circumstances," her aunt decreed. "For that I will need his address so I can send a footman round with this letter for him. He must surely be worried about his only child."

Thinking Papa was probably still snoring and not worrying about her in the least, Verity meekly wrote the address of their rooms on the outside of the letter, and her aunt sealed it with a blob of red sealing wax that looked a lot like congealed blood. Why she was thinking like this, she had no idea, but the sight of it made her stomach churn.

Or perhaps that was because she felt she was being coerced by circumstance, and her own inability to prevent this, into doing something she didn't think she wanted to do. Her aunt seemed to be under the impression she'd not only already agreed to all of this, but also that she was pleased about it, and for some reason Verity didn't have the energy to fight. It would be easier to do that later. Let her aunt have her way for a while.

And perhaps a lonely, love-starved part of her liked being this small whirlwind's center of attention. She'd never had that before from a woman in a maternal position, and she had to admit that she liked it. Plus, just being with her aunt was giving her a sense of belonging, of being part of something she hadn't known she'd missed, and of a certain degree of security. If she told her aunt she had no intention of marrying Lord Dunster it would all vanish away and she'd be back with Papa, lurching from one game of cards to the next and one city to another, further one. And she found she didn't want that either.

Aunt Josephine hadn't shown her the contents of her letter, but before he left to go back to Lord Dunster's house, Walter had confided in her that he was sure it would be putting her papa in his place and telling him off for what he'd done to his only child.

"The mater is nothing if not outspoken," he confided in her in the hallway as he retrieved his hat and sword stick from a footman. "My advice is never to cross her. Do as she says and you'll be fine, and she'll be happy. Best for everyone when the mater's happy." He pulled a rueful expression. "I speak from thirty-two years of experience."

"She seems very kind to me," Verity ventured, glancing over her shoulder towards the parlor as the footman opened the front door. "I quite thought when she heard my story she would be shocked and want to turn me away. I know nothing of the history between my papa and his family, but to hear him speak, I always thought they hated him and threw him out."

Walter shrugged. "I don't know about that myself, Coz. I

don't remember your papa at all." He frowned. "To be honest, don't recall much before I went away to school when I was thirteen. All sort of a blur. I'm not so good at remembering anything from that long ago."

He did indeed seem the sort of young man for whom a childhood on an estate as lovely as Somerton would not have been appreciated nor remembered with clarity. A young man who lived for the moment, and did not dwell on his past over much. What a shame. Verity recalled her own time spent there, at the Dower House, with pleasure, perhaps because of the uncertainty of her life after her grandmother had died and her parents had come to take her away to France with them. In her life, that time glowed like a beacon of security and happiness. Not that she'd missed out on happy moments while with Papa, because of course she hadn't. But she wasn't about to disclose any of this to Walter.

He fidgeted, stick in hand. "I'd best be off now, Coz, or the mater will be hot on my trail. If she tells you to do something, you have to do it or risk her wrath. And I'm not about to do that. Learnt that lesson a long time ago."

Verity nodded. "I won't keep you, Cousin Walter. I shall be fine here now." Perhaps more was called for as he seemed to be hesitating. "And thank you very much for bringing me to the safety of your mother's care. I appreciate your kindness." She leaned forward and kissed him on the cheek, mainly because he was looking so flustered and she thought he needed reassurance. The kiss didn't work. His whole face suffused in color and he backed hurriedly out of the door.

The impassive footman closed it behind him, and Verity wandered back into the parlor her aunt had vacated in order to set about her new quest with alacrity.

She went to look out of the window. The road was busy, but she caught a glimpse of Walter's tall form as he hurried around the corner, purpose in his stride.

Perhaps marriage to his friend would enable her to regain the security she'd had with Grandmama. If she was honest with herself, her need for security was probably the only thing preventing her from turning tail right now and bolting back to Papa. Whom she really needed to go and see so she could explain to him in person how everything had turned out.

Perhaps she could do that tomorrow, when hopefully he might not be quite so foxed. Lately, he'd taken to breaking his fast with more of what he'd imbibed the night before. Odd how he could afford to buy brandy but not food nor better lodgings. The footman bearing the letter was going to turn his nose up at their meager rooms and then the servants would gossip about her below stairs. She wouldn't think about that.

She sighed. What did she care if they did? She would do what Papa had always done—she would live for the moment. And right now the moment was this.

She would make the best of what life had thrown at her, as she had done so many times before. And perhaps she would go ahead and marry this man. At least if she was married to an earl, even one as conceited and dissolute as this one, she wouldn't have to worry about where their next meal was coming from, nor where she would lay her head at night. Everything that marriage entailed was a small price to pay for that, and perhaps, if she was lucky, she might be able to help Papa as well. In fact, she would insist on helping him.

She let her thoughts wander back to her meeting with Lord Dunster. Her husband-to-be. How odd it was to think of him like that. If Walter had not arrived in time to recognize her and save her virtue, what would have happened? The earl had clearly cherished the notion that she would perform better on her back than in an office with his accounts or with a mop in his kitchens. Would she even now be lying in bed with that scoundrel who had fleeced Papa last night at cards? Hiring her as a maid had not been in his mind as he'd looked her up and down so acquisitively. Would she have given herself to him in the way he had so obviously wanted her to? Until Walter arrived, that was.

Yes, she would have done, horrible as the thought was. To save Papa. But had it been right of him to expect that of her? He must have known, even as he'd suggested she could perform some menial task for the man who'd won her at cards, that what a man like Lord Dunster would want of her would not involve books or mops. And yet he'd sent her.

Until this moment, she would have done anything for Papa. He'd been her sole family, her sole friend, her sole support, and he'd taught her well how to make the best of things. And if the best of things had been to surrender her virtue to a stranger to repay a debt and keep Papa out of the debtors' prison, then she would have done that. Against her will, teeth gritted. Only now she'd met her aunt and seen her horrified reaction to this, she had to ask herself if Papa had done the right thing. She'd never questioned his actions before, but in the raw light of the daylight her aunt had cast upon him, she began to doubt.

She looked round at the beautiful parlor. At the family portraits on the walls, the rich silk wallpaper, the exquisite Chinese rugs on the polished floor, the ornate furniture, the candelabra and chandeliers, all of it proclaiming the wealth of the family Papa had run away from. Of course, she'd seen houses like this before, but never in her wildest dreams had she envisaged staying in one. Nor that such a house could be a part of her life. And Lord Dunster's town house had been much the same: lavish, opulent, rich. A house that was to become her home. And really, he was, she supposed with reluctance, more than passably handsome with that wild dark hair, black as a raven's wing, those intense eyes, those broad shoulders, and long, muscular legs. A girl could do much worse, especially one in her position. Although...as Grandmama had been wont to say, beauty was only skin deep, and so far she did not much care for what lay beneath Lord Dunster's skin.

That made up her mind. If she could offer herself up to pay a debt then she could offer herself up in legal marriage to attain the security she'd so long craved for. Tomorrow afternoon she would walk round and call upon Papa. She needed his advice, for what it was worth.

THE OBJECT OF her dislike was at that precise moment in time reclining in the desk chair in his study, his long, booted legs stretched out in front of him and wondering how he had got himself into such a pickle. After all, what was a game of cards for if not for winning or losing money? Hadn't he lost plenty of it himself in the past? Although he could afford to. No one should enter into a card game, especially not a game of Faro in an establishment renowned for its clientele having deep pockets and making large and ostentatious bets, if they didn't have the money to pay their debts if they lost. And that fellow, that Anthony Farrington, that old drunk, had done just that. This was all his fault. Damn him to hell and back.

Now he'd had time to recover a little, a few wisps of memory had returned to him concerning the previous, fateful night. He'd allowed Walter, yes, Walter, who should not be considered blameless in this, to persuade him to join him at the Lyon's Den, a gambling house of repute, not always good. He'd been there before, of course, and much enjoyed both the gambling tables and the company of the upstairs ladies. But last night had been different.

One of the ladies of the house had been with him, leaning over his shoulder, her scent, thick in his nostrils, a hint of promise. He couldn't have recalled her name if he'd tried, but he could remember the heady smell of her. The temptress. She'd encouraged him to drink more than usual, no doubt on the instructions of the house, and in a state of extreme inebriation, a lot worse than foxed, he'd accepted that old reprobate's daughter in payment of his substantial debt. He'd never have done it if he hadn't been so Ape-drunk.

He aimed a kick at the desk but this only served to hurt his foot.

And now he was engaged to be married to someone who

might, if he were unlucky, have a very insalubrious past. Never mind might, she almost certainly did have an insalubrious past. After all, she possessed a father who had, without a qualm, as far as he could remember, calmly offered up his daughter and her virtue to pay a debt. What sort of father did that, and, was he not, therefore, the sort of father who had done that sort of thing before? Did his now affianced bride actually have any virtue to offer up? Might she be a veteran of such bargains? Even though he himself was the sort of man for whom morals were optional, and who had bedded most of the available and some of the apparently unavailable women of the ton, the thought that the woman he was now to marry might not be virtuous and untouched rankled. He pushed aside his initial assessment of her as being pure with determination.

He clenched his fists. Was there no way he could extricate himself from this? The idea that her father might have sent her to his house with the express aim of tricking him into marriage now arose. Had he been snared by a man less drunk than he'd appeared to be? Or was this all horrible chance? He, like Verity had he but known it, was going to have to make the best of the situation. Although, unlike Verity, he was not used to having to do so. Years of being the spoilt only son, first as the heir and later as the earl, with everyone obeying him and pandering to his every wish, had not prepared him for putting up and shutting up.

He slowly unclenched his fists and put his hands on his thighs, fingers spread.

However, she *was* very pretty... Imagine if she'd had a face like a horse and still been Walter's cousin. He'd have had to marry her, come what may, or Walter would have called him out. And she'd probably have produced a string of horse-faced daughters. Horrible thought. If he had to marry someone, he was glad it was to be someone pretty, because he couldn't bear the thought of having ugly children. To someone as spoiled and handsome as he was, physical beauty meant everything. Even his servants had been vetted for their looks, much as his father had done in his time.

So that was a good thing.

Was there anything else good about this? He racked his brains.

At least he didn't have to do any preparations for the marriage himself. He could leave that to Walter. This thought led him to wonder how he might be faring in introducing Verity to his mother. As it had been Walter's own idea to do so, he had no feelings of sympathy for his friend. And it neatly took care of what to do with the young lady until the wedding could be organized. How long did it take to do that sort of thing? How much freedom did he have left? He had no idea. Most of his friends were as single as he was, with the same lifestyle as his, and a healthy abhorrence of matrimony. They were going to be surprised to find him leg-shackled before any of them. Although, he had no intention of letting marriage and a wife get in the way of his pleasures. No. None whatsoever. His father, damn him to hell, had managed it, so why shouldn't he?

He smiled to himself a little grimly and his hands formed back into fists.

He usually liked the idea of shocking his friends, but not in this way. Teesdale, of whom he was not in the least bit fond, in fact whom he had hated since Eton, was going to be cock-a-hoop to find he'd had to marry the girl he'd accepted, mostly as a joke, in payment for a debt. Now he'd recalled it, the memory of that man's leering face as he witnessed the signing of the promissory note would not leave his head. But with it came the very odd sensation that at least old Anthony Farrington hadn't been forced to hand his daughter over to the impecunious and unpleasant Teesdale. Ugly, too. What a terrible punishment that would have been for any girl. Even one with a face like a horse.

What was he thinking of? He couldn't deny that he had the same inclinations towards women as Teesdale. He would have seduced Verity without a second thought, made her want him, and taken her up to bed that very morning if Walter had not arrived so opportunely and put a stop to that. He would have deflowered her without compunction, always supposing she hadn't already been deflowered in the past. He would have kept her for a while for his own amusement and then most likely cast her aside with a sizeable pay off. Was Teesdale any worse than that? The only differences were that Teesdale was older by four years, possibly poxed, and certainly ugly. This latter, alongside Teesdale having bullied him in his first year at school, being another good reason Jonathan, with his love of all things beautiful, didn't like the man. Hated the man.

Surely one shouldn't hold his ugliness against him? The bullying, yes, but possibly not his heavy-jowled and heavy-browed face, his thick lips, and uneven, tobacco-stained teeth, all of which, bar the teeth, he must have inherited from his parents.

Well, yes he could. The man offended every sensibility and should keep himself like a hermit instead of frightening society with his looks and turning up when not wanted at respectable gaming houses and clubs. It wasn't as though the fellow had money to burn, because he didn't. Now Jonathan thought about it, Teesdale seemed set on the same road to ruin Anthony Farrington had long ago taken, and would one day end up as drunk and impoverished as that sad old man.

Good. He deserved it.

This was a very confusing day. He'd be glad when it was over.

Chapter Six

BARELY A DAY later, in what could only be described as a seedy backstreet drinking den which happened to be in Cheapside, two very much out of place gentlemen sat at a grubby table nursing pewter tankards of beer. One of them was Thomas Teesdale, the former school bully Jonathan had hated since his days at Eton. The man who had gleefully witnessed his careless drunken agreement to accept Anthony Farrington's daughter in payment for the debt. The other was a much older man who bore an uncanny resemblance to the portrait of Jonathan's father that hung over the fireplace in his town house's parlor.

Sylvester Wintringham, the old earl's younger brother and uncle to Jonathan, might once have been called handsome, but time had not been kind to him. Ten years younger than his brother Edward, he'd grown up full of resentment in the domineering shadow of a brother who had seemed to excel at everything he turned his hand to.

Even when he'd reached manhood himself, via a less than an industrious career at first Eton and then Oxford, where he was supposed to have been learning to become a clergyman, Edward had overshadowed him in everything he did. He'd been taller, broader, more handsome, more successful with women, a better and braver rider to hounds and a better shot. And, to cap it all, he'd been the treasured heir, while Sylvester had very much been the spare and brought up expected to know his lowly position in life and take up the living of St Mary-in-the-Vale, the church nearest to Luxborough.

Of course, one living had not been enough for a man with Sylvester's expensive tastes. So, much in the manner of younger sons for hundreds of years, he had procured himself a good half dozen other livings, all of which he employed poorly paid curates to run for him. Pocketing the majority of the income from all these livings, Sylvester had been able to take up residence in a modest house in London with his family, a hopeful son and two plain daughters, where he managed to just about maintain the sort of lifestyle he considered he was owed.

And whilst doing so, he had been able to observe his despised nephew from a distance, just as he had his hated father. Which had meant much brooding over the unfairness of birth that had left him a mere second son, and brother to a man who had seemed to boast annoyingly good health. And who, with the French woman he'd married in his late thirties, an act that had ruined Sylvester's hope that his brother would die unmarried and childless, had produced a robust young heir. An heir who was still at Eton when he inherited the earldom, granted, where accidents could easily befall daring youths.

Which had been a couple of years before Sylvester and young Thomas Teesdale had become acquainted.

Thomas was the son of one of Sylvester's own old school-friends, a man who had not long afterwards taken his own life when he'd been ruined by Jonathan's father in one of his final acts as earl. This ruination had been undertaken with supreme disinterest and no consideration for Teesdale senior's wife and family. But, before this occurrence, the father had invited Sylvester and his wife, herself a woman brimming with spiteful ambition for her husband and son, to a house party. A house party at which the young Thomas, who was in his final year at Eton and was itching to leave his school days behind, was present.

Something about the angry young man had spoken to Sylvester and, on the second day of the house party, he'd found himself alone in the gardens with Thomas, who of course knew exactly who he was. Conversation had turned with surprising speed to the fact that both of them knew young Jonathan, who'd been fourteen at the time. Thomas from school, and Sylvester because he was the boy's uncle. And it hadn't taken them long to work out that neither of them liked him, although possibly for different reasons.

A somewhat unholy alliance had formed between the two of them, with one aim in mind—the downfall of both young Jonathan and his father, and Sylvester's accession to the earldom, which he'd promised would benefit Thomas monetarily. As a consequence, before Thomas had finally left Eton considerably richer than when he'd started, one or two not quite accidental misfortunes had befallen young Jonathan, none of which had resulted in permanent damage and all of which had been written off to boyish high jinks. Luckily for Thomas.

Eighteen years, and a very unexpected accident on the stairs at Luxborough leading to the sudden passing of the 5th earl, had passed since that house party, and their mutual dislike of the now 6th earl had forged an even more indelible bond between the two men. Teesdale was no longer a callow youth attempting to enjoy the fleshpots of Oxford on a shoestring budget, and Sylvester, father of a hopeful son and two younger daughters, had only grown more cynical and resentful of all his nephew owned, which for some indefinable reason he considered should have been his.

And now news had come to him that the young man he'd taken for a confirmed rake, who would probably die unmarried and childless in a duel or from being stabbed in a dark alley one night, was about to marry. Teesdale, who always knew the gossip, had been the bearer of this atrocious news.

Sylvester occupied a table in a shadowy corner of the inn with his back to the wall and fumed. If he'd fumed any more, smoke would have been issuing from his ears. He'd chosen this table and this seat on purpose, for he was a man of immense caution. From here, he could see all who came and went whilst they could not see him. The last thing he wanted was for anyone to be able to say they'd seen him in conversation with the man he hoped would rid him of his irritating nephew.

His elegant, long-fingered hands, not unlike those of his nephew, had wrapped themselves around his beer tankard and, with his shoulders hunched forward and his brows lowered, everything about him spoke of menace. If anyone had looked at him, they would have turned away in a hurry. But no one did. He'd chosen this inn wisely as it was full of the most disreputable of back street scum—thieves, vagabonds, pickpockets, and women of the street. Not that he feared any of them setting upon him, for a glance from that grim face would have been enough to put them off. And he never went anywhere unarmed.

Thomas Teesdale, seated opposite him, could not but relish the hatred spilling out of his companion in nearly visible waves. Since Jonathan had started at Eton as a raw but over-confident thirteen-year-old, and had been assigned to Thomas as his fag— basically a slave for one of the seniors—he'd nurtured a strong jealousy of this sprig of nobility with a fat silver spoon poking so obviously out of his mouth. A whole canteen of silver spoons in fact. Whenever he met up with Sylvester, their conversation always gravitated towards the young Earl of Dunster, and tonight had been no different.

"It was Walter Farrington who told me Dunster's going to marry the girl he won in that card game," Thomas said, his upper lip curling in distaste. "His story is that they've been affianced for a number of years, but you and I both know that's a complete faradiddle. Not a chance of it being true."

Sylvester gave an angry snort. "News like that travels fast." His eyes narrowed. "I rather wish I'd been present to see that card game." He sniggered. "What sort of a man wagers his daughter on a game of chance? For that is all cards are. Games of chance for those with more money than sense and those desperate and foolish enough to try to improve their fortunes that way. Which never works." He grunted. "Which is why I don't indulge in any form of gambling. It does not befit a man of the church."

As Thomas did indulge and had been doing so on that particular night, although not at Dunster's table, he made no comment. One of his less appropriate skills was his handling of cards. He could cheat, but as a wise man, he never chose to cheat anyone who might notice he was doing so. Which meant he could make a nice living at the card table. Perforce, he'd not been at the same table as old Anthony Farrington and the Earl of Dunster, the latter of which would have spotted him cheating in an instant.

Sylvester tapped his fingers on the gnarled surface of the table. "And of course, we both know what my nephew marrying will lead to."

Thomas pulled a dismissive face. "Not necessarily. I think you're getting a sight too worried about what could be many years down the road. Not every woman is able to produce an heir. And if she does produce a child, odds on it'll be a girl."

Sylvester shook his head. "I never leave anything to chance. If he marries and gets himself a son, my chances and those of my own son will vanish." He bared his teeth in a savage snarl that rendered his face even more frightening. Age had sloughed away the flesh he'd once had and left him remarkably skull-like in appearance, with a nose like a fierce beak jutting above his thin-lipped mouth. Thomas would not have liked to have come upon him in a dark alley.

Sylvester almost spat his next sentence. "This wedding needs to be prevented."

Thomas rubbed his bristly chin. Being so swarthy, he was a man for whom shaving twice a day was a requirement, and after Sylvester's note had been delivered, he'd not had the opportunity to do so this evening. "I don't know how you think you can stop it. I heard from Walter Farrington that it's to go ahead next week. They seem to be in an inordinate hurry to make it look as though everything is above board." He shrugged. "Although for the life of me I can't see why Dunster would even consider marrying that girl." He sniggered, like Sylvester had, but his snigger was more lascivious. "After all, from what I saw of the occasion, he was getting a girl handed to him on a plate with whom he could do just as he liked. No need to put a ring on her finger whatsoever."

"It turns out she's young Farrington's cousin."

Thomas, for whom this would not have mattered a jot, gave a dismissive shrug. "And? Why does that matter? A girl's a girl, after all, and they're all the same in bed. And if she turned up on his doorstep the day after the debt payment was agreed, which I'm told she did, then he had carte blanche to do with her as he wanted." He sniggered again. "I would have, and be damned to Walter Farrington's sensibilities."

Sylvester picked up his tankard and examined the dregs sloshing about in the bottom. "Perhaps he did. Who knows? Perhaps Farrington forced him into the marriage when he caught them in flagranté. They are friends, I believe. Whatever occurred, the unpleasant result is that my nephew is to be wed in barely a week, and if he did deflower her before Farrington arrived, then she may already be nurturing my nemesis."

Thomas shrugged. "And if she is, the chances remain that the child will be a girl. There's only two choices, after all. A boy or a girl. And I've often noted how many noble families seem to throw out girls more than boys. It seems a fact of life." He grinned. "And a boy child often dies... Weaker than girls, I gather, until they're grown. You only have to look about you at how many mothers are touting their frumpy girls on the marriage mart. More than there are suitable young gentlemen to oblige."

Sylvester shook himself. "Whatever child she might have, I want this marriage stopped. I've waited long enough in the wings to get my hands on what should be mine. I thought my brother would never abandon life as a rake, but he did for long enough to get his new wife with child. I prayed for his wife to give him only girls, but he got himself a boy. I prayed for that boy to die as a baby, and he grew stronger. I prayed he wouldn't marry and it seemed the gods had heard my prayer as he followed in his father's footsteps in a life of debauchery. I dreamed my time would soon come, and yet now, it seems I'm to be thwarted again." He banged his fist down on the table, making heads turn. They must have seen his face for they quickly turned away again. "And now," Sylvester hissed, lowering his voice. "Now is the time for you to fulfil the promise you made me all those years ago. Do not forget how I've been subsidising your income all that time. And don't forget your longing to avenge your father."

Thomas glanced over his shoulder but no one was now looking at them. He leaned towards Sylvester. For the last eighteen years, Sylvester had been supporting Thomas's lifestyle, grooming the younger man, whom he would never have honored with the title friend, and molding him into the weapon he feared he might one day require. "What do you need me to do?"

Sylvester also leaned forwards, putting his mouth close to Thomas's right ear so he could whisper. No one should hear what he had to say. There must be nothing that would come back to haunt him.

CHAPTER SEVEN

Staying with Aunt Josephine proved to be the most enjoyable thing Verity had ever done. Not since she'd lived with Grandmama had she experienced being waited on hand and foot in the way her aunt's cheerful servants did. She was given the bedroom her aunt said had once belonged to her older cousin Emily. This was the cousin she couldn't remember at all, as she'd left home to marry when Verity had been only six years old, and before that had been mostly in London as she participated in all the events of the London Season.

In the dining room a portrait of Emily, painted just before her wedding, showed a petite and pretty young lady, very much a younger version of her mother. She was wearing the fashion of twenty years ago and standing in a curtained alcove holding a small bouquet of white violets. "For her purity, candor, and modesty," Aunt Josephine said, with more than a hint of pride. "It would be a good idea for you to learn the language of flowers, I think. Far more use to you than being able to speak Russian." Walter had informed his mother of Verity's linguistic prowess and she'd been unimpressed. Conversational French, she'd opined, was quite sufficient for any young lady to know. She'd have been most surprised at her niece's fluency in the patois of France.

"Where is Cousin Emily now?" Verity asked.

"She married Sir Richard Hughes when she was nineteen,"

her aunt replied, a hint of sadness in her eyes. "Dear Dickie, such a charming man. I miss my lovely Emily still, though. She was such a good companion to me. Such a breath of fresh air compared with the two boys and their rumbustious play. Even Robert's, for he's never allowed his health to hold him back. But I'm glad to be able to inform you that she has a very happy marriage, so I'm happy for her." She cheered up. "She and her husband live at Liston House, near Winchester, with her family. She has four beautiful daughters and is at this moment anticipating a fifth arrival." She sighed. "She and her husband are hopeful of a boy, this time. Dickie is most keen for her to provide him with an heir." She looked sideways at Verity. "Something your husband will no doubt be hoping you will be able to do. Every title needs an heir in order to provide for its continuity."

Verity bit her lip but the heat still climbed up from her neck to her cheeks. She didn't want to think about what being married entailed, even if she might have been prepared to give herself up to Lord Dunster before. Somehow, as the days had passed and she'd settled in to her aunt's town house, the specter of the marriage and in particular the marriage bed had seemed to grow out of all proportion.

Three days had passed during which Aunt Josephine, aided by Walter, had acquired the necessary Common License and arranged for the vicar of St James's church in Piccadilly to conduct the wedding four days from now. Those four days seemed a very short barrier between Verity and the joys, or more likely the perils, of marriage.

With only those four days to go, Hesketh, her aunt's butler, sought her out to inform her that she had a caller. He found her sitting in a shady arbor in the verdant garden reading a book, a pleasure she'd never been able to indulge in before. Her absent uncle, who was due to arrive from the country on the morrow, possessed a formidable library, no doubt full of history and dull tomes, but her aunt had a small collection of her own—of romantic tales. And it was these Verity was devouring, perhaps in the hope that reading about romance might render her readier for marriage than she felt. It wasn't working.

Hoping her visitor was Papa come to enquire about her health and perhaps mend the broken bridges that existed between him and his estranged family, she hurried inside, the book forgotten. It was indeed high time he made an appearance and she had a mind to give him a telling off for leaving it so long.

Her caller was awaiting her in the parlor where she'd first encountered her aunt, standing with his back to the door and staring out of one of the long windows. Tall and powerfully built, it was not Papa.

Even though she couldn't see his face, she knew without a doubt that it was Lord Dunster. And quite a different Lord Dunster to the one she'd encountered four days since.

Hearing the door close behind her, he turned around.

She stared. She couldn't help it. If she hadn't already known who he was, she would not have recognized him. However, she kept her face expressionless, a must for anyone who liked to gamble.

He wore an immaculately cut coat that hugged his broad shoulders like a second skin, over a brocade waistcoat, and figure revealing breeches. His top boots had been polished to such an extent she was sure she might be able to see her reflection in them. His mane of black hair had been brushed back from his face and arranged in an artless disarray that was most certainly not artless. Heavy eyelids drooped over those black eyes in the manner of a panther, a creature she had seen in a zoological garden in Hanover, eyeing up his prey.

Gone was the pasty-faced drunkard she'd first encountered, and in its place stood a man supremely confident of his animal attraction, of his success with women, of his place in society that was so much higher than hers. None of this made her like him any more.

She hesitated, caught by that mesmerising and disturbingly hypnotic stare. And all she could think was that he was the most handsome man she'd ever seen, and also the most dangerous.

But she was a girl who'd escaped Venice in the middle of the night in a gondola, who'd ridden helter-skelter over the Pyrenees to get out of Spain while pursued by a furious Spanish don eager to kill her father, and who'd once tricked a prince out of his golden crown. She was not afraid of a mere earl, even if he was a rake who had his eyes set on getting her into bed. She'd met men like him before, including that prince, and fought them off with great success. She could do it again.

She sank into a modest curtsey, dropping her gaze, wary of allowing him any insight into her thoughts. He had about him the appearance of someone for whom reading minds would not be a chore. "Good afternoon, my lord."

He bowed with a definite flourish. "Miss Farrington."

What a show off.

Now what? Perhaps they'd better sit down. They could hardly stand here staring at one another for the entirety of his visit. Although she had to admit that he warranted being stared at a lot. Not that she was going to let him know that. She'd met handsome men before, that prince, for instance, and she was not going to be swayed in any way by this one.

"Won't you be seated?" she asked, gesturing to the array of choice provided by her aunt.

He took a seat on an upright, high-backed chair, one leg tucked under it, the other extending into the room like some dominating, male intrusion. How could one leg do that? It drew her eyes and made her want to look at it rather than anything else in the room. Most annoying. However, it was a very shapely, muscular leg...

She tore her eyes away and took a seat as far away as she could from him, perching herself on the edge of an over-stuffed settee, her back ramrod straight, and looked at him expectantly. He would have to make the first move.

It seemed he was doing the same thing. Expecting her to speak first.

She waited, well aware of his gaze resting on her in an almost accusatory fashion, his black brows slanting as though in annoyance.

The silence grew.

She could wait forever. She hadn't grown up with a father who gambled without learning the efficacy of both waiting in silence until the other person had to speak, and of keeping a face so still it betrayed nothing of her inner thoughts.

It worked. It almost always did. She had, as her father had often said, the patience of a saint.

He cleared his throat. "I thought I had better call on you," he said, his voice a little gruff, but pleasingly deep. "As we are to become husband and wife in a few days' time."

She bowed her head a fraction in acknowledgment. "Thank you. You are most welcome." And wondered why he'd not called sooner. Three days was a long time to ignore your affianced bride.

He gave a slight nod. "I trust you are comfortable here, with your aunt?"

She nodded. "Most comfortable. My aunt has been nothing but kind to me. She has even taken me to her dressmaker and ordered me a number of new gowns." She paused. "You have no need to fear that I will show you up on the day of our marriage by appearing in a less than respectable gown."

Two red spots showed on his cheeks. "I didn't think that for a moment. I'm sure your aunt will be proud of your appearance. And I'm sure between you, you will have chosen a suitable gown for a wedding." A hint of tension had made itself known in his voice. He probably, no, certainly, had been thinking she would have nothing to wear that was suitable. Touché.

But these spots of color proved to be a revelation. He was nervous! The realization hit Verity in the face. He was more nervous about this than she was, despite his façade of not caring, of hardened rake, of man about town whom nothing could trouble. For the first time, she felt a small pang of sympathy for him instead of the contempt she'd been feeling since her father had told her what he'd done.

"You will have to wait and see," she said, bestowing a gentle smile on him.

His forbidding expression softened a little. "As we are to be married, I wondered if you would care to take a drive in my curricle with me? There would be no impropriety in accepting. I have it waiting at the door, if you would like to ask your aunt if you may accompany me."

How very proper of him. And what a temptation.

She stared. This was not what she'd been expecting. A ride in a curricle. She'd seen people pass on the street in such vehicles, drawn in the main by two horses but sometimes by only one. What fun they looked to be, especially to a girl like her who loved horses. Of course she would like that. What adventurous young woman would not? But, ask Aunt Josephine's permission to go? Why did she have to do that? She wasn't used to asking anyone's permission to do anything. Papa usually did as she told him, unless gambling and drinking were concerned.

A little frown settled between her brows as she realized that being proper was the right way to go now she was a young lady of the ton. "I suppose it would be polite to tell her where I'm going."

"And inquire if she has no objections."

There it was again. For some reason he thought her aunt might object. Oh. Of course. He was a rake, and a well-known one at that. Would it be a bad thing to go for a drive in a two-person vehicle with a man like him? Although...Cousin Walter had been busy putting it out that she was engaged to marry Lord Dunster. So surely anyone who saw them would know, and surely it was permissible for an engaged young lady to take a drive with her husband-to-be? She could come to no harm in so open a vehicle.

Oh, how she wished she knew more about etiquette. She might have learned some useful tips about swindlers and habitual gamblers in her time with Papa, but she'd learned nothing from him of how to behave in polite society. However, asking her aunt seemed to be the polite thing to do as she was at present residing in her household.

She nodded. "I'll go and ask my aunt."

WHEN SHE'D DEPARTED, Jonathan leaned back in his seat and stretched both legs out in front of him. Was this what one did when wooing a prospective wife? An affianced wife one did not know, but whom he thought it might be a good idea to get to know. To exert his charms on.

He wasn't sure. All the wooing he'd done so far had been with one aim in mind—getting the object of his desire into bed. Although of course, getting Miss Farrington into bed would be a pleasurable side effect of wooing her for marriage. And he could begin that wooing today, as it seemed fate had decreed that he would have to marry her. Her prettiness went a long way to softening the blow. And he really did need an heir to the earldom, so it would please his grandmother, if she could be brought to understand what he'd done. He dismissed thoughts of what his mother would think.

So wooing, which he was good at, was what he was going to have to do. After all, his pleasure would be all the greater if he could get her to want him as much as he'd now decided he wanted her. And having taken a better look at her without his vision being clouded by a haze of alcohol, he'd decided that was definitely his intention. He would view her as yet another conquest to be made, a mistress to be added to his string of mistresses, but a mistress he would have to keep. Not so hard, surely?

The only thing that obscured his vision of a rosy horizon was the fact that she seemed a trifle...what was it? Determined. He was used to his women quickly becoming putty in his hands, and succumbing to his undeniable charms without too much effort on his part. A smoldering look, a suggestive lick of the lips, a roguish smile: All of that usually served to persuade even the most prudish of ladies it would be a good idea to allow themselves to become his latest prey. And of course, he made it worth their while. Not for nothing did he have a reputation not just as a rake but also as a lover. Women fell over themselves to cross his path. Not mothers of hopeful daughters, obviously, as what they wanted for their daughters were husbands. But those same mothers were often not averse to offering themselves to him, in order to sample the delights he could provoke in them.

Yes, he felt quite certain he could persuade even this determined young lady to fall at his feet in a swoon of delicious desperation.

After a liquid breakfast, he'd dressed with care, perhaps with an inkling that Miss Farrington might be harder to win over than most. He'd had Arnold arrange his hair to a level of perfection Walter would have approved of, and had been deliberately standing silhouetted against the light from the window when she entered, just so she could see and appreciate, as surely she would, his perfect, manly outline.

For some strange reason she had seemed unmoved by his artifice. Disappointing. In fact, never had he seen someone left so unmoved by his physical presence. She must have a heart of stone. Or be short sighted. Although, her lack of reaction only served to strengthen his resolve to make her want him. She would fall for his charms, if it were the last thing he did. It struck as an insult to his masculinity and he couldn't abide that.

She kept him waiting a long time.

He was just beginning to feel irritated when footsteps sounded and the door opened, framing her elegant figure. Was that one of the new gowns she'd mentioned? Why hadn't he noticed before and remarked on it. He was getting careless. Commenting on a lady's attire was one of the ploys he was fond of using, although he preferred them in a state of nakedness and sprawled on his bed in open invitation.

She smiled that gentle smile again, although he had the impression she was no more gentle than Walter's estimable mama. "Aunt Josephine has said it is perfectly acceptable for me to go for a drive with you, as you are my betrothed, but that we are not to be above an hour. She says the park will be perfect."

The park be damned. And the hour. He had no intention of curtailing his ambitions by sticking to public areas. Besides which, his horses, a pair of real high steppers, were much in need of a good run. Out along the Bath Road would be perfect for them. Miss Farrington would not be able to prevent him once he had her aboard, and her aunt would hopefully never know, as by the time they returned he intended Miss Farrington to be putty in his hands.

He bowed his head. "Of course. Allow me to offer you my arm."

With no hesitation she took his arm and they headed for the front door.

This was going to be fun.

CHAPTER EIGHT

T HE VEHICLE AWAITING them in the street outside Aunt Josephine's house was everything Verity could have hoped for. One of her aunt's footmen and a small Tiger in his uniform stripes who surely couldn't have been more than ten years old were holding a pair of matched bays of immaculate appearance and evident good breeding. They looked as though a flat-out gallop might well be their preferred pace. The curricle itself was spotless, shiny, and very sporting with a high perch seat for the driver and one passenger and a step behind for the Tiger to balance on.

It was the sort of vehicle she'd looked at with envy more than once or twice when she and Papa had taken a stroll in Hyde Park. Although the drivers of these vehicles, young bucks all of them, had not been sedately promenading along the Row and raising their hats to passing matrons. Oh no. They'd been belting hell for leather along the Uxbridge Road, driven by young men whose sole aim in life must be to be dubbed a Corinthian by their friends.

What a good thing Aunt Josephine had not bestirred herself from her parlor. If she'd laid her eyes on this curricle and the horses hitched to it, she would have doubted whether Lord Dunster intended to take her niece for a respectably sedate ride in the park. It did not look like the sort of vehicle, nor the horses the sort of horses, for a quiet drive anywhere, let alone in a park. Her aunt might well have vetoed the whole outing, and Verity did not want that to happen.

She was a girl who had frequently lived dangerously, and besides, she'd always wanted to ride in one of these dashing vehicles, with their capability for great speed. On top of that, she was quite capable of looking after herself where his lordship was concerned. This was going to be fun.

She fastened the ties on her bonnet a little more firmly and accepted the help of the footman up onto the high seat beside Lord Dunster, who had already gathered up the reins in his strong and capable hands. The little Tiger, who'd still been holding the horses, ran around to the back and jumped onto his small perch, and the horses sprang forward in their eagerness to be off.

Their shod hooves clattered on the road, and Verity just managed to stop herself from seizing hold of the armrest for security. She didn't want Lord Dunster thinking he'd affianced himself to a woman of feeble heart, as she was anything but. And, as he looked as though he was far more familiar with the ribbons than any of those would-be Corinthians, she had no need to be frightened. Not that she ever was where horses were concerned. But she'd always been sensible, and she would not have relished a ride in such a vehicle had the driver been of lesser skill. She had to admit, a little unwillingly, that he'd just gone up a notch in her estimation.

He turned the horses, who were champing at the bit in their eagerness to be given their heads, north into Fitzroy Street then west onto the New Road towards Paddington. This road, still in remarkably good condition and for the most part free of wheel ruts, ran along the northern edge of the city, butting up against the tall trees of Marylebone Park. Once on it, the horses set off at a spanking trot, covering the ground with ease, the rush of wind caused by their speed making Verity glad she'd tied her bonnet so securely. Most invigorating, but they could surely go faster than this. The wicked thought arose that she would like to see what Lord Dunster could really get them to do. And that she would like a chance with the reins herself. What fun to drive a pair such as these two fiery beasts. She would bide her time before asking.

At Baker Street, which was crowded with other vehicles to the point where crossing the street would have been hazardous, they headed south with the horses held on a tight rein, and Lord Dunster stayed silent, concentrating on controlling his vehicle and horses. When they reached the Oxford road, they turned right, heading towards the northern boundary of busy Hyde Park.

Perhaps they were indeed going to take the decorous ride Aunt Josephine had envisaged…although that seemed most unlikely. Lord Dunster didn't seem the sort to do anything decorous. Flushed with enjoyment, Verity decided not to object. She'd had so little in the way of fun and excitement since she and Papa had arrived back in London, this opportunity needed to be seized with both hands and appreciated.

The horses tossed their heads in impatience and snatched at their bits, clearly keen to go faster, but Lord Dunster held them under close control. She had to admire his skill as a whip, even if it was out of the corner of her eye so he wouldn't know she was doing so.

Heads turned as they passed, both of pedestrians and of those in other equipages. Men must have been admiring Lord Dunster's team, and women were looking at his passenger with curiosity. Verity sat up straighter and tried not to think of how people must be talking about her and what they might be saying. Although if Walter had been true to his word, most must already know she was to marry the man by her side. Which probably meant they were all wondering exactly who she was and how she'd come from nowhere to marry an earl. Let them wonder.

All too soon, the open spaces of Hyde Park passed them on their left, with Lord Dunster making no attempt to pass through its gates. Verity caught a glimpse of water between the trees that must have been the Serpentine, on whose banks she'd walked only last week with Papa. How long ago that felt and how much her life had changed in so short a time. Traffic was still heavy, so she made no attempt to engage His Lordship in conversation, knowing how he had to give all his attention to his horses.

She was quite glad they weren't about to sedately drive up and down on Rotten Row, which would have been both boring and exposed to public view, but where were they going? Was there another park a little further along this road? She had no idea. However, she had the feeling no parks were to be involved this afternoon. Perhaps she should ask him, now they were leaving the heaviest of traffic behind them.

The horses broke into a canter and the curricle began to sway a little alarmingly.

"Better hold on," Dunster said, speaking at last but keeping his tone terse.

This was sound advice. She held on to the edge of her seat as the wind whipped tendrils of her hair loose and tugged at her bonnet with determination.

But as the horses were evidently still under his control and she was safe, curiosity soon got the better of her. "Might I enquire where we are going, my lord?"

"To give my horses a much-needed run." He hadn't even looked at her and seemed preoccupied in preventing his pair from breaking into a gallop, which surely would be detrimental to health and safety, even on this smooth road. Although tempting. "They haven't been out for several days, so a few laps around the park would not have been sufficient for them."

"They're fine animals." The wind snatched her words away.

He threw her an appraising glance and nodded. "The best. I will only tolerate the best in my stables."

Why was she not surprised?

They were going very fast now. The world flashed past them at increasing speed, but she wasn't afraid. Instead, she felt the stirring of her blood just as she did when riding at a gallop, a pleasure she'd not often been afforded. Was this what he did every day? She had to admit she'd been right and it was fun. The blood zinged in her veins and she couldn't hide the smile growing on her face. Was this what life with Lord Dunster would be like? If that were the case, she might almost bring herself to like it. Life at the gallop. Not unlike the life she'd led in Europe.

One hand now holding onto her bonnet and the other gripping the seat, Verity gazed at the English countryside rushing up on them, for she'd seen so very little of it since her arrival back in Kent aboard a ship from Boulogne. Only the road up from Dover, by night, and the crowded streets of London, in fact. Now she saw the true rurality of England that lay so close to London: the thatched cottages, the countless small market gardens with high and thick hedges, small clumps of woodland, farms, church spires, men driving farm carts who hurriedly got out of the curricle's way, geese, cows, sheep grazing, and even pigs rooting away in pens. Scrawny chickens scattered before the curricle's wheels, squawking their indignation. Once or twice she caught a glimpse of water in the distance, which must surely be the lazy River Thames itself, so very different from the Seine in Paris.

The horses seemed not to tire, their breath coming in angry snorts and their long strides eating up the road. Which thankfully was in good condition, no doubt due to its proximity to London, much as the roads in Paris improved the nearer one drew to the capital.

Dunster was still giving them all his attention, as was necessary, without even a sideways glance for her, his long-fingered hands firm on the reins, his eyes on the road ahead. A glance over her shoulder showed her the little Tiger hanging on with both hands, a grin on his impish face.

What would it be like to drive a pair such as these at such speed? She'd done a fair bit of driving in her time, most often of horses of a much more mundane and workmanlike breeding, but she knew how to handle the reins and whip. The desire to ask him to pass the reins over arose again. However, a glance at his stern expression made her shelve that idea. For now. She could just hang on firmly and enjoy this sortie into the countryside for what it was.

Eventually, though, their madcap pace slowed and Dunster brought his horses to a walk, their sides heaving and steam rising from their sweat-slicked coats. "This is as far as we'll go," he said, finally turning to look at her. "Any further and we'll be on Hounslow Heath, and even though any highwaymen who remain would be unlikely to strike in daylight hours, there could well be footpads lurking. If I were alone, this would be of no moment, but I refuse to take a lady into danger. We'll turn for home now and to give the horses time to regain their breath. They deserve it."

He swung them around with a little difficulty due to the narrowness of the road and headed them back at a walk in the direction from which they'd come, giving them a longer rein so they could stretch their necks. They took advantage of this and visibly relaxed, their need to run quenched.

He needed a compliment for this display of his driving skills, especially if she were going to request a turn with the reins. "That was the most exhilarating ride I've ever had. I've never seen horses handled so well. You are a veritable Corinthian." In her experience, men were always susceptible to praise, and in this instance, he deserved it.

Lord Dunster was apparently no different. A smile curved a mouth she suspected could, if he wanted, look as cruel as that of the man in the portrait in his parlor. "Thank you. I have a reputation as a noted whip and have had the pleasure of that soubriquet you so kindly mentioned."

And probably a reputation for having a big head too. But men who liked flattery were often easy to control. A tactic she'd employed many times while at the card table with Papa. With Papa himself, in fact.

They passed a cart load of hay drawn by a pair of oxen, but the horses paid it no heed.

Verity took the opportunity to survey the view now it wasn't passing her by so quickly. The sun was high in the sky and the day was warm with a light wind stirring the branches of the roadside trees. In the small fields, barley, wheat, and oats bobbed in the breeze, rippling like water. Most of it was beginning to change from green to gold, and the heads hung heavily in promise of a good harvest. Not so very different from the countryside she'd experienced in countries such as France, Germany and Italy, although with a lot more hedgerows and no mountains. Over there, in the warmer regions, she'd been more used to seeing fields of vines and lavender as well as orange groves and olive trees. How different was the world and yet how similar. The people working in the fields and gardens could have been the self-same people she'd seen in villages and on farms all across Europe. The only difference being the language in which they spoke to one another.

They passed an orchard heavy with ripening fruit, the fat geese grazing beneath the trees guarded by a small, barefoot boy. Doves fluttered up from the roof of a barn then resettled on a farmhouse, cooing to themselves. Ahead a daring flock of chickens scratched on the dusty verge.

England. The place she'd dreamed of so often in her exile abroad with Papa. The place she'd longed to return to. And now she was here, at last, it seemed to be fulfilling all her childish dreams. If she could have preserved this day forever, she would have.

Lord Dunster broke in upon her thoughts. "How are you finding staying with Walter's family? Your family, I should say. He's told me a little of your history, which I imagine he's had from his mother. You have had an unusual upbringing." His tone was one of interest in what she might have to say.

She tore her gaze away from a millpond dotted with a large number of ducks, some with tiny, fluffy ducklings, the wheel on the old mill beside it idle. "I am most grateful to my aunt for taking me in." Best to stick to polite pleasantries. He was virtually a stranger to her, after all. "As I am grateful to you for agreeing to help me avoid disgrace." Although it would have been his disgrace as well. Only she had a strong suspicion he didn't much care about what people thought of him. And she still wasn't sure she wanted to be avoiding disgrace this way. Who would care or even know about it if she and Papa returned to the Continent? Then she remembered Papa trying to disguise how poorly he was. If she was married to an earl, then she could buy Papa all the treatments he needed from the best physicians in the land.

Lord Dunster had let his strong, gloved hands rest on his knees as the horses ambled back up the road, the reins slack. "It was the least I could do, as Walter so wisely pointed out." A trace of irony tinged his voice.

Let him be ironic. If he hadn't accepted her in payment of a debt, he wouldn't be in this position now. And he could have refused to continue playing cards with Papa very easily, but he hadn't. So it was his own fault, really. She had no sympathy for him.

He was looking straight ahead and not at her, showing her his profile with its firm chin and slightly Roman nose. No hint of any kind of emotion. What had she expected, though? Nothing.

Did he regret accepting her in payment for Papa's debt? Most likely. A sense of annoyance rose in Verity's breast.

A life on the road had stripped her of needing to guard her words. "I take it you are not the marrying sort."

Now he did look at her, his black brows slanting and giving him a devilish appearance. Despite not having been long in London, she'd heard the whispered, and quite ridiculous, rumors that he'd sold his soul to the devil, or even that his true father had been Satan. Perhaps he'd started them himself. She wouldn't have been surprised.

He smiled, and she couldn't deny how charming he could make himself, soul sold to the devil or not. "You have it correct." If she wasn't careful she was going to fall under the charms of the magnetism that seemed to radiate from him, which would have been such a shallow thing to have done. She must not be taken in by his undeniably attractive appearance and remember he was, at present, a wolf in sheep's clothing.

Two could play at that game. "And you will perhaps be surprised to discover that I too am not the marrying sort." She wrinkled her nose. "I have not led the sort of life that would have encouraged me to find a suitable husband. And let me assure you, Lord Dunster, that when I called on you three days since, I had no intention of forcing you into marriage." Which was quite true.

Those eloquent brows rose. "You did not?"

Did he think she had?

She shook her head with vehemence. "Nothing of the sort. I am not in the habit of forcing gentlemen into matrimony."

He returned to frowning. "So you came without hope of anything…respectable?"

She shrugged. "I am skilled with numbers, and I was hoping you might make use of me to keep your books, or if not that, as a housemaid. I have been used to managing my father's household, such as it is, and I would have made an excellent maid. I am also skilled with a needle and thread, if you were ever to need anything darned." She paused, reflecting how very unlikely it was that he'd ever worn anything that had been darned. "But I am a loving daughter. You must know I would do anything to help my papa. To save him from ruin"

He appeared to be ruminating. "So," he said, his voice speculative, eyes narrowed. "I presume you have done this sort of thing before? To help your father?"

What? For a long moment she couldn't believe what she'd just heard. Been accused of. What was in his mind. What he thought of her.

She stared at him, shock making her heart thud. All she could think was that he was accusing her of having done before what he'd so clearly wanted her to do before he'd realized who she was. The import of this question sank in like a lead weight on her heart, and fury rose in her breast to replace the annoyance. How dare he ask her this. How dare he think this. How dare he put it into words with such casual disdain. How bloody dare he.

On an impulse she grabbed hold of his hand and yanked on

the reins. "Stop the horses at once." Her voice and hands were shaking. Perhaps because she had indeed been ready to do what he'd wanted in order to save Papa, and would have done it before had he ever asked it of her. But he hadn't. And now she stood accused of it. Such little words, but such hurtful ones.

Looking taken aback, he halted his horses and she released his hand.

Still carried away by anger, and without a second glance for him, Verity climbed out of the curricle and landed squarely on the side of the road, glad she hadn't stumbled in front of her accuser. A large hedge reared over her and up ahead an oak tree spread its branches in an oasis of shade. This far from London nobody was about and no other traffic was visible even in the distance. She glared up at him. "Thank you very much for the ride, my lord, which I enjoyed, but I think I will walk back from here." Her voice was stiff with hatred.

The horses seemed quite happy to take a rest. Flies buzzed around their heads and their ears twitched at them. Tails swished, and one of them stamped a back foot.

He was staring at her in open astonishment as though he couldn't understand what he'd said to offend her. The oaf. "What on earth do you want to walk back to Town for? It must be all of eight miles to your aunt's house. You can't walk that far. Not in those shoes." He waved a disparaging hand at her dainty footwear, which her aunt had bought her along with the new gown and bonnet she had on.

Verity looked down at her feet. Damn it. He was right. This made her even more angry. "Do not concern yourself. I shall beg a ride on some passing wagon. I am well used to looking after myself."

How dare he imply she'd given herself to someone before in order to pay off Papa's debts. In fact, the implication was that he thought she'd done so many times. How bloody dare he. More anger bubbled up in her, almost impossible to control. She would have liked to have slapped his cheek, had she not so precipitately descended from his curricle. Or dealt him a proper facer, something she'd had to do to that lustful prince.

Lord Dunster's handsome face took on an air of even more intense bewilderment. Had he no idea how much he'd just insulted her? Was he more of an idiot than she'd at first assumed? "Whatever do you want to walk back for?"

She glared at him. "You-you have no idea, do you? You sit up there in your expensive curricle behind your expensive horses that you'll drive back to your enormous house and leave your servants to look after while you go inside and sit down and drink a bottle of-of port or brandy until you're in your cups and then go out and gamble as much money as you like because you have oodles of it to spare. And you judge me?" She had to stop to take a breath.

No sign of comprehension dawned on his face. He continued to regard her in deep confusion. This was a man who had no understanding of how others less well off than he lived. He'd lived a life of luxury and indulgence. He'd never had to worry about what he would eat the next day, or where he would lay his head.

What an absolute idiot. An overindulged, spoiled idiot.

"I cannot believe you don't realize how much you have insulted me," she snapped, and forced herself to take another steadying breath. "You have had the temerity, the utter temerity, to suggest that this is not the first time I have been prepared to surrender myself to some…some *man* in order to pay my father's debts." She would not say gentleman because she didn't think he was one. "Well, let me tell you that is absolutely not true. Not true at all. This was the first time my father had ever done this. The first time I was ever asked to offer myself in payment." She would have stamped her foot in rage but caution prevented her. "And had you been a gentleman, you would have found me employ in your house as a maid. But you are not a gentleman. And your implication that I am not a lady cuts to the quick. I am horrified by your suggestion. Horrified. Mortified. Disgusted that you might think such a thing of me." She had to pause for breath. "I am untouched, I can assure you, and I fully intend to remain that way."

Realization dawned on his face. "Oh."

The Tiger was trying hard not to smirk.

"Yes. Oh. Now you understand, do you? Is that why you brought me out here, all alone, instead of taking me for a quiet ride in the park as my aunt specified?" She disregarded how happy she'd been at the outset to be going for a proper drive at speed. That didn't count. "Did you think that because I wasn't a lady, which I repeat that I am, it would not matter? You could perhaps importune me when no one was about to see?"

Those black eyes flashed between his winged brows, giving him more than a passing look of Satan himself. Again. She could quite see why his nickname was the Black Earl and why the rumors about him had circulated. "I can assure you, Miss Farrington, that I had no other intention than to exercise my horses and give you the pleasure of a drive in the countryside. We are, as you are well aware, about to be married, so there would be no incentive for me to forestall the ceremony by seducing you in my curricle. Which you will note, I am driving and which needs both my hands on the reins for safety's sake. How you imagine I would importune you, I have no idea. Plus, we have Samson riding behind us." He shot a glance at the Tiger who ducked his head to hide his mirth.

Clearly it did not go unnoticed. "And you can wipe that expression off your face or you'll find yourself walking back with Miss Farrington and looking for another appointment." The Tiger sobered in a moment.

Verity glared back at Lord Dunster, barely mollified, but all too aware of the disadvantage at which she'd put herself due to now being so low down. He towered above her on the curricle's seat. She gathered her slightly scattered wits. "Your intention today is irrelevant. It is the insult you have cast at me that makes it impossible for me to return with you. I cannot in all honesty sit beside a man who thinks so badly of me."

He sighed but the frown didn't lessen. "Then I apologize for that insult if that will get you back up here so I can return you safely to your aunt. I fear her considerable wrath if I don't do so."

Not having expected to receive such a ready apology, Verity could only glare at him. The thought that she'd acted far too impulsively reared its ugly head. Eight miles was too far for her to walk, even if she'd had her boots on, and especially as she didn't know the way. And probably it was dangerous too. If England was anything like Europe, any of the people she'd observed on their outward journey could be waiting to attack and rob her once she was alone. Common sense won as her anger began to subside. She was going to have to accept his apology.

He must have sensed her capitulation, unwilling though it was. Bending towards her, he held out his hand.

After a moment of tumbling emotion, she took it and he half pulled her back into her seat. Without another word, he shortened up the reins and clicked his tongue at the horses who broke into a trot. Perhaps he didn't want to give her a chance to change her mind. After all, it would be difficult for him to explain to her aunt where she'd got to if he abandoned her.

Settling beside him, but as far away as possible, Verity fumed in silence. Never for a moment had she imagined that she might develop such a dislike for the man she was to marry. Gone was her admission of his charm. In fact, he no longer seemed the least bit charming to her.

This was an insult she was not going to let him forget.

CHAPTER NINE

THE VERY NEXT day, Verity decided to walk around to her father's lodgings in Bruton Street. She refused point blank Aunt Josephine's offer to accompany her, mainly because she didn't want her aunt to see what sort of lodgings Papa had. However, her aunt put her dainty foot down and insisted she accept the services of one of the footmen to make sure she remained safe. "So many disreputables about, my dear. I couldn't bear it if anything were to happen to you now we are so happily reunited."

Marrying her off to a disreputable didn't seem to be bothering her much though. Just because he had a title and a huge income.

Verity gave in with polite good grace. And she forbore from telling her aunt how she'd negotiated the dangerous back streets of cities like Venice, Rome, Florence, and Paris in her travels, almost always alone. She also didn't reveal to her the fact that she was in the habit of carrying a slender knife tucked into the side of her boots and a small muff pistol in her reticule. Such a revelation might have come as a shock to so gently bred a lady.

She'd been less adept at preventing her aunt from insisting on providing her with a wedding trousseau, probably because she'd rarely had any new clothes and the whole idea of a complete new wardrobe was intoxicating. "I have only the one daughter who is now long married," Aunt Josephine exclaimed, wagging an admonitory finger at her niece when she protested that it would be too expensive. "None of her beautiful daughters, my grand-children, are as yet out, and I have several years to wait until even Eleanor, the oldest of them, will require my services. So you must, you simply must, allow me the pleasure of dressing you for your wedding. It is a mother's duty, and as you no longer have one, I would consider it an honor if you were allow me to undertake that role."

Faced with such an onslaught carried out in so beseeching a manner, and coupled with the knowledge that Papa's nonexistent resources could not have furnished her with even a pair of new gloves, Verity had agreed. And pushing aside her misgivings about just about everything, she had relaxed enough to enjoy the sensation of being looked after by someone else. She'd been the one doing the looking after for so long, each time her aunt did something nice for her, or spoke a kind word, she inexplicably found herself tearing up. She had to get a grip or she would turn into one of those awful weepy women she so despised.

So it was that after a morning spent at her aunt's dressmakers, as three new gowns were simply not enough, followed by a light luncheon in the parlor, Verity set out, in the company of a tall and sturdy young footman called George, in the direction of Papa's lodgings.

The house in Bruton Street had been divided into numerous rooms let to the less well-off who might aspire to occupy the fringe of society. Older men like Papa who were down on their luck, young men, often younger brothers, just come up from Oxford or Cambridge in the hope of snaring a rich wife, and a few merchants who were in town to do business, so were frowned upon by those who did not need business in order to survive. However, despite having lived there for several weeks with Papa, Verity had encountered none of them.

Papa's rooms were on the third floor up a staircase that had seen better days when this house had belonged to one family. With George following in her wake, Verity climbed the stairs and tapped on Papa's door.

Nothing.

She deliberately counted to a hundred in her head, to allow him time to get up, shuffle across, and answer the door, before she knocked again, a little more loudly.

This time she heard the distinct sound of something being knocked over and some swearing. Beside her, George's expression remained politely blank, although he must be wondering where it was she'd brought him.

The door opened.

Papa, dressed in the same banyan he'd had for years and which was more threadbare every time she saw it, took a moment to recognize her. Unsurprisingly, as she could smell the alcohol on his breath even from six feet away. His eyes were bloodshot and red rimmed, and his still-thick white hair stood out from his head in a fuzzy halo, giving him the appearance of a puzzled cherub.

"Verity?"

She sighed. Did he not know his own child?

She nodded to George to remain outside and stepped through the door. Having closed it behind her, she looked Papa up and down. Much as she loved him, she couldn't deny that most of their problems were due to his behavior. To his refusal to believe that he couldn't make their living from playing cards and conning people. Although, to be honest, he was considerably better at conning people than he was at cards. If only he wasn't in the habit of taking the money he made in a con and frittering it away on cards, life might have been a lot easier for them both.

But it was no use crying over spilled milk, as her grandmother had liked to say when something went wrong.

"Papa." She gave him a quick, hard hug, and pulled him over to sit at the table. The room was furnished with a bed, a wardrobe and this table, with just the two chairs, one of which was wobbly. Her own tiny boxroom, from which Aunt Josephine's emissaries had collected her meager belongings only a few short days ago, was next door.

She took the seat opposite his and covered his gnarled old hand with her own. Having been away from him now for longer than they'd ever been parted, even that time he'd been clapped in jail in Vienna, it came as a shock to her how she felt she was seeing him anew, as if through Aunt Josephine's eyes. Instead of her wonderful Papa, she saw an old, broken man, turning to drink to drown his sorrows. A sick old man with a cough he couldn't shake off, lurching from one desperate attempt to make money to the next. It was surprising how even so short a separation could render them almost strangers.

She didn't like the way it made her feel one bit.

His eyes crinkled in a gentle smile and in an instant he was no longer a stranger she felt sorry for and was back to being her beloved Papa. "Verity, my love. I didn't think to see you again now I hear you've moved into high society with such ease." The slight slur in his words betrayed his inebriation, and his hands shook. As with many drunks, it took a lot to get him slurring.

A lump rose in Verity's throat. "How could I not come to you? You are my dear Papa and I love you above all else." She squeezed his hand. "You know you are." He'd been the center of her world for so long, how could he not be now? She could forgive him anything, even handing her over to a stranger to pay his debts.

His smile widened. "And I find all has worked out well, as I knew it would, and you are to be married. To an earl, no less. The gods are smiling on us at last. On you, and through you, on me also."

She wasn't quite so sure about that, not with what her husband-to-be clearly suspected her of. That was no way to begin a marriage. Indecision wracked her. What she had come here wanting was for him to tell her everything would be all right and that they could slip away to Dover and the Continent and she wouldn't have to marry a man who despised her. But, now she was face to face with his obvious happiness that she was to move up in society, she couldn't bring herself to ask him to do that. He seemed so happy at what had happened to her, did she dare burst his bubble? But she needed someone's advice and she had no one to turn to but him.

She took a steadying breath. "I have to inform you, Papa, that I do not much care for the gentleman everyone seems to want me to marry."

His faded-blue eyes widened for a moment before narrowing. She'd seen that obdurate expression many times before. "Frankly, my dear, I do not in any way see that as a barrier for marriage. Especially not as good a marriage as this one. It is not considered essential to love one's spouse. That will surely come when you get to know Lord Dunster better."

"I did not say I don't love him, although I most certainly do not. I said I do not care for him. Perhaps I should be more blunt and say that I do not like him at all."

Papa's expression barely changed. He patted her hand as though in encouragement. "I am sure that will pass. It's natural that on short acquaintance you might mistakenly think you do not like your betrothed. When you get to know him better, all will change."

"Papa! He is a rake. His nickname is the Black Earl and people say he's sold his soul to the devil. I have to tell you that I do not think he is a nice man at all."

That obdurate expression hardened into mulishness. "Now, Verity, do not vex me. I think you should be thanking me for having procured you such an advantageous marriage."

What? Verity had to bite her tongue to prevent herself from being rude to her father. Did he truly believe that he was responsible for her impending nuptials? That marriage could follow on his using her to pay a debt, just as the sun follows the moon? Was he addled in the head? She looked down at his shaking hands. Probably.

She set her jaw, but she had the long habit of doing what he told her, and rebellion did not come naturally. No, maybe not addled. Just drunk. And like many a drunkard he had an inflated idea of his own importance. And now he saw himself as a matchmaker it would be nigh on impossible to dislodge that idea.

For a long moment she considered her next move. It would be of little use to ask for his help now he had assumed the role of father of the soon-to-be countess. How could she ever persuade him to destroy that vision and bolt for Dover and the Continent? And then he coughed. Not a little clearing of the throat, but a paroxysm of breathlessness that bent him double and required the application of a handkerchief he whipped out of his waistcoat pocket and held to his mouth until he could breathe again.

The thought that he might have done this deliberately had to be pushed aside. He was not that manipulative. Was he?

He straightened up, his face flushed but not in a healthy way, the handkerchief screwed up in his hand as though to hide its contents. She had no need to see. He'd been coughing up specks of blood for the last three months. Again, she thought of the treatments she could procure for him if she married so rich a man as Lord Dunster.

"I know you loved Mama," she said, keeping her voice as gentle as possible even though it longed to rise in protest. "Would you have been happy to have been married to someone else whom you neither loved nor liked?"

His hand twisted in hers. "That is a ridiculous suggestion that I cannot possibly answer. Your mother and I…we had something that transcended all else. We were soulmates, my child."

So very true. It had been a bond that had precluded all other love and that had inspired them to abandon their only child as a baby with her grandmother for nine long years. Only grandmama's death had brought them back to retrieve that child. Despite temptation to throw it in his face, Verity forbore from mentioning that. How could she, when he was so ill?

"Try to put yourself in my position," she said instead. "Thanks to your having lost so much money at cards, I found myself in the house of a dreadful rake who, I must tell you, had no intention whatsoever of marrying me at first. I am not a fool, and I've had enough men try their hand with me in the past to recognise lust when I see it and to be able to resist it."

"Sensible girl." Papa's expression was one of pride. "You kept him at a distance and bargained for the blessing of the law. Just what I would have done."

What he would have done? She almost burst out laughing.

Instead, she kept her expression serious and shook her head. "But I *would* have done what he wanted, if it meant saving you from the debtors' prison. And that is wrong. You should not have put me in that position, a position I now find it impossible to extricate myself from."

Her father's bushy white brows rose. "Why should you wish to extricate yourself from a situation that has been turned to our advantage? If I taught you nothing else, I taught you to seize every opportunity. And this is an opportunity beyond any other we've ever encountered. Thanks to me, you are to become a countess, daughter. How can you object to such a rise in your social status? He has a house in London and an estate in Oxford-shire. A vast estate. I have it from a reliable source that he has no less than fifty thousand a year. A veritable fortune. You need never want for anything again." He coughed again, less dramati-cally, and she was sure this time it was an artifice.

"Only love," she muttered, but Papa ignored her.

His eyes blazed with enthusiasm. "If you won't do it for your-self, then do it for me." As if all that coughing had not been to reinforce this very thing.

She fought down the impulse to rage at him. How unfair to suggest that to her. Had not everything she'd ever done been for him, and yet now, he wanted her to make the ultimate sacrifice.

How could she say no? Her shoulders sagged. "I was going to beg you to flee with me, back to Paris, perhaps, but now I see you mean me to stay here and go through with this."

"Is he so monstrous you can't bring yourself to like him, just a little?" He smiled. "He is very handsome."

Verity frowned, conjuring up the arrogant, self-centered face of her husband to be. "I suppose I will allow that he could be called so." She paused. "In appearance if not in his personality. But looks are not everything, Papa. If he were not such a rake, such a spoiled, arrogant creature, I could bring myself to like him if he were quite ugly. You know me. I am nothing if not adaptable." She shrugged her slender shoulders. "But he is, as far as I can ascertain on such a short acquaintance, a man who has been spoiled and pandered to his entire life, with disastrous results."

Papa pursed his lips, a familiar expression of dogged determination settling on his visage. "Everyone has at least one redeeming feature, Verity, and for your sake, I hope you can find his." He cleared his throat and a smile of satisfaction settled on his face. "I have been invited by your aunt to attend your wedding, which you must understand is a difficult thing for me as my brother will be there." He frowned. "As you know, we did not part on good terms, and I am sure he has as little desire to see me again as I do him. But for you, and for your immense good fortune in obtaining such a match, I will put the past behind me for your special day." The frown became a smug smile. "And it will be worth it to see his face when it is my daughter and not his who becomes a countess."

Was that all that mattered to him? It was like talking to an immovable rock. She'd come here today to see him, expecting to receive sympathy. A title had never been important before, lest it had been for achieving a better con. And yet now he seemed to have changed so much he wanted to tie her down to becoming a countess. Although she had to admit that fifty thousand a year must look more than tempting to him.

"I doubt very much that Lord Dunster is the sort who gives handouts to impecunious relatives," she snapped, immediately regretting her sharpness of tone.

Papa's mouth drooped. "I don't like you referring to me in that way."

She frowned, the inclination to be belligerent large. "But it's true, isn't it? You want me to marry him because you think it will make you better off. Don't think I don't know it, because I do. It's exactly the same as you giving me to him in place of the money you owed him. Just because I'll be putting a wedding ring on my finger, it won't make it any less venal. I shall be marrying for money and position, not love." She wasn't about to reveal to him how she'd dreamed for years of meeting the man of her dreams and falling in love. Every young girl's dream, she supposed, but one few of them could attain. And it seemed she was destined to be one of that number.

Papa's face fell further. "Please don't look at it like that, Verity. See it the way I see it. That by great good fortune, and some manoeuvring on my part, you have found yourself set in front of a man of means, an earl no less, and you are now to marry him. Haven't I always taught you to make the best of things? Haven't I? That is what you must do now, and I know that you can be happy." He gave her a small, hopeful smile. "I only want you to be happy, child."

Verity heaved a sigh. There was no support coming a man who equated happiness with money. She'd been a fool to think there might be. Everyone was ganging up on her and she was going to have to do as they said. Even Papa, with whom she'd had some of the most glorious, and sometimes terrifying, adventures. If he wasn't on her side, no one was going to be.

She was going to have to do as he said and make the best of things.

CHAPTER TEN

LEAVING WITH A heavy heart as she knew Papa was about to continue the day's drinking, Verity walked home, her head in a whirl. She scarcely noticed George assiduously guarding her lest any disreputable person might approach, not that she would have noticed any. She was too busy going over her visit to Papa and wondering if it could possibly have gone any worse.

Arriving back at her aunt's house, she was about to hurry up the stairs to her room in search of some time alone, when Aunt Josephine emerged from the parlor.

Drat it. Living in a house with members of one's family was not exactly easy. There was always someone about requiring one's attention, mostly Aunt Josephine, who had proved to be inordinately fond of her newly returned niece. While Verity returned her fondness, it would have been nice, for once, to have escaped for an hour or two of peace.

Aunt Josephine's face was wreathed in smiles. "Verity, my dear. I was hoping it would be you. You will never guess, but my darling Adolphus has come up from Somerton as promised and he's brought my oldest granddaughter, who lives not far from our home, with him. You must come in and meet them immediately. You will like Eleanor, I'm sure. She might be young, but she is such a sensible and charming young lady. I often cannot believe she's only sixteen still."

There being no excuse Verity could politely make, she removed her bonnet and allowed her aunt to usher her into the parlor.

Uncle Adolphus, a man who would have made two of Papa, lurched to his feet, his broad face glowing an almost fiery red. In no way did he resemble her father. Where Papa was scrawny with age, Adolphus had ballooned to gargantuan proportions. Where Papa was white-haired, Adolphus wore a gray horsehair wig, which, she was to discover, disguised the fact he possessed a head as hair-free as an egg.

"My dear child," Adolphus opened with, holding out his pudgy hands. "This is such good fortune. I can scarcely believe my eyes. I had held out no hope at all of ever seeing you again." He squeezed her hands. "You were such a taking little thing when you were living with Mama. I own that I was most disappointed when my brother arrived so promptly after Mama's death and snatched you away from us. I had quite been thinking that it would have suited us well to take on your care. Wouldn't it have, Josephine?"

Aunt Josephine made noises of agreement.

Uncle Adolphus galloped on. "And you are such a taking little thing nowadays as well, I must say." His eyes, a little disguised by his chubby cheeks, twinkled at her. "And I hear you have captured yourself an earl. I am not at all surprised. With the Farrington good looks, how could you not have aimed so high?"

Aunt Josephine cleared her throat in what sounded like impatience. "Come and take a seat beside Eleanor, my dear," she finally managed to get in, and Verity saw for the first time the girl on the striped settee.

Eleanor, who must have been Walter's sister Emily's daughter, was the image of her grandmother. Petite and dark haired and pleasingly plump, her still youthful countenance held the promise of real beauty. Just as Aunt Josephine must have looked forty years since. She rose to her feet and curtsied, her lovely eyes cast down in modesty.

Verity bobbed a return curtsy encompassing everyone in the

room. One she surely should have made on entering, had not Uncle Adolphus waylaid her so swiftly. She sat beside her new cousin and smiled at her.

"Eleanor has come up with her grandpapa especially to be your bridesmaid," Aunt Josephine said. "As the wedding is to be done in something of a rush, then it would be best not to be too ostentatious, I always think, and one bridesmaid will be sufficient. Do you not think? It is so handy Eleanor is of an age to oblige and that dear Adolphus could escort her to us."

As Verity had discovered early on that if Aunt Josephine asked what she thought of something, the response she always wanted was to agree, she did that this time as well. "Very proper." That phrase had been coming in handy as her aunt bowled along with wedding preparations.

"I have never been a bridesmaid," Eleanor ventured. "My sisters are quite envious, but I pointed out to them that they are far too young to fulfill such a responsible task. And of course, they are desperate to meet you, Cousin. My mother has been telling us all about you."

"And I have never been a bride," Verity said, refraining from adding that it was something she did not wish to become under these circumstances, and that her betrothed was not at all to her taste. She had an uncomfortable feeling that the time for withdrawing from the arrangement was long past. Not to mention she would get no support from Papa if she did so. Being a young woman of few means was not an easy thing.

"Why don't you girls take a turn in the garden?" Aunt Josephine said. "Get to know one another. Adolphus and I have much to discuss and I'm sure you will only find it tedious. The roses are all out, Eleanor, and I know how much you like the scented ones."

A few minutes later Verity and Eleanor, each wearing a light shawl in case they might catch a chill from the gentle breeze, emerged into the garden. It was walled and not large, but the scent of the roses was strong. At the end of the garden, out of sight of the house, a little wooden arbor had been constructed with a bench and climbing roses festooning it.

The two young ladies sat down in its leafy shade.

Eleanor immediately overcame her apparent shyness. "I had no idea I had a cousin until the other day," she began. "Mama was able to tell me a little about you, but on the way here from Somerton, Grandpapa told me he and your papa had fallen out many years ago and that he'd never liked to speak about it."

"My papa has never spoken to me about it either," Verity said. "I knew he and Uncle Adolphus didn't get along, but I've never known why. Families can be very difficult." Couldn't they just. She smiled. "For most of my life it's only been Papa and me, so I have no idea how having a bigger family might work."

"Where is your mama then? Is she here with you?"

Verity shook her head. "No. She died when I was nine. Not long after my papa came and took me away. After Grandmama died. You were probably a baby."

Eleanor frowned. "Which would explain why I don't know you, I suppose." She brightened. "But now you are here and I am to be your bridesmaid, we can be friends, I hope. And you are to be married to an earl. Mama, who could not accompany Grandpapa and myself because she's in a delicate condition again, is quite green with envy that you have snared an earl, even if it is one with a dreadful reputation." She wrinkled her nose. "Does that bother you? His reputation, I mean."

What a blunt young woman she was.

Verity, liking Eleanor immediately, gathered her thoughts. "I have not been long back in England, you must understand. However, I've been here long enough to have heard of the Earl of Dunster and to know that people do not say good things about him." Why was she feeling as though she wanted to defend him? That was silly. For a start, he was not worthy of being defended. And yet her instinct was to try to point out his good points. But did he have any?

"He's very handsome," she said, aware that this sounded feeble.

Eleanor nodded her enthusiasm. "So I hear, although Mama says looks are not the first thing one should look for in a gentleman." She leaned closer as though she thought someone might be eavesdropping. "Mama says that a title and a good income are the most important things in a gentleman, although in my opinion I would require him to love me, and for me to love him. I haven't told her that. She might be cross with me and we're not allowed to vex her when she's increasing."

Verity chuckled. "And I must confess that since I was your age I have cherished a similar notion—that I would find true love and happiness. His Lordship's title and money are of no import to me."

"But you *are* going to marry him. Is it a match your papa has made for you? As you have no mama to do it. My mother is intent on making matches for me and my sisters even though we're all still in the schoolroom. I swear she already has gentlemen lined up." She giggled. "For all I know she might have had Lord Dunster on her list. Which makes me very glad you have already snared him. Handsome or not, I do not think I would like to marry a rake such as he." She paused for breath. "But of course, you know him. So tell me what he is like. I should love to hear. Until I come out, I am only allowed to enjoy such things vicariously."

That was a question. What was he like, this man she was engaged to marry? Until this very moment he'd been an ogre in her head. Now, she had to take stock and properly consider him. She frowned and thought back over the very short time she'd known him, and the even shorter time she'd spent in his company. As her father's assistant, it had fallen to her on many occasions to assess their mark and pick out his or her weak or strong points. Why not do that for Lord Dunster?

"I would say," she began, weighing her words with care, "that he is a gentleman too used to getting his own way and with too high an opinion of what he sees as his charms."

Eleanor smiled. "Is that not just men in general? I must point out that I don't speak here from experience but rather from listening to what Mama has to say on the point, and she says they love flattery far more than we women do." She giggled. "She advised me on more than one occasion that it is best with gentlemen to let them think they are getting their own way, even when they are not, and always to tell them how clever you think they are. Even when it is an outright lie."

"Your mama sounds very wise."

"She is. Since she bestowed that advice on me, I have taken to watching her with Papa, and I believe she is right. Papa always thinks things are his idea and that she is just a silly little woman with no ideas in her head, but in truth, everything he does has been her idea first. She just lets him think he formulated the ideas all by himself."

Verity chuckled. "I should very much like to meet your mama so she can give me some advice."

Eleanor seemed pleased with that remark. "I'm sure she would also like to meet you, once I have a new baby sister or brother in the nursery. But go on. There must be more to your betrothed than just him being a typical man, must there not?"

Verity bit her lip. "You say he's like a typical man, and you're correct in a way. I have encountered a wide variety of men on my travels in Europe with my father, not all of them gentlemen by any means, and, in the broad spectrum, I would say he fits in with them." She wrinkled her brow in deep thought. "I would also say, however, that his behavior goes considerably further than is normal. This is on very short acquaintance, you must understand, but his behavior is, in many ways, exactly like that of a spoiled child, and I would hazard a guess that his every wish has been pandered to since early childhood. And this, I would say, has caused the faults in his character. It is very easy, I believe, to spoil a child's character by overindulgence."

Eleanor nodded with vigor. "On the way up from Somerton in the carriage, I asked Grandpapa to tell me everything he knows about Lord Dunster, and what he told me inclines me to think you are right. He didn't want to tell me, of course, but I am learning from Mama and I soon wheedled it out of him, although I daresay he left out all the more salacious bits." Her shoulders slumped in evident disappointment at this omission.

Verity glanced back towards the house, only the upper windows of which were visible. "Might I prevail upon you to tell me what you gleaned? You probably know more about his background than I do. The only thing gossip told me before I met him was his nickname."

Eleanor beamed. "I thought you'd never ask." She settled herself more comfortably. "He is an only child and always has been. I mean, no dead brothers and sisters as is so common in most families. Mama always says it is not good to only have one child. They become spoiled and unpleasant."

"I am an only child."

Eleanor waved a dismissive hand. "I suppose it doesn't apply to everyone. Probably especially not us ladies. Men are much more inclined to being spoiled if they're the only son."

Verity nodded. "Indubitably."

"Well, as I was saying, he was an only child and his father died when he was still at school. He fell down the stairs at Luxborough one night. My papa knew his papa apparently, although not well. Grandpapa told me the old earl was probably in his cups. He does rather like a bit of gossip."

"I daresay inheriting a title and estate and everything else he now owns in such a sudden manner and at a young age did not do him an ounce of good."

"Just what Grandpapa said. Too young and too much. Those were his exact words."

"And then?"

"Grandpapa said Lord Dunster refused to return to school after he became earl. Declared he'd educate himself in all he needed. Grandpapa tut-tutted and said it was in all the wrong things for a boy his age. He also said he threw himself into a hedonistic lifestyle with total abandon, just because he could.

That bit is also his exact words. I'm not sure what a hedonistic lifestyle is, but I'm sure it's not good, and he refused to elaborate."

"A hedonistic lifestyle is not good. It's what spoiled, rich young men do. They indulge all their vices."

Eleanor shook her head. "I'm also not at all sure what vices they might have."

"And I'm not going to tell you."

She frowned, looking intrigued. "But you know? How is it you know?"

Verity glanced again at the house, not at all sure she should be telling an impressionable sixteen-year-old anything at all about the sort of vices Lord Dunster might have indulged in, might still be indulging in, might continue to indulge in even after his marriage to her. "Well," she said, with caution. "Gambling would be one of them. My own papa is fond of gambling." A mild understatement.

"Just gambling? I hear Lord Dunster has a fortune so that surely wouldn't matter would it?"

Gambling so very much mattered, Verity wasn't sure what to say to this for a moment.

"What else?"

"Er, drinking, I should think." She leaned closer. "My own papa is fond of both vices, I am afraid."

"As is my papa. But he doesn't count them as vices, I'm sure. Mama might, I suppose…"

"Both can be done in moderation," Verity said, struggling to find the right words. "Your papa perhaps does both in that way, but my father does not. And neither, I gather, does Lord Dunster." No need to mention what she'd heard despite her short stay in London about his womanising. Not a subject for an innocent young girl.

"Oh." Eleanor nodded sagely as though she understood. It was likely she did not. No one could understand what living with a gambler and a drunk was like. The uncertainty, the worry, the constant fear of being left penniless. No one.

They sat in silence for a few moments as Eleanor digested this information. Then she looked up, her eyes questioning. "Do you mind if he has these vices? I mean, do you think you can come to love him? Despite them? I would like to think that you will be happy in your marriage, something for which I'm sure all young ladies hope."

Another big question. Could she? After what he'd said to her? Perhaps. But he needed to learn his lesson first and make reparations. And she had a good idea what that lesson was going to be.

She smiled at Eleanor's open face. "I shall have to see."

And so would he.

CHAPTER ELEVEN

THE DAY OF the wedding, four days after the disastrous carriage ride, dawned dank and dreary despite the fact this was supposed to be the height of summer. It was London, after all. Heavy cloud overhung the city as though the weather had sensed the foreboding Jonathan was feeling. He should, he supposed, have been anticipating this marriage with excitement, but he was not. The fact that his bride appeared not to like him one bit and was immune to his charms had a lot to do with this. Somehow, he had allowed himself to stumble into an alliance he did not want, and from which there seemed to be no escape. Although…she was quite beautiful now her aunt had taken her under her wing and started dressing her well.

He rose at what was for him an unearthly hour, especially since he'd not returned home from the card table before four that morning, and took a light breakfast in his room. In no hurry to dress, he donned a gold silk banyan with velvet collar and cuffs over his night rail and sat barefoot at the small table set in one of the large windows.

Had he felt cheerful enough, he could have looked out upon the verdant gardens in the center of Cavendish Square with the splendidly martial statue of the Duke of Cumberland astride his horse. Somewhat bedecked in pigeon droppings, but definitely impressive.

As it was, he refrained from glancing outside and picked in a desultory fashion over his food. With a bride who had refused to see him since his perceived insult on what he'd wrongly antici-pated would be a pleasant and seductive drive out of London, he had a nasty feeling today was not going to be a good one. Perhaps she might not even turn up.

He was somewhat crapulous from too much drink, having celebrated much of his last night as a bachelor with a group of friends at White's. His head was thick and aching, and what he most craved was another shot of brandy. Although he was not suffering so much as he'd been on the day he'd first encountered Verity, he was, nevertheless, not quite on top form. Not on top form at all, if he admitted it to himself.

At nine-thirty Arnold, who seemed annoyingly chipper, ar-rived to shave and dress his master and, by half past ten, he was donning his coat and reaching to take his beaver hat, a Welling-ton, from Trubshawe in the front hallway of the house, looking the epitome of a young man about town.

At a nod from his master, Trubshawe swung the front door open to reveal a smartly dressed Walter already on the doorstep, his hand reaching for the bell pull. For a moment, his comical expression of shock at having been so preempted almost made Jonathan laugh. But not quite. It was going to take a lot to make him laugh this morning. The fact that had it not been for Walter's inopportune arrival a little over a week ago, he would not now be about to set out to solemnise his marriage in a church to a young lady who seemed immune to his charms, weighed heavily on his heart.

"Good morning to you, Walter," Jonathan said, keeping his tone curt. "I had thought we had arranged to meet at the church." He raised his eyebrows at his friend.

Walter, his eyes sliding sideways to peer at Trubshawe, bri-dled. "Thought I'd come here and walk along there with you. Lots of footpads about, you know, even in broad daylight. Dreadful daring, some of them." He waved an airy hand at the perfectly respectable passersby. "You never know. Best to make sure you get there safely."

Jonathan, choosing to ignore this ridiculous excuse, took his cane from Trubshawe and settled his hat with so little care on his immaculately arranged hair that Arnold would have been horrified. "No need for you to trouble yourself. I have my trusty swordstick." He raised the cane. "And I have my reputation. Or perhaps that's why you've decided to walk with me—so that I and my reputation can keep *you* safe?"

Walter's cheeks reddened. "That's it. Need you to keep me safe. Should've said that to start with. Craven coward, that's me."

Jonathan was not fooled. Walter had called around to make sure his friend was going to show up at the church. Since that disastrous carriage ride, the only contact he'd had regarding the wedding had been with Lady Somerton and he'd not dared ask her anything about Verity.

After maintaining a stony silence on their return journey, his bride-to-be had dismounted from the curricle, still in frosty disgust, when they'd arrived back at her aunt's house. He'd called the next day with a plan to attempt to mollify her, on Walter's suggestion, but been informed by a flustered Lady Somerton that her niece was indisposed. He'd not been fooled then, either. Despite his apology, she'd not forgiven him, and seemed determined not to give him the opportunity to ingratiate himself. So why would he bother further? If she wanted to sulk, let her. What did he care? He was quite good at sulking himself.

Only it seemed he did care, or he wouldn't have been in such a miserable mood today. And the fact that he cared what she thought of him made him angrier and moodier than ever. Since childhood, as the cherished heir and then, after he'd inherited the earldom at barely sixteen, as the earl, he was not used to being thwarted. He was, as Verity had rightly concluded, suffering from having led a spoiled and indulged life in which few people had ever crossed him, had he but known it.

That she had been insulted by his careless words didn't occur to him, for no one had ever had the temerity to tell him he was wrong. He was also well versed in justifying his own point of view. And she was, after all, what his late grandmother would have called an adventuress. Surely she couldn't refute that. So of course he was going to suspect she wasn't as pure as she wanted him to believe. He still wasn't convinced she'd told him the truth when she'd denied having been used to pay off prior debts. If she had been, would she have told him the truth? Probably not.

The fact that he himself was in possession of a highly chequered past which he would have disapproved of, had it been her past, never once occurred to him. For a man, it didn't matter, and indeed could be said to be desirable, or that was what he'd always believed and heard his father use in justification of his own lifestyle on several occasions.

But he'd said he would marry her, so marry her he would, even if she remained in high dudgeon with him. He felt confident he could win her round.

With Walter beside him, like a broody hen with one chick, he stepped out onto the square and turned down Holles Street, heading south. A brisk walk would do both of them good and blow away the cobwebs of last night's drinking.

They crossed Oxford Street in silence and progressed down Roxburgh Place into Hanover Square, then on into George Street, still heading south. The pavements were quiet at this time of the morning, although a fair number of equipages rumbled past them. Conduit Street contained smaller houses and led on to Bond Street which in turn became Old Bond Street and from there they turned into Piccadilly.

As they drew nearer, and the momentous occasion approached, Jonathan felt his sense of foreboding growing, despite his earlier confidence that he could bring Miss Farrington round. She hadn't wanted to see him when he'd called at her aunt's. He'd sent a message around the day after and received no reply from her. He had an uneasy feeling she was holding his faux pas, his perfectly reasonable faux pas, against him. Or was she playing hard to get? Was it all a game to her? A game she might well have played before.

He couldn't make up his mind.

Damn the woman. She'd upset his equilibrium more than any other woman ever had. His brows lowered and his step lengthened, forcing Walter, whose legs were shorter, to scurry to keep up with him. There was no getting out of this. He'd have to make do with the hand fate had dealt him, even if it meant marrying a woman who so obviously didn't like him. At the moment.

Walter, by his side still, remained judiciously silent.

St James's, a church very popular with members of the ton, nestled between Piccadilly and Jermyn Street, a few hundred yards to the east of the junction with Old Bond Street. As they approached it, Jonathan took out his fob watch. The time was five minutes to eleven.

The rector, Mr. Gerrard Andrewes, was waiting in the doorway, an expression of some agitation on his heavily lined face. An elderly gentleman, he wore a horsehair wig over what, from the look of the wispy white hair escaping it, might well have been a balding pate. His expression changed to one of relief when he spotted Jonathan and Walter approaching. Maybe he'd thought they wouldn't turn up.

"Lord Dunster?"

"Him, not me," Walter said with far too much satisfaction. "Not daft enough to get myself leg-shackled to a piece of skirt. Not yet, at any rate."

The Reverend Andrewes's bushy white brows shot up almost into his wig and a frown of extreme disapproval settled on his face. He was, after all, a man of the cloth. "Holy matrimony is not a thing to be joked about, sir. Today is a very solemn occasion." He cleared his throat and the frown became a threatening scowl. "I do not have the pleasure of your name."

Walter, who had probably spoken before he thought about it, colored. "Walter Farrington, cousin of the bride. Here to act as best man and witness for the groom."

The Reverend Andrewes bestowed another hard stare on him and turned to Jonathan. He bowed. "My lord. If you will step this way we will approach the altar. If we linger here the bridal group will be arriving, and you should not see them yet or it will bring bad luck."

Hadn't he had enough of that already?

And did rectors even believe in bad luck? Wasn't that a little un-Christian? Having endured what he considered some very bad luck recently, Jonathan decided adding to it might not be a good idea. He followed the rector into the church, Walter on his heels.

The interior was gloomy after being outside, but he paid scant attention as he and Walter followed the rector up the wide aisle. At the top, just before the altar, they halted and the rector turned to face them. "If you would take your position here, my lord, to my left, so you will be on the right hand of your bride when she approaches."

Feeling oddly detached from the proceedings, as though this was all happening to someone else, which he rather wished it was, Jonathan did as he was told. Straightening his back, he kept it turned away from the doorway. For a man usually brimming with self-confidence, especially where women were concerned, nerves seemed to be getting the better of him. Supposing she didn't come?

Time ticked on.

With difficulty, he resisted the temptation to take out his fob watch and check how long they'd been waiting. Beside him, Walter, who had possession of the ring, fidgeted and kept glancing back towards the door, but Jonathan refused to do so.

The rector, who'd taken up a position in front of the altar, like a sentinel, was looking down the aisle towards the open doors at the bottom, a resigned expression on his face. Perhaps he frequently presided over weddings where one or the other of the bride or groom didn't turn up. Jonathan was just beginning to think he'd had a lucky escape, when the rector's coming to attention alerted him to the arrival of his bride. This time he couldn't resist temptation. He turned his head to look down the aisle.

Verity stood outlined in the open doorway, her image shimmering in the light as though illuminated from behind by a thousand candles. How was the gray and dismal daylight doing that? Or had the sun come out in order to bless her? In a gown of pale cream, the bodice thick with embroidery, and a headdress of matching flowers set in her rich auburn hair, she looked like nothing less than a princess. He couldn't help the comparison and the inescapable response of his body. Maybe this wouldn't be so bad, after all. In fact, it could be quite good fun. He'd never been married before, so who was he to turn his nose up at the institution?

Behind her, figures he couldn't make out were bending to arrange her gown for her, smoothing down the skirts and twittering like so many broody hens in a farmyard. On her right-hand side a thin and bent elderly gentleman he recognized from the night of that fateful card game stood a little to one side, his expression bemused, as though he wasn't quite sure what they were all here for. No doubt not accustomed to having a daughter who was about to become a countess, all because he'd accrued for himself a debt he couldn't pay.

They had themselves organized at last, and Verity slipped her hand into the crook of her father's elbow. They began to walk up the aisle, followed by Walter's oldest niece, Eleanor, a pretty schoolgirl Jonathan recalled meeting some time ago when she could only have been eleven or twelve. She must be the bridesmaid. Behind her came her grandparents, Lord and Lady Somerton. So, Walter's father, who was renowned for his dislike of London and all the season entailed, had bestirred himself to come up here for the marriage of his black sheep of a brother's daughter. Interesting.

Jonathan dragged his gaze away from the vision approaching him up the aisle and turned back to look at the rector, standing up straighter and squaring his shoulders. Yes, he could do this.

FOR VERITY, THE wedding ceremony passed in a blur of words

that seemed at the same time to tumble over themselves at a gallop and also to take an interminable length of time to be said. Words that seemed to mean nothing emerged from the rector, and repeated vows from Jonathan and herself, hers formed automatically as though some strange outer power had taken control of her voice.

However, what kept churning through her mind throughout the whole ceremony was that she didn't want to be here. For her father she was marrying a man who thought she was little better than a common…no, she could not repeat the words even inside her head. Because that was indeed what he thought she was, she was certain. His apology had meant nothing and had been inspired only because he didn't want the problem of leaving her to walk eight miles home on her own. This was no basis for a marriage. A husband who thought her worthless.

She didn't look at him once, but she could feel his immense, masculine presence brooding by her side. Only strong words of intervention from not just Aunt Josephine but also Papa and Uncle Adolphus, who for once seemed in accord, had persuaded her to come to the church. Strong words had also flowed between Papa, who of course had already fortified himself with a copious liquid breakfast, and her uncle, who'd not seen each other in over thirteen years and didn't seem pleased by their reunion. These strong and loud words had been mainly in Uncle Adolphus's study, but everyone in the house had been able to hear. Only Aunt Josephine's intervention in this altercation had prevented these two from coming to blows, even at their advanced age. Two angry old men.

Not an auspicious start for a marriage.

So it was a very much discontented wedding party that had arrived in two carriages at St James's church some twenty-five minutes late. Luckily, Uncle Adolphus had traveled in a different one to Papa or they might never have got there. This lateness had been due to Verity having yet another bout of not so much nerves, but more open rebellion as they left the house. It had taken Papa's putting down of his foot and ordering her to get into the carriage with him to bring her to what Aunt Josephine, who couldn't understand why a girl might not wish to become a countess, called her senses. Although Verity wasn't at all sure right senses came into this.

Even at the door to the church, she would have turned tail and run had she not been so hemmed in by her determined family. And now she was stuck. The only thing that had kept her going was her vow to teach the insufferable Lord Dunster a lesson.

At last the ceremony ground to an end and the old rector declared them man and wife with an air of distinct relief. Had he perhaps picked up on the atmosphere of disunity amongst his small congregation? Whatever his opinion, it was now much too late for changing her mind, or at least that was what Aunt Josephine would have said.

She slipped her hand into the crook of Jonathan's arm, feeling his impressive muscles tense beneath her touch, and they proceeded down the aisle again, as a couple this time, her triumphant family behind them. And it was only then that Verity realized Jonathan's family had been conspicuous by their absence. Did he not have a family any longer? Or, what was worse, had he not told them because he was ashamed to be marrying a nobody whose father had forfeited her in payment for a gambling debt?

Heat rose up Verity's cheeks at the thought, only serving to bolster her conviction that he should indeed be taught a lesson he would not forget. She set her jaw in determination and glanced up at him, but his handsome face was expressionless. Well, not quite expressionless. More stern. Possibly not the moment to enquire where his family had got to at such an important moment as a marriage. What a bad-tempered old grump he seemed to have turned into, as well as someone who thought so much of himself and so badly of her, as though she were the one in the wrong for objecting to his insulting behavior.

Yes, she would take great pleasure in teaching him this lesson.

Handsome he might be. Rich he might be. An earl he might be. And spoiled and indulged he certainly was. But he was not going to get his way with her. No. She would make sure of that.

That'd show him.

Chapter Twelve

THE WEDDING BREAKFAST, such as it was, over, the guests, few as they were, departed, Verity found herself at last alone with her husband. The man who thought he'd been forced into marriage with an adventuress, a woman of low morals, and possibly also a fortune hunter, this latter one she'd added for herself. The man who no doubt assumed she would be an easy conquest.

They were sitting in the parlor where she'd first encountered him just over a week ago. At least she was. He was standing by the hearth, his masculine presence dominating the room, just as he'd done on that fateful morning. How long ago that seemed now. So much had happened. She wasn't the same young lady who'd come here prepared to give herself to him if it meant keeping Papa from the debtors' prison and if he refused to take her on as a servant. And she was most definitely not at all prepared to give anything to him.

The door opened and his butler, Trubshawe, entered. "Dinner is served, Your Lordship. Your Ladyship." His expression gave nothing away: not surprise at his master's now married state, nor shock that he'd married a nobody, which he probably thought she was. The most exemplary of butlers.

Dinner. Of course, they had to eat dinner. One more protective barrier between her and having to face the what the rapidly approaching evening would bring. Dinner with her husband. Not that she felt as though a morsel could pass her lips. However, she smiled as politely as possible at Jonathan and rose to her feet as he held out his arm for her to take.

Beneath his coat sleeve she became aware yet again of the size and tautness of his muscles. This was a very strong man who could, if he so wished, take what she didn't want to give and was accustomed to a lack of opposition. She would have to be clever and plan ahead. No doubt, with his supreme sense of entitlement, it would not have crossed his mind that she was about to refuse him. That anyone would refuse him. Well, he was about to find out that such a thing could indeed occur. Not every woman could be called putty in his hands.

They proceeded into a splendid dining room where the table had been laid for two in a far too intimate arrangement, his seat at the head of the table, hers to his right. She would have rather sat as far away as possible at the foot of the long table, but she wasn't about to let him know that. Instead, she took her seat as an impassive liveried footman held it out for her and Jonathan settled into his presumably customary place.

Dinner arrived, and Verity applied her attention to the food.

The first course was red mullet and fricandeau veal with a sorrel sauce, as well as white soup. None of which she fancied.

She picked at her food but it all tasted the same. Of sawdust. The cook would not be amused that she could not eat. She was not amused herself because she'd never seen such fine food, not even at Aunt Josephine's, and never when living with Papa. And before that, with Grandmama, her meals had been of the plain and simple nursery variety.

"Are you not hungry?" Jonathan asked, although, in truth, he also did not appear to possess much of an appetite. He must be anticipating their wedding night in a slightly different way to her.

She raised her eyes from her rapidly cooling soup and wished she hadn't. His eyes, which on close inspection were really a very dark brown, not black, could be described in no other way than smoldering. She didn't need to guess what he was thinking about.

She swallowed. This would make her planned revenge even more humiliating for him. Well, let him be humiliated, because that was how he'd made her feel and she was not about to forget it. Papa could have verified, had Jonathan thought to ask him, that Verity was not a girl who forgot an insult.

She stiffened her spine, determined to resist those eyes. "I indulged myself with the wedding breakfast." Something that wasn't at all true as she'd barely nibbled at it. She had to remain calm and collected, but the only thing that occupied her mind was the possibility of the angry scene to come when she turned him away from her bedroom. Thinking about doing so was easy enough, but succeeding might not be nearly so. Her heart beat a rapid tattoo beneath her stays, and not just because she feared the coming altercation. No, she wouldn't like to admit it, but a very small part of her was hoping he might insist on his conjugal rights. Dislike, no, hatred, was a strange thing, especially when it involved someone of such personal magnetism as His Lordship, who could, with a mere look, turn her stomach to a quivering jelly.

Oh my goodness. Was she that shallow? Did she want him to take her in his arms and bruise her lips with passionate kisses? Was she just like the other women in his life?

No. She was not. She dragged her eyes away and regarded her soup once more, leaving him visible only out of the corner of her eye.

He inclined his head. What a profile. She'd met handsome gentlemen before, of course. She'd moved within circles where a plethora of young men existed, although none of them of the sort she would ever have considered worthy of marriage. But he was the most handsome man she'd ever seen.

No. She must not think of him like that. He was just a spoiled schoolboy who needed taking down a peg or two. Or three. Or maybe twenty.

"Your aunt has told me you are an accomplished horsewoman." He took a sip of his wine. "I must admit, some of the things she was able to tell me about your life on the Continent are quite hair raising."

An easy topic of conversation and one to which she turned in relief. "That was most kind of her. I would not be so bold as to describe myself thus." She must keep it formal and polite.

His eyes crinkled in the most attractive way as he smiled. "I believe she had this from your esteemed papa."

Of course. Papa was inclined to sing her praises to anyone who would listen. But was his tone mocking?

"I like horses and I like to ride." She eyed him aslant, considering her words. "I also like to drive horses and would very much like the opportunity to drive your curricle with your splendid pair of bays." Not that he was ever likely to allow this once she'd humiliated him. It was just another easy comment to make, and, after all, it was true.

He raised his elegant brows. "A veritable whip?"

"Hardly, but I am considered competent." She'd driven a pair of far lesser breeding across the Pyrenees, on occasion along rough tracks on the edges of precipices, with Papa lying addled in the back, unaware of their danger.

"Merely competent? I had heard otherwise directly from your papa." His smile held promise. Of what, she had a good idea. The thought was a little intoxicating. Being so close to him was a disadvantage, and she could feel her resolve wavering.

No, she must not allow herself to fall victim to his notable charms. Difficult. This was a man from whom something almost tangible emanated in waves. Almost hypnotic in its strength. No wonder women flocked to him and threw themselves at his feet. In another age people might have called it magic. She was not about to join their number.

She gave him a sweet smile. "Others are quick to bestow praise where praise is not deserved."

Was he too convinced of his own charms to realize she meant him? Probably.

"But praise should be accepted where praise is due."

Perhaps he wasn't so dense as she'd thought. "If so, it should not be allowed to go to one's head."

He let out a guffaw of laughter so spontaneous that it took her by surprise. "Touché, madam. Or, now that we are officially married, might I call you Verity?"

She bowed her head in mock humility, desperate not to fall under his hypnosis. "You may." The temptation had been to say no, but that would have been silly on her part, sinking to the pettiness he stood accused of.

"Such a beautiful name," he said, his voice lowering to a seductive purr. "For such a beautiful woman."

Of course, she'd had people, men, tell her she was beautiful before, usually when they were after something. But none in so alluring a fashion as His Lordship. She gave another little bow of her head, her eyes fixed on her soup bowl. "Thank you, Lord Dunster."

His hand slid across the table and covered hers before she had chance to withdraw it, in an unexpected move that had her heart hammering even faster. Hopefully he couldn't feel her pulse. "Please, let us cease these formalities. I am your husband now, and all who know me well call me Jonnie."

His hand was hot on hers and, for several moments, Verity could think of nothing to say as she fought with the twin contradictory inclinations to both snatch her hand away and relish the feel of his touch, which could not be accomplished in concert. But no, she must remember he was just exercising his well-known powers of seduction. Powers he must have used on so many ladies in the past. For him, she was just to be another notch on the bedpost and she refused to acquiesce. If she was to be married to him, as she now inescapably was, he must either leave her well alone and continue his lifestyle, or he must come to value her as she felt she should be valued, and abandon his old way of life. She was a person, not a toy for him to play with and then throw aside. And his first lesson in this was soon to come.

She removed her hand from beneath his and set it in her lap, where he could no longer reach it.

The footmen and butler cleared the first course and brought neck of lamb in a braised cucumber sauce and ripoles of pullets, none of which Verity had any appetite for.

Once they'd been served, Jonathan returned to his assault. For that was what it was, she saw clearly. A part of his seduction of her that he thought would end in the bedroom. A man who knew women found him irresistible exercising all his efforts to add her to their number. Or was this just the way he wanted women to see him? The upkeeping of a hard-won reputation.

"You must tell me about your adventures on the Continent," he said, his food untouched on his plate. "Your father gave me very little information other than a list of cities you'd visited with him. I had wanted to make a Grand Tour myself after I left school, but circumstances at the time were not favorable." A little frown settled on his forehead. "My father died while I was still at school, and I was the only heir, you understand. Both my mother and grandmother insisted that I not leave the country. Not with war in Europe going on."

That this had vexed him was apparent. "My father and I were able to pass ourselves off as French," she said, before she had time to think. In truth, the less she confided in him about her past, the better, but it was too late now.

"An admirable skill and one that I respect."

"My mother was French. Papa and she always spoke it together as she had no English she was prepared to admit to. I learned it myself with alacrity when all I could hear spoken around me was French. And a little Breton."

"My mother is also French." Bitterness edged his voice. For a moment the veil she'd already suspected he'd constructed to hide himself from others dropped, and she saw the real Jonnie before her. A Jonnie she liked a lot better than the rakish one.

"Then you also speak French?"

He frowned. "I prefer English."

"Mais, tu es bilangue, comme moi?"

The frown deepened. "I would not claim so and have not spoken the language since I was a child. Since before my father died." His tone indicated his desire to halt this line of conversation and a silence fell between them.

Not for long. He pushed his food around his plate as though it held no interest for him. "Tell me, Verity, what was the most interesting country you visited? I am quite envious of your travels, you must know. I had hoped to see Rome, at least, and Vienna. Perhaps Athens, also, with its classical ruins."

This was easy for her to talk about. Glad to be able to fill the air between them, Verity, whilst omitting all things personal, recounted descriptions of all the cities and countries she'd visited, which were many. She told him about the natives, about the buildings and countryside she'd seen, and never once did she let slip anything of what she and Papa had thought or felt or done in those places. He must never know what they'd been up to. She could create as good a veil to hide behind as he could.

He seemed content to listen to her and interject a few apt questions now and then, so, in the end, their dinner that had begun in so constrained a fashion ended on a note of conviviality. He'd recounted a few funny incidents himself, laughed at some of the things she'd said, his whole demeanor one of a man hanging on the words of the woman he loved. Only she knew it was all a sham, and love had nothing to do with it. However, his open interest in what she told him had her almost liking the man.

Until dinner was over, that was, and they were alone again.

His smile, which had been up until now one of amusement and interest, suddenly changed. "And now," he said, his voice a purr once more, "to bed, I think."

Perhaps he assumed he'd charmed her enough to make this easy for him. And her. There must be many women for whom this would have been true.

A cold feeling, like a wet shawl, settled on Verity, as she suddenly became aware that she'd been allowing her wall of dislike to slip in a disastrous fashion. Had all of this smiling and laughing and listening to her talk been just a ruse to put her at her ease? Of course it had. The man was subtle. The man was accustomed to wooing women who might have been as unwilling as she was. And he thought he had her.

Well, no he didn't have her. But she had to deliberately re-kindle her distaste for what he'd said to her or she might slip and succumb. And that would never do. Although, after time spent with him and the discovery that he could be a pleasant dinner companion, so interested in what she had to say, she began to hope that being taught a lesson might be beneficial to their relationship. That she might in some way retrain him, like a recalcitrant puppy or a wild colt.

She rose to her feet and bestowed a smile on him. "I will retire to my room now, I think, if you would like to take some port." Papa was very fond of a glass of port before bed, and Uncle Adolphus and Cousin Walter had indulged after dinner every night when the ladies had withdrawn.

He had stood as well and now he took her hand, and, bowing over it, pressed his lips to her skin. "I shall not be long."

An unexpected wash of heat rose through Verity's body at his touch, but she managed not to snatch her hand back a second time. Let him think she would be waiting for him, ready to welcome him to her bed. That would teach him. Although a tiny, and slowly growing, part of her couldn't help but wonder what it would be like to allow him entry.

She pushed that rebellious part of herself away with firm determination. This would only work if she was adamant and remained so. If she gave in now, she would always be what she feared—yet another notch on his bedpost and the provider of his heirs. And he would move on to other women's beds.

On legs that were a little weak at the knees, Verity hastened from the room and hurried up the stairs, power, along with determination, returning to her as she went. A tug on the bell pull in her room brought Bessie, the new maid supplied by her husband, hurrying, all girlish smiles, to help her prepare for bed.

Once she was in her nightgown, which was new, and her hair brushed and braided, she sent Bessie away, always the nagging fear that he, Jonathan, might arrive before she had time for what she planned.

The room possessed two doors, neither of which boasted a lock. Furniture would have to do. She'd already assessed how to put her plan into action while Bessie was busy doing her hair, and now, starting with the door to what must be his bedroom, which fortunately opened inwards, she pushed the heavy chest of drawers along the wall until it was up against it. Then, heart pitter-pattering with anxiety as she feared her time might run out, she pushed a large chest against the door into the corridor. Only then could she sit down on the edge of her bed and take a breath.

She didn't have long to wait.

The opening of the door into his bedroom on the other side of the chest of drawers blocked door alerted her to his presence. Was he undressing? Putting on his nightshirt? Or would he just come barging in, or rather, trying to barge in, fully dressed, or worse, naked?

She clasped her hands in her lap and waited.

He tried the door. The trusty chest of drawers, which had taken an inordinate amount of strength to position, didn't shift. The latch rattled again. "Verity? I can't open the door."

On legs that had become wobbly again, she approached the door.

"Is something blocking it?" He sounded puzzled.

"Yes, something is blocking it," she managed, struggling to keep her voice steady and determined. "For I am quite certain you will not want to come into the room of a woman you consider to be little better than a common street walker. I myself have barred the door. And it is no use trying the one from the corridor as I have barred that one as well." She took a deep breath. "We are married, but I have no intention that we should consummate this union, as you so clearly have indicated your scorn for me. Dinner, I know, was just a ruse to lull me into a false sense of security and a somewhat feeble attempt to persuade me to like you. It didn't work. This will be a marriage in name only and I trust you as a gentleman to abide by my conditions."

Silence.

She found she was holding her breath.

The latch rattled again. "I have apologized for the way I spoke to you, Verity. Was that not enough?" He sounded calm. Perhaps he still thought he could persuade her.

She bit her lip. "An apology holds no weight when it is not sincere."

He sighed. "I am your husband. It is your duty to let me in." Where pleading hadn't worked, he clearly thought being firm with her would.

"And you have a duty as a gentleman not to force me. Or am I wrong in thinking you a gentleman?" Not quite true. "I ask you to respect my wishes and not force yourself upon me. Unless, that is, you are no gentleman and the forcing of a woman is something you consider acceptable. If you try that, you will find me unresponsive."

Silence again.

A long silence. He must be thinking.

"Very well." His voice had lost the purr and instead was tight and curt. "If that is how you feel, then I see little future for us in being together. I will send you down to Luxborough in the morning, for there is no reason for you to stay on in Town if you are not to be my wife in more than name."

Luxborough. His country estate. Yes, she could do that. Although at some point he would be bound to turn up there. And then...?

Sensing victory, however ephemeral it might be, she stood up straighter. "Thank you, my lord. I shall sleep peacefully knowing you do not intend any violence towards me." And she turned away from the door to head for her bed, not without a perplexing sadness in her heart that she couldn't quite understand.

CHAPTER THIRTEEN

THE CARRIAGE JONATHAN had ordered pulled away from the front of the house in Cavendish Square and rumbled across the paved roadway. From his position at the window of his study, on the first floor, he watched it until it turned out of the square, heading westwards, before turning back into the room with a grimace of disgust.

Good bloody riddance.

It was the day after the wedding, and his mood could not have been worse. Why on earth he'd allowed himself to be coerced into a marriage he didn't want, he had no idea. He could only put it down to having been much in excess of three sheets to the wind almost continuously for the last week and taken in by the astonishing good looks of his bride. He'd been more than looking forward to consummating that marriage, and not just because she was so pretty. No. Also due to her feistiness. The pleasure of the chase and the winning over of a reluctant bride with his charms had enticed him, as it always did. And he'd thought they'd worked.

Until bedtime last night.

His ruminating was interrupted by the study door bursting open and Walter precipitating himself into the room, cheeks flushed and hair awry. Not quite the immaculate Walter he was more used to seeing. In fact, since his friend had virtually forced him into marriage, Walter had been looking decidedly flustered.

Obviously organizing a wedding, even with the assistance of one's mother, was a flustering experience.

"Did I just see your carriage heading off piled with luggage and with Cousin Verity aboard?" he spluttered. "Stap me, Jonnie, but where's she off to? You can't be fed up with her already, can you? Not even you could have such a short attention span."

Jonathan glowered at his friend, thoughts of how much easier it would have been to have refused to marry Verity and to have bloody well killed Walter in the ensuing duel tumbling through his head. Easier than this, for certain. "On the contrary," he said, keeping his voice as measured and calm as possible. "It is she who is fed up with me."

Walter froze. "Fed up with you?" At least he sounded amazed, as though wondering how any woman could be fed up with his friend. A sop to Jonathan's dented pride.

Jonathan nodded. "Yes. Fed up with me. Need I speak more clearly?"

Walter's brows shot up. "What on earth did you do to her last night?" A glint of salacious curiosity shone in his eyes. He was clearly flipping through his list of heinous crimes that could be undertaken on a wedding night with a blushing bride.

"Nothing," Jonathan said. "Nothing at all."

Walter, after a moment's pause while he no doubt digested this, gave him a sly grin. "Come now. It can't be true that she don't like you. All women like you. Did you shock her with the size of your splendid manhood? Frighten the girl? You must have done *something*." He was almost wheedling.

Jonathan ignored the flattering reference to his manhood and shook his head again. "I mean nothing when I say nothing. My bride took herself off to her bedroom shortly after we dined together and refused to come out. She barred the door against me, if you must know." He paused, hesitating to reveal the extent to which he'd been shown up. "There has been no...consummation. I can assure you she departs *virgo intacta*, or so she would like me to believe." He gave an angry shake of his head. "I've decided to apply for an annulment. Immediately."

"I say," Walter said, taken aback. "That's a bit stiff. You have to give the girl a chance. She's my cousin, don't forget, and she's not like one of your light o' loves, you know. And not like the girls we meet at balls and such like. Been brought up different. And besides which, annulments aren't exactly ten a penny. Damned hard to get one. Look at old Carstairs. Stuck forever with that horse-faced wife his parents promised him to as a child and he don't like."

Jonathan sighed, mainly because he knew Walter to be correct. An annulment between two healthy people would not be an easy thing to arrange. And if she wasn't *virgo intacta* and was examined by a doctor, it would look as though he was responsible for her state. Nonconsummation could be a nonstarter.

He shook his head in frustration. "She might be your cousin, Walter, but she's proved herself a vile temptress. A hussy. Please don't be offended, but I fear she and her pestilential papa dishonor your family name. I'm sorry to have to say so." He refrained from stamping his foot, as he had been wont to do as a child and which had mostly worked as everyone had been obliged to pander to his temper tantrums. "The blame must lie with her renegade father. He's caused her to lead some kind of itinerant lifestyle and now she does not possess the same morals as we do."

Walter bristled at this mention of morals. "I say, Jonnie, no need to insult my family. She *is* my family, you know, even though no one's laid eyes on her for years. So I can't have you saying things like that about her." But he didn't sound as though this was anything more than a lip service objection. He shook his head as though to clear it. "So where has she gone off to in your carriage?"

"Luxborough."

"Whatever for?"

Jonathan shrugged. "Because I decided she shouldn't remain under the same roof as me…" His voice trailed off. Had he sent her away because he was just angry with her? Or had it been to get her out of his sight, and therefore rid himself of the temptation of her presence, which had grown ten-fold since her rebuttal of him. He had no desire to repeat what they'd said to one another. Mainly because if he did repeat it to Walter, he might get that duel after all.

Walter had no need to know he'd actually implied to Verity that she wasn't the virgin she claimed to be. Although, from her reaction, he might have been wrong in his initial assumption. A little voice at the back of his mind kept saying that she'd deny his accusation even if he'd been right, though. Why was life so damned hard where women were concerned? Far better to have a mistress than a wife. One could just cast a difficult mistress adrift on a whim, but not a wife. He was stuck with her now for the rest of his life. Or hers. Although, as he almost never went to Luxborough, he'd as good as cast Verity adrift this morning.

"And?" Walter's tone was insistent.

"And?"

"You still haven't given me a good reason for sending her off on her own. Why didn't you go with her and…do a bit of that wooing everyone says you're so good at. Live up to your reputation. Surely you can get her to like you? Every other woman you smile at does. Can't understand it myself. A smile from you and their tongues are hanging out and they're ready to jump into bed with you." He paused. "Did you try smiling at her?"

Jonathan grit his teeth for a moment, then gave a dismissive shrug. "Of course I did. Do you think me an idiot?" He gave an angry shake of his head. "No wife of mine is going to show me up. She can kick her heels at Luxborough for a while until she gets lonely and bored and comes to realize being married to me isn't such a bad thing. And I'm going to continue with my life here in London without a thought for her. Mark my words. Being married is not going to be a barrier to resuming my old ways."

But did he really want to do all of that? Frustration rising to the fore, he kicked one of the legs of his desk and then regretted it.

Walter frowned. "Not sure you'd ever given them up. I don't think I ought to be condoning all this, you know. She *is* my cousin, after all. Not some gal I don't even know. What would the mater say if she found out? You don't want to go putting her back up, Jonnie. She's taken young Verity under her wing and loves her like a second daughter, even though she's only known her a little over a week."

Jonathan shrugged. "Quite frankly, I don't care. She's made a fool out of me and as far as I'm concerned, she can rot down there in Oxfordshire. I rarely go there, so I'll have little need to see her."

Walter pulled a disbelieving face. "You're sure that was a wise move? What with your sainted grandmother being down there, and your sister? What d'you think they'll say when she turns up there? Have you even told them you're married? I really think you should go down there post haste and attempt to win your wife over. Yes. Much the best idea."

Jonathan scowled. "I have no intention of crawling to her like a beggar after the crumbs from her table. And as for letting them know, you'll be happy to hear I sent a note down a few days ago informing them of my decision to marry and telling them they had no need to bestir themselves and attend. None of them would have, anyway. My grandmother is half the time out of her wits, my mother wouldn't have cared and is housebound nowadays, as you know, and as for Kitty…well, I couldn't have her coming up here, now could I? Too many questions would have arisen." He paused. "And, before you bestow more of your wisdom on me, I have no idea if it's a wise move and nor do I care. All that bothers me is getting my wife out of my hair. So let us repair to White's, shall we? I have need of an exclusively male retreat. I've had my fill of women for now. Wives especially. Let's go."

And with that, he swept past Walter and out into the hallway.

IT TOOK VERITY quite some time to settle into the journey

westwards to Luxborough. For most of the earlier part of it she remained slumped in a corner, suffering from an excess of emotion and a night spent awake and waiting for an assault on the defenses she'd erected against her bedroom doors, despite his promise not to bother her. But that assault had never come, and she'd lain awake in bed puzzled by her own disappointment at the lack of it. Which had in turn annoyed her to the extent that sleep had eluded her for most of the night. Which meant now she was exhausted.

When she at last pulled back the blind from the coach window, the countryside at first seemed to be much as she'd seen it from the mail coach that had brought her and Papa up from Dover just a few weeks since, only this time viewed in daylight. The day being cloudy with no sign of the sun, she had no way of discerning in which direction they were traveling, so for a while settled back into silent repose. She had a lot to think about before she and Bessie, who was asleep in a corner, reached their destination.

The road sign to Oxford finally alerted her that much time had passed and they must be nearly at their destination.

She turned to her new maid, who'd woken some time ago. "Bessie," she made her tone curt, as she was not feeling in the least bit generous to anyone associated with her new husband. "Do you know how much further we have to travel?"

Bessie, a pretty little thing who seemed very young for promotion to lady's maid, turned wary eyes on her new mistress. "To Luxborough, milady? I'm not very good at knowing places, I'm sorry." She also peered out of the window. "I don't see nothing I can recognize yet, so I don't think we're close."

Verity pointed out of the window. "I think you'll find we are approaching the city of Oxford right now."

Bessie's eyes widened. "We are? Already?"

Verity nodded. "We have just passed a road sign at that last crossroads declaring that Oxford is only ten miles off. My knowledge of the geography of England is admittedly poor, and I have no idea on which side of the city the Luxborough estate lies. Do you? Do you know the estate at all, or are you London born?"

Bessie looked pleased she could answer a question at last. "I do know where Oxford is, all right, on account of it's being near Luxborough Park, where I was brought up. Not in the house, I don't mean. You see, Your Ladyship, my ma and pa work a tenant farm on the estate. One of my brothers is a footman in the house. Very proud of him my ma and pa are, and they will be of me, too, when they see I'm a lady's maid now."

Verity swallowed. "Is Luxborough a very large estate?" Of course, it had to be, when one considered the fortune Jonathan had at his disposal annually. Silly question, but it was nice to talk to someone who knew it.

Bessie nodded with vigor. "Yes, milady. Very big. Huge. Biggest in the county, my pa says. His Lordship's got another up in Yorkshire, but I've never been there. My job was up at his town house. I've only ever been there and at Luxborough where I started as a laundry maid when I were twelve."

Verity compressed her lips into a thin line. Of course, she'd seen many large houses, and one or two palaces during her adventures with Papa. But it was quite another thing to be rapidly approaching one that was to be her new home. She would feel like a gauche intruder, not meant to be there, she was certain.

She looked out of the window again at the fields and woodland flashing past. The coachman was maintaining a spanking pace, which must be why they'd arrived here so quickly. Behind the clouds the sun would be starting to head towards early evening, and here and there, through a break in the cover, rays slanted down to illuminate the fields and verdant woodland. A pretty sight, especially to a girl brought up in many of the more arid areas of Europe.

She looked back at Bessie, who seemed quite cheerful to be returning to the place of her birth. No doubt, as she'd said, she was looking forward to seeing her family again and showing off about her promotion to lady's maid. "Do you know where

Luxborough is? Which side of Oxford?"

Bessie shrugged apologetically. "I couldn't tell you, milady. All I know is it's about a five mile walk into the city from my ma and pa's farm, and that's about a mile from the big house." She gave a rueful smile. "It's a right big house. Like I said, I was laundry maid, which was a lot of work, then underhousemaid there before his lordship had me sent up to London to work in his town house as a housemaid. My ma and pa weren't so happy about that. They'd have preferred me to stay at the big house, they said."

Verity sank back into her seat. Jonathan had sent her to his house in Oxfordshire. Well, at least he hadn't sent her to the one Bessie had just told her about—in Yorkshire. That, she assumed, although she wasn't quite sure due to her lack of English geographical knowledge, was much further away. But Oxford, which it seemed was a long way from London, would not be close to Papa, whom she'd hoped to be able to visit. She grit her teeth. How constraining being a countess was. She much preferred the life she'd led with Papa, with no one able to say no to her if she wanted to leave.

There was nothing she could do about this now. Yet again, she'd have to make the best of what life had thrown in her way. And at least she wouldn't have to see the despicable, but disturbingly handsome, Jonathan every day and sleep with her bedroom door barred. That was one blessing. Ever practical, she shoved aside her fury and allowed herself to ruminate on what Luxborough would be like. Hope burgeoned that it would be similar to living in the Dower House with Grandmama, a period that had taken on almost magical qualities in her mind during her enforced exile on the continent with Papa.

Yes, she would make the best of this new exile, and she would like it.

IN THE SAME seedy Cheapside alehouse as they'd used before, Sylvester Wintringham, man of the cloth, sat head-to-head with

Thomas Teesdale. He was not happy, and his face reflected his mood so no one, not least Thomas, could be in any doubt as to his displeasure.

"What went wrong?" he hissed at Thomas. "My nephew is married. I thought you were going to do something about it before the wedding occurred."

Thomas glanced over his shoulder but the rest of the alehouse's dubious clientele was busy ogling one of the women who was singing a ribald song near the bar. "I couldn't get near him. The man doesn't like me. It's not as if we move in the same circles. He's been surrounded by his friends all week."

"You were meant to stop this wedding. You assured me you could."

Thomas, who nurtured a real fear of his mentor, suppressed the shiver that had crept up his spine. "I could only have done what we planned if I'd been able to engage him at cards. You knew that."

Sylvester frowned, which only added to the menace of his countenance. "Damn it, man. You promised me you'd deal with this at long last. Just when there's an emergency you've let me down. I've a mind to engage someone else to carry out my plans." He nodded at the men cheering the singer on. "I'm sure more than a few here would be glad to help me if I asked them and probably for a cheaper price than you."

Thomas swallowed. He did not want to lose the nice stipend Sylvester had been paying him. "I'll get it done, mark my words. I'll get it done."

Sylvester rose to his feet, snatching his beaver hat from the table. "Then do it, before any more time passes. Or I just might employ some of the men here to not only do it for me, but also to remove you from my way. Good day to you, Teesdale."

Thomas sat there for a few long minutes after Sylvester had left. At length, he turned in his seat and also regarded the alehouse's customers. Perhaps Sylvester was right. Perhaps, instead of letting Sylvester turn to them, he could do it himself. It might be a sight easier than his own plan which had been to challenge Jonathan to a duel, as he was himself a crack shot, when Jonathan caught him cheating at cards. Yes, some of these cutpurses and vagabonds might come in very handy indeed. Yes. Now, how many would he need. Half a dozen might be best.

He rose from the table and approached the revelers.

CHAPTER FOURTEEN

A BARE HALF an hour later, the carriage bearing Verity and an increasingly excitable Bessie turned off the main road to Oxford and headed into much deeper countryside, a countryside awash with greens of every hue. High hedges framed the narrow, potholed road, enormous trees cast looming shadows, stark and strong in the bright summer sunshine, and their branches muttered indecipherable secrets in the slight breeze. Everything seemed brighter and clearer than London had, but without the fierce glare of the hot European countryside.

Verity realized she was approaching a different world to the one she was familiar with in the gaudy, vibrant cities of Europe and the crowded streets of London. A world of verdant greenery, fields of gently rippling standing crops, and of countless animals grazing behind the thick hedges, glimpsed every time they passed a rickety gate.

Ten minutes of jolting, but enjoyable, progress brought them to where the most impressive entranceway she'd ever seen shouted the start of Luxborough Park. Beneath what seemed worthy of nothing less than a Roman triumphal arch, ornate metal gates stood open in welcome. Beyond them, a long, woodland-edged drive rose away from the high road, seemingly heading into the far distance with the intention of holding their destination close and hidden. To either side of the gates, tall, octagonal gatehouses topped with ogee roofs stood sentinel. She had the distinct impression that they were leaning threateningly towards her like the trees, daring her not to breach their guard. An imposing sight. If this was the gatehouse, whatever would the house be like?

She found out soon enough. Eventually, the wide, graveled and pothole-free drive left the woods behind to curve across what looked like hundreds of acres of rolling open parkland. Far off, browsing in the shade of yet more woodland, a herd of sun-dappled deer seemed tiny. Verity, caution thrown to the wind, leaned forward to peer out of the window at the awe-inspiring vista as it spread out before her, her heart beating to the same rhythm as the sweaty, trotting horses. Horses that must surely be tired after such a long journey.

And then she caught sight of their destination.

Luxborough House occupied the center of this sweeping, open landscape as though it had stood there for centuries and would do so for many more, an immovable rock against the tide of time. It stood four square and sturdy, yet exuded an undeniable elegance. Whoever had commanded this house to be built had possessed more than just good taste. Foresight, perhaps, and a grand idea that he'd caused to become reality. Towers rose in pinnacles, reaching towards the arc of the sky, their ogee roofs perfectly echoing those on the gatehouses and giving the whole place an almost fairy-xrtale appearance.

For a brief moment the thought that all of what was happening to her was just a vivid dream arose, only to be dismissed. No, this was real enough. Not a dream, but the reality of another world she was now going to be part of. A world into which she feared she would not fit.

The carriage bowled along the drive until it reached another set of gates, smaller this time but also standing open, which led onto the vast circular driveway that lay at the front of the house. To the left stood what might be service buildings and stables, themselves only a little less splendid than the house, and ahead, a vastly ornate loggia looming out of the face of the building marked the main entrance, itself bigger than any accommodation Verity had ever inhabited. Steps led up to huge doors flanked by elegant pillars, and above the whole thing rose two further stories to battlements decorated with aggressive, pointed spires. As though whoever designed this house hadn't been quite certain they didn't have to keep undesirables out.

The carriage rolled to a halt, the gravel crunching under the wheels.

She was here.

Casting a quick, sideways glance at Bessie, Verity swallowed down her nerves. She would have to brazen this out with all the artifice Papa had instilled in her.

The doors in the loggia swung open and a bevy of servants hurried to attend their arrival. Someone opened the coach door and let down the steps, and someone else held out a gloved hand to her. A liveried footman, bewigged and attentive. After a moment's wary hesitation, Verity took the offered hand and stepped down onto the gravel.

The footman who'd offered her his hand was strikingly handsome, and she couldn't help but notice how he filled out his livery to perfection. Of course, she'd come across footmen many times in her travels, and Aunt Josephine had possessed them too. Most footmen were chosen for their looks and height, and this one, as he executed a perfect bow to her, was no exception. No wealthy homeowner wanted their guests being greeted by short and unattractive young men, and this one was both tall and handsome.

He released her hand and stood back, his expression bland and giving nothing away. The realization that no one here might know who she was dawned, and color rose to her cheeks. What was she supposed to do? Introduce herself? This was followed by the awful possibility that they wouldn't believe her when she did so. After all, they must know that Lord Dunster was not the marrying kind.

The butler, another handsome man, this time with iron-gray

hair that indicated he must at least be in his late forties, came to her rescue. He made her a deep bow. "Lady Dunster, I presume. Welcome to Luxborough. His Lordship sent word a few days since of his intention to marry, but we had not thought to be blessed by your presence so soon. I must apologize in advance if the house is not quite to your taste. Given more warning, we could have prepared everything to your liking more efficaciously."

So Jonathan had warned his country house servants of his marriage plans. How thoughtful of him. Possibly. Although perhaps he hadn't thought they would be meeting their new countess so soon.

The butler put a hand to his own chest. "Allow me to introduce myself and your servants to you. Lucas is my name. Mrs. Burke is your housekeeper. Mrs. Lovell your head cook." He went on, naming the servants where they stood in line, one or two of the younger ones a little flustered as though they'd been summoned in haste when the carriage was seen approaching, but the names were meaningless to Verity. All she could think of was the fact that he'd called them all *her* servants. She, a young lady who'd never had anyone other than the nanny at Grandmama's Dower House, now had a house brimming with staff. All of whom merged with no difficulty into a blur of unrecognizable faces.

She caught Lucas glancing surreptitiously at the carriage. Was he looking for his master? Perhaps she ought to say something.

She cleared her throat and concentrated on him as the one person whose name she could remember. "Lord Dunster has not accompanied me, I'm afraid, Lucas, but I'm certain I will find no fault in the house." She tried a smile in what she hoped was a friendly fashion. A mere week at Aunt Josephine's had not been sufficient to accustom her to dealing with servants, especially not upper servants.

"I'm sure I will be most happy here," she added, wondering if she was lying. The whole house, beautiful and impressive as it was, looked far too large to be welcoming and cozy. She already felt out of place and clumsy and she wasn't even inside the front doors yet, as if everything she was doing might be wrong. If only she were back with Papa in their small, safe lodgings. They seemed very far away. Her stomach did a convulsive flip and she sensed tears forming at the corners of her eyes. Tears for the life she'd never have again. Despite all its difficulties and problems, it suddenly took on the mantle of safety and normality.

Lucas did not appear to have noticed the threat of tears, or if he had, he was tactfully ignoring them. "If you would be so gracious as to step this way, my lady," he said, and she preceded him up the steps and into the loggia.

If it had been open all the way through once, it was not now. On the far side, doors gave onto what looked like an enormous courtyard, but this was not where they were going. Instead, the butler guided her, as though he were a shepherd herding a refractory sheep, into a vast entrance hall.

Without a doubt, the inside of the house was even more splendid than the outside. Whoever had chosen the contents must have had bottomless pockets. It made the house in Cavendish Square look sparse and shabby by comparison, and Aunt Josephine's house like a humble hovel. Although perhaps she was exaggerating that comparison a bit due to the awe the place was inspiring in her. This was like a palace. Like Versailles, which she had seen as a child and vaguely remembered. Like somewhere a queen should live, not a humble young woman such as herself.

Followed by Bessie, who to do her credit did not look at all overawed, she crossed the marble tiles, the clacking of hers and Bessie's boots loud in the silence, to where a pair of wide staircases, one on either side of the hall, rose to meet each other on the floor above. A shadowy galleried landing surrounded the empty space, and an ornate, highly decorated ceiling hung over everything, light allowed in through a vast glass dome.

Never had she seen such splendor, even at Versailles. Every

wall was covered in paintings of people in old-fashioned clothing who had to be past earls and their families, and she had to do her best not to stare like some kind of country bumpkin. The trouble was, though, that she *was* a country bumpkin, no matter the family she'd been born into.

In the long hours she'd had since leaving London behind, she'd had time to speculate as to what Luxborough House would be like, and her imagination had never furnished her with such a spectacle. Without doubt, she would never fit in, even if she were to live here forever, quite alone and never bothered by her new husband. This was not somewhere she could ever call home. Not somewhere, she feared, that could ever be a home for anyone. She began to have an inkling as to why Jonathan was the way he was.

Running footsteps echoed from above in the gallery. A slight figure appeared at the head of the stairs, leaning precariously over the wrought iron bannisters. A girl, long dark hair streaming over her shoulders and framing a pert, elfin face. With a squeal of delight, she straightened and hurled herself down the stairs at a run. At the foot, she skidded to a halt in front of Verity and stared up at her.

She was short, but, from her blossoming figure, perhaps fifteen years of age, with large, dark eyes, that seemed somehow familiar to Verity, brimming with excitement. "Are you she?" she asked, a trifle breathlessly. "Tell me you are." An abrupt introduction if ever there was one, but Verity was not taken aback. She had experience in meeting young girls such as this one.

Having no idea who this girl was, though, nor what she was talking about, she could think of nothing to say in answer to her question.

The girl reached out and caught hold of her hand. "You must be my new sister, I am sure. Jonathan wrote to Grandmama several days since to inform us of his coming marriage, but I had no hope that he would come down here to see us at last, and bring you with him." She peered past Verity. "Where is he? At the carriage still? Did he perhaps ride one of his horses down? I cannot wait to see him." She released Verity's hand and ran to the door. But the carriage had gone, presumably round to the stables. And of course, there was no sign of Jonathan.

The girl turned back, her expression abject. "He is not here, is he?" Her shoulders sagged in eloquent despondence. "I thought it too good to be true that he would come." She met Verity's curious gaze. "And it seems he has condemned you also to exile here at Luxborough."

Exile. Was that what he'd sent her here for? Did she even care?

Those eyes. Of course. They were Lord Dunster's eyes. "Might you be His Lordship's sister?" she asked.

The girl nodded in delight. "His half sister, if we are to be honest with one another. And as we are to be friends, a matter I have already decided, then honesty is by far the best option. I am certain you will agree with me on this."

"Half sister?"

The girl nodded. "And in the interest of complete honesty, I must inform you that my mother was not married to my father, so I am not precisely legitimate."

She had such an air of confidence about her that Verity could not possibly have held this against her. Besides which, she very much wanted a friend herself. She smiled. "But what is your name, if we are to be friends? Mine, as you perhaps already know, is Verity."

The girl laughed, a joyous peal that echoed round the lofty hallway, managing to sound very much out of place. "And mine is Katherine. Although of course, you may call me Kitty, as almost everyone does. Even Grandmama, when she can remember who I am." She wrinkled her nose. "Which is not all that often nowadays."

"Delighted to make your acquaintance, Kitty." The sensation that she was going to need a friend loomed large, and this frank and open girl seemed an ideal candidate.

"And yours." Kitty shook her hand with vigor. "And delighted to at last have someone young living here apart from the maids. This place is like a mausoleum. Everyone here is so old."

Verity took a glance at the butler, who fulfilled this description admirably, and the footman, who did not. Perhaps if you were only fifteen everyone over twenty looked old. Did Kitty think her new friend was also old? A disturbing thought.

"Now," Kitty declared, as though she'd just reached a momentous decision. "I will take you up to your room. As countess, it will be the best bedroom, of course, beside Jonnie's when he is home…" Her voice trailed off. "Not that he ever is. But we won't think about that. Come along. Send Bessie off to retrieve your luggage and I'll take you up." She seized Verity's hand again and hurried her up the stairs.

The best bedroom was, in keeping with the rest of the house, large and splendid. A velvet-canopied bed stood halfway along one picture-hung, paneled wall and a Chinese rug covered the floor almost to the edges of the room. Every exquisite piece of furniture, from the chaise longue in the window to the footstools and dressing table, must be both old and valuable. Would she even dare to use such beautiful objects? Never had she slept in a room such as this, not even when Papa had been flush with money after a particularly successful ruse.

"You like it?" Kitty asked. "It is my favorite bedroom of all. In fact, I have on occasion sneaked in here to spend the night. My governess, Miss Bligh, has no idea I do that, or she would be most annoyed."

"You have a governess?" Not something Verity had ever had. Everything she knew she'd learned either from her own grandmother or from Papa.

Kitty wrinkled her nose and nodded. "She attempts to teach me French and reckoning and music and how to write a polite letter, but she says my head is always in the clouds and I don't listen." She beamed. "I fear she may be correct in that. Luckily for her, and me, of course, she's only expected to teach me in the mornings. She is the unmarried sister of our local vicar, so she returns after luncheon to the vicarage to assist her brother in doing things like writing sermons and visiting the sick and elderly. Which is why she is not here, keeping an eye on me." She dimpled. "To my utmost relief."

Verity went to the window and looked out. Wherever they were in the house, this window gave onto a sweeping slope down to a long lake. "Who else lives here then? Just you and your grandmother?" Who must be Lord Dunster's grandmother as well.

"Just us," Kitty said with a deep sigh. "And I suppose you could say all the servants, too. Shocking how many we require just for two of us. But I'm not allowed to associate with them." Did the twinkle in her eye betray the fact that this was not a rule she followed? She chuckled. "Which is why it's so boring. Of course, there's also Jonnie's mama, but she lives in the Dower House, and we never see her and someone told me she's a witch." Her smile widened. "She is not all that fond of me, you see, which I consider a witch-like thing."

Verity ignored the fact that Kitty thought Jonnie's mother a witch. But her dislike of her husband's illegitimate offspring made sense. But what was she doing being brought up in this house as though she was one of the family? Verity had come across more than a few illegitimate offspring in her adventures, and none had been provided for as this girl had been. Best not to enquire about that though. Not yet, at any rate. Kitty seemed the sort of girl given to confidences, so no doubt she would find out soon enough.

She scanned the extensive parkland. "Where abouts is the Dower House?" Where her mother-in-law, who didn't like this vivacious girl, lurked. Possibly a place to be avoided. She could foresee no scenario where this woman would like her any more than little Kitty.

Kitty pointed to the right. "Off over there. I never walk or ride in that direction, and Lady Dunster never comes to the house. I've heard she can't. And she doesn't get on with Grandmama, which might be because Grandmama supported Jonnie in letting me be brought up here in the house. Or it might just be because she's a mean old witch, as I said. One of the maids told me that because she's friends with a maid at the Dower House." She gave an expansive shrug. "Although, of course, you are now Lady Dunster so she is now just the Dowager Lady Dunster. The second of that name, as Grandmama is also the Dowager Lady Dunster still, I suppose." She beamed. "I find I like it that Jonnie's mama has been demoted somewhat."

Three Lady Dunsters within a very short area. And she, Verity Farrington, was one of them. Only she was Verity Wintringham now. She mustn't forget.

Even though she'd not met the younger dowager, Verity found herself agreeing with her new friend. Meeting her mother-in-law might well be something to be put off indefinitely. Although she had a sinking feeling it would be bad manners to do so. She'd think about it. "I think I will be keeping to the house and this part of the park, in that case. Thank you for the warning."

Kitty shrugged. "She may take to you, I suppose, as you have married her precious son. Last time Jonnie was here, I heard him telling his friend Walter how angry he was with his mother because she kept asking when he was to be married. He laughed and said he'd far rather seduce young ladies than marry them." She frowned. "Which means, in that case, that you are going to have to reveal to me how it is that he chose to marry you rather than just seduce you. I need to know everything, you know, or I shall not be satisfied."

Her ingenuous smile removed the import of her words, and Verity discovered that she had a burning urge to unburden herself to another human being who might not be so biased as Aunt Josephine or Papa or Walter. Someone who might put her own happiness before the perceived benefit of marrying an earl and all that entailed. Her family probably hadn't foreseen her exile to Jonathan's country estate when they'd been doing their plotting.

CHAPTER FIFTEEN

Bessie's arrival with the luggage forestalled the confession already brewing on Verity's lips. This might have been a good thing. After all, she'd only just met Kitty and had no idea whether so young a girl could keep such a secret. And from what she'd seen of her so far, this felt like a wise decision. For now.

So she sat in the window while Bessie unpacked and Kitty made appreciative noises about the wardrobe Aunt Josephine had furnished her with in such a short time. Gazing out at the vista of the apparently endless parkland, which seemed to stretch to a hazy, tree-covered green horizon, she began to wonder if life here might not be too bad if she had a friend such as the expansive Kitty.

At last, she was able to send Bessie off to go and sort her own accommodation and unpacking out, and Kitty joined Verity in the window. She sat down and seized Verity's hand. "I've noticed you have some very beautiful gowns, but I'm afraid you'll be disappointed as we don't dress for dinner here. In fact, we eat in our rooms. Grandmama cannot leave hers, for she's too feeble to walk far and has to use a Bath chair which no one can be bothered to get down the stairs, and I'm not considered important enough to merit a meal being served in our rather grand dining room." She wrinkled her nose. "In fact, the only time we ever use the dining room is when Jonnie comes to visit. And as I've already said, that's not often. I think it might still be under dust sheets, unless Lucas has ordered them removed so you can dine there."

Verity patted Kitty's hand, heaving an inward sigh of relief at what seemed the informality of the dining practices. "I confess that is a comfort to me, as I am not at all used to formal meals in big dining rooms. I'm sure I would show myself up in front of the servants, so I think I should tell Lucas not to bother just for me." Papa's instructions on etiquette in this direction had been somewhat lacking, and the occasion to partake in a formal meal had scarcely ever arisen while they'd been in Europe. It had been difficult enough at Aunt Josephine's, with the vast amount of cutlery laid on the table for dinner, and she'd been dreading it being worse here.

Kitty cocked her head to one side, spaniel-like. "Oh." She paused, as though considering how to respond to this admission. She opted for tact. "I'm quite sure you wouldn't show yourself up. You've clearly never watched a mad old lady eat." Her grandmama, no doubt, who sounded as though she might well be senile, not mad at all. "But in that case, would you be happy if we were to eat together? In one of our rooms? I should love it if we could. Eating alone is so boring."

Verity nodded. "I would go so far as to say that I'd prefer it."

This made Kitty smile broadly, showing her small white teeth. "Back to being honest, I'm afraid. I just wanted to confess that you are not at all what I was expecting. Not the sort of wife I was afraid Jonnie might choose. Not at all. Of course, I've had no one to discuss this with as I'm not allowed to fraternize with the servants, so most of my speculation since I heard Jonnie had married has been inside my head." She wrinkled her nose. "And Miss Bligh is a bit of an old stick who doesn't like to gossip, so I get no succor there."

Verity smiled at this dismissal of the as yet unknown Miss Bligh. "She *is* a vicar's sister. Probably, not gossiping comes with the position. Vicars are supposed to be able to handle confidences."

"I thought that was only Catholic priests. And she's only his sister."

"I imagine it applies to a vicar and his family too." Curiosity got the better of her. "What sort of wife did you think he would marry, then?"

Kitty gave an unladylike chortle of mirth. "Well, not one like you, for certain. I know he likes lots of ladies, although Grandmama told me most of them are *not* true ladies at all. Not in the sense of being ladylike, at any rate, or they wouldn't allow themselves to be seduced by Jonnie. Once, when she was having a good day, she told me she thought Jonnie prefers having mistresses because he's afraid of commitment." She frowned. "Although I don't precisely know what she meant by that. But I did understand when she said he's never grown up properly. When he comes down here he's such good company and treats me as if I were just the same age as he is. When I was a child, he played all sorts of games with me, and he lets me stay up late and he even taught me to swim in the lake. I didn't tell Grandmama because she'd have said it was unladylike. We had to swim in our underwear and she'd have told me I was a hussy for doing that."

She laughed again. "I'm afraid Grandmama thinks every part of having fun is not very grown up. Although…on her good days she often plays cards with me, and sometimes chess. She says I'm a card sharp. I'm not at all sure what that means, either, but I think she says it because I always beat her. I can assure you I don't have to cheat. I'm just good at cards. Lucky, too. She also says I take after my father. So I suppose mine and Jonnie's father must have been as lucky at cards as Jonnie and me."

Verity burst out laughing. "I must say that I agree with a lot of what you say. My impression of my husband, so far, is that he's a little immature."

Kitty nodded with vigor. "Grandmama says it's his mother's fault."

Her grandmama might well be right.

Kitty, whose attention span seemed alarmingly short,

shrugged this conversation off and leaned forward. "If I tell you something, will you promise not to tell Grandmama, or...or Jonnie if he ever deigns to visit?"

Outside, a peacock in full display plumage strutted across the grass. How decadent. Wasn't this the same sort of decadence that had led to the French Revolution and the aristos having their heads chopped off by the guillotine?

Verity nodded. "We are friends now, are we not? Of course I won't tell anyone."

Kitty's eyes twinkled. "Well, in that case I will confess that I do have one other friend. Meggie. She's my maid. She's the same age as me and we are special friends and have no secrets from one another. None whatsoever. So when I want someone to talk to, I find her. But I'm not supposed to be friends with a servant, as she's not of the same class." She gave an eloquent shrug. "Although my mother was a servant here in this very house, so really, I am half servant myself and fail to see what the problem is. Clearly my father had no problem fraternizing with the servants."

Verity's interest was piqued. "Where is your mother now?"

Another shrug. "I'm afraid she died when I was born, so I never met her. Actually in the act of giving birth, so Grandmama told me. I don't miss her as I've never known what it is to have a mother. And after I was born and she died, Jonnie insisted that I should be brought up here in the house, not be handed over to one of the tenant farmers' wives to bring up as their own. He insisted I was one of the family, even though his mother wanted me gone." A flush of pleasure warmed her pale cheeks. "Grandmama said so too. She backed Jonnie up against his mother even though he was hardly older than I am now."

That was a bit of a revelation. Jonnie, as she was now beginning to think of him, had certainly been nothing more than a boy himself when that happened. That a boy who had just come into an earldom would want his father's by-blow to be treated as one of the family was interesting. Not the act of an immature person, but more one of accepting generosity. Perhaps he wasn't quite so bad as she'd thought. But no, she wasn't going down that avenue.

Kitty must have read her mind. "My real father was dead, you see, long before I was born. He was the Old Earl. He fell down the stairs right here in this house. It wasn't the fall that killed him, but the landing at the bottom—Grandmama told me that. Broke his neck. So he never laid eyes on me, and Jonnie declared I was not to be forgotten. He said he would rather forget his papa than me. And he was the new earl then, you see, so everyone had to do as they were told." She smiled again. "Even though he wasn't yet seventeen himself, he put his foot down. He told me that." She paused. "He's very good to me, you know." Her face softened into a smile. "I love him dearly and wish he came to visit more often."

Verity smiled. "That's a very dramatic tale." But she was still wondering about Jonnie's concern for his little, orphaned half sister. Somehow, it didn't seem to fit with the impression he'd given her in London. There, she couldn't have imagined him caring for anyone except himself. And yet, here...this child seemed to view him as her lifelong benefactor.

Kitty nodded. "And I suspect yours might be as well. So, before your maid comes back, tell me how you managed to persuade Jonnie to marry you. I can't quite believe he's changed his mind about marriage. Isn't there a saying about the tiger not changing his spots?"

"The leopard, not the tiger." Verity swallowed. Who was this child going to tell if she revealed the whole sordid mess behind her marriage? No one. Well, perhaps her maid. And servants were renowned for their gossip. "I will tell you," she said, "if you promise me not to even tell Meggie."

Kitty nodded. "I promise faithfully that whatever you tell me shall remain between just the two of us, so help me God." She crossed her heart with a flamboyant wave of one hand.

She certainly had a flair for the dramatic.

Verity glanced out of the window again but the peacock had

gone. "Well," she said, "it all began with a game of cards."

AFTER A QUIET supper in the entertaining company of her new friend, Verity retired to bed early and slept until the morning, her dreams troubled only from time to time by the tall dark stranger to whom she was now married, wide lakes, and a house whose corridors stretched on forever.

She awoke to find her heavy curtains were being thrown back to fill the bedroom with bright morning light. Kitty, dressed in a flowered muslin gown that might have fitted her well two years since, bounced onto the end of the bed with disturbing enthusiasm.

Verity sat up and rubbed her eyes. Thanks to Papa's nocturnal lifestyle, she was more used to late mornings, and the last thirty-six hours had been draining. However, now she was awake and the bright day glimpsed beyond the window appeared to be so promising, she might as well stir herself. At heart she was a girl who preferred the mornings, and she'd only adapted herself to suit Papa's vagaries.

"Good morning, Verity." Kitty bounced up and down on the bed a bit more. It was a very soft and bouncy bed, which had contributed to a mainly good night's sleep. Verity's dreams receded into dim shadows and vanished away.

"And a very good morning to you, Kitty." She pushed her covers back and slid out of bed, the silk rug luxurious beneath her bare feet.

"I came to wake you up and bring you down for breakfast," Kitty said. "I, I mean we, take it in the breakfast room. Just me mostly. Grandmama eats in her room, as you might imagine. She hasn't been downstairs for years." She threw open the wardrobe. "And after breakfast, I want to take you exploring. What are you going to wear?"

Verity eyed the opulent selection Aunt Josephine had purchased for her and let her eyes slide past it to her few faded, and beloved, old gowns. If she was going out and about, as Kitty so obviously wanted her to, then one of them would do best. She didn't want to risk damaging the smart gowns from the London dressmaker. "Ring the bell for my maid, then, and I'll get dressed."

An hour later, with breakfast behind them, they were free. "It's Saturday," Kitty explained when asked about Miss Bligh. "She doesn't come on Saturdays or Sundays. Thank goodness. She has to help her brother those days. I keep wishing he had more parishes, because then she'd have to help him more and couldn't be here so often. Last time Jonnie was here, I asked him about finding them some, but he only laughed. I don't think he appreciates how dull it is to have to sit in a classroom all by oneself when outside the window the world is passing one by. He went away to school, you see, and I have a suspicion that might be more fun than being taught at home. All by myself. I should very much like to have friends." For a moment she sounded melancholy before she brightened. "Although now I have you as a friend, as well as Meggie, things will undoubtedly look up."

Well, the world had never passed Verity by, but had rather thundered along with her caught in the middle of it. "Then let us make the most of your days of freedom," she said, her heart lightening by the moment. "And as it is such a beautiful day, perhaps you could show me the outside of the house, not the inside. I have never lived in a house with gardens before and have always wanted to."

Kitty bounded with further enthusiasm, like a skittish colt just turned out in a lush meadow. "Exactly what I think. The insides of houses are full of such boring things. You have to be careful not to knock things over and break them, you're not allowed to slide down the bannisters—which you must allow are immensely inviting—and even opening a window is frowned upon by Mrs. Burke."

"Remind me who Mrs. Burke is, please."

"The housekeeper."

Of course. Verity vaguely remembered her introduction

when she'd arrived.

They passed out of the door into the shady loggia. "I think perhaps you'd better tell me the names of the staff again, so I don't get things wrong. They were introduced yesterday but the only one I can remember is Mr. Lucas, the butler. And perhaps a little bit about them, which will help me to remember who is who."

Delighted, Kitty rushed into a rather indecipherable description of everyone residing and working within the house and gardens, that Verity had to struggle to make head or tail of. As they walked around the extensive and beautiful rose garden, she finally began to put names to posts, in between her informant giving her unnecessary information about the roses.

She learned that Mrs. Burke, the aforementioned housekeeper, was a woman Kitty did her best to avoid, for fear she would be told off. Mr. Lucas, on the other hand, was, according to Kitty, a sweetheart. Then there were the footmen—all four of them, which seemed a bit excessive. "All very handsome and very dull," Kitty sighed, plucking a large pink rose with delicate finger and thumb. She removed the thorns with neat pincer movements of her nails and set it behind her ear. "I am quite certain Jonnie has ordered them never to speak to me on pain of death. And I'm also quite certain he would carry out that punishment without batting an eyelid. He can be so very stern when he gets cross."

He could indeed. However, possibly a wise move on his part with so pretty a sister and a bevy of handsome young men working in the house.

Then there was Mrs. Lovell, the cook, for whom Kitty nurtured a deep fondness. "If I go to the kitchens, which I'm not supposed to do, Mrs. Lovell always has cake for me. I'm also not supposed to *eat* the cake, on Grandmama's orders, but as she's batty, I have no qualms about disobeying her. I mean, no cake? Whatever for? And Mrs. Lovell is quite happy in aiding and abetting me. She's a dear."

The housemaids were called Rose, Mary, Kate, and Janet, and

one of them, but Kitty wasn't sure which, was having a love affair with one of the footmen. She also didn't know which footman, but had heard the girls all talking about it together one morning when they didn't know she was up and about. "Whoever it is, they're going to get into dreadful trouble," Kitty said, with a wise shake of her head but a hint of salacious enjoyment. "My mother was a maid too, but she didn't waste her time on a footman, otherwise I wouldn't be here now."

"So she caught the eye of the Old Earl? She must have been almost as pretty as you." Which was true, for Kitty was quite the prettiest child Verity had ever met, with her dark hair and eyes and pale, unblemished skin.

Kitty nodded. "That's why I'm Jonnie's half sister, you goose." She clapped her hand over her mouth. "Oh. I shouldn't have called you that. I'm so sorry. Miss Bligh would be cross with me. I have such a habit of speaking before I think, she always says, and I fear she's right. You are a countess, after all, so I shouldn't call you a goose."

Verity laughed, something she hadn't felt like doing for over a week. For longer, in fact, as life with Papa had not often been inducive of merriment. "That's quite all right. I don't feel in the least bit like a countess, and you know exactly why not. If I am a goose, then you're more than welcome to point it out to me. I've so much going through my head that I'm getting it all muddled." She took Kitty's arm. "Is there a portrait of your papa, perhaps? I would very much like to see it if there is." What she really wanted to find out was how much Jonnie resembled his father, although she wasn't about to admit that even to herself. Surely that had been his picture on the wall in the house in Cavendish Square.

For some reason, Kitty's face took on a worried frown. "Of course. I should also like to show him to you. Only, also of course, you must remember I never met him. But if I had, I know quite well that I would have loved him, even though I know Jonnie didn't."

If that portrait in the house in Cavendish Square was one of her father, Verity wasn't convinced, having observed his stern expression and cruel mouth, that anyone could have loved him. And if Jonnie hadn't…

They linked arms. "It must have been hard for you growing up without mother or father." Verity might not have had her own parents until she was nine, but at least she'd had Grandmama before that, who had not been senile and bedroom-ridden, and Papa after that. She barely remembered her own mother, a woman who'd shown no interest in her for the brief time they'd known one another. The clearest memory of her she had was of the day she'd died, and how Papa had sobbed at her passing. And how he'd pushed her away when she'd tried to comfort him. The sensation that she was never going to be enough for Papa had begun then.

Kitty nodded, turning back towards the house. "I suppose it was quite hard, but I had dear Nanny Jarvis, which was like having a mother, I think. She'd been Jonnie's nanny too. She looked after me from when I was a baby until I was six, when Jonnie decreed I had to have a governess instead, because I was too big to be treated as a baby. Mean thing that he can be. But Nanny Jarvis lives in one of the estate cottages. She's a very old lady now, but I visit her every week and take her cakes from Mrs. Lovell. And other things…" Her voice trailed off. They were at the house now and entered through double doors off the wide terrace.

Verity found herself in a long hall with a huge stone fireplace, empty now, halfway along the opposite wall, and dark wood paneling on all the walls. "The Great Hall," Kitty said, lowering her voice to a whisper. "It's very old and said to be haunted. I don't come here very often." She shivered.

Verity glanced about the gloomy hall, half expecting to see some phantom emerge from the oak panels. "Who is it haunted by?" She kept her own voice down as well, perhaps fearful of disturbing otherworldly inhabitants.

Kitty's voice dropped further and she leaned closer. "One of my ancestors. Lots of greats but a grandfather of some kind. Legend has it he was the man who built this house. I think, or rather I've heard, that he stole the land from a monastery or abbey or something like that. They say the old abbot cursed him and he was haunted for the rest of his life by the ghosts of the dead monks, until he threw himself off the battlements because he couldn't stand their whispering any longer."

"Oh." Verity glanced over her shoulder at the still open doors where a shaft of bright sunlight was spilling in, but not daring to venture far. The rest of the gloomy hall seemed to have dampened its effect. Was it her imagination or could she herself hear faint whispers echoing around the walls? Might that be the ghostly monks? She shook herself free of the idea. "Is this the room with your father's portrait?"

Kitty nodded. "That's him, over the fireplace."

Verity looked. The portrait was large and ostentatious.

The Old Earl, Jonnie and Kitty's father, was portrayed sitting at a table, a pen in his hand, caught in the act of writing a letter, his expression faraway and pensive, as though his whole attention was on what to write. His free hand rested elegantly on his left leg and he wore a rust-colored banyan over a silk waistcoat and neckcloth. His graying hair was tied back from his face, revealing a man with a long nose and chin and a wide, intelligent forehead. Yes, this was the man whose portrait Verity had seen in Cavendish Square, only in this one he looked less stern and his mouth less cruel, and was clearly some years older than in the other painting. Perhaps it had been done not long before his accidental death.

But, now she knew Jonnie better and had another of his offspring to study, she saw he looked nothing like Kitty, nor much like the image she could conjure of Jonnie. Kitty's face, with her little pointed chin, pert nose, and wide eyes was quite a different shape to her father's. Jonnie was more like him than his sister was, but, even so, there must surely be more of his mysterious French mother in him than his autocratic-looking father. A little odd that Kitty was not like either of them, but perhaps she took after her own dead mother.

Kitty had moved on. "And this," she said, in tones of deep gloom, "is the new dowager countess. The one living in the Dower House who doesn't like me."

Verity followed her and halted in awe. The Dowager's portrait, which was smaller than her husband's, took her breath away. It had clearly been done when its subject was very young, for the woman in the picture glowed with the bloom of youth from her jet-black tresses via her alabaster skin to her suggestively parted, ruby lips. She was a beauty by anyone's standards, and by the look of her, she knew it. Her knowing, dark eyes held promise, her whole bearing enticed the watcher to drink her in and be impressed. Verity had the sensation that the artist had captured her very soul with his brush, perhaps soon after her wedding. The only other time she'd seen a woman with such obvious allure had been in a high-class brothel in Florence. And that woman had been one of the main attractions for the rich clientele.

Easy to see this was the same woman whose portrait she'd seen in the Cavendish Square parlor with the little boy at her side. A boy who'd grown up to be her husband. Only that portrait had been bucolic in comparison, and very much a portrait of a mother. This one, by contrast, was the sort of painting a man might commission of the love of his life. A man besotted, perhaps.

But the most interesting thing about this portrait was how very much Kitty resembled the woman who was not her blood relative, although in a softer, more innocent fashion. Jonnie's mother had the same wide eyes and tilt to her nose, and her chin was just like Kitty's. How very odd.

"She's French," Kitty said, as though that explained everything, interrupting Verity's ponderings.

Verity nodded. "My own mother was French as well. Breton, in truth."

Kitty pursed her lips. "So you and Jonnie have that in common, at least."

But it was most likely the only thing they did have.

CHAPTER SIXTEEN

THAT AFTERNOON, HAVING partaken of a light luncheon together in the only drawing room not under dust sheets, Kitty insisted on taking Verity to meet her grandmother. "Grandmama will be vexed if I don't take you up," she said, when Verity attempted to resist. "She might be confined to her bedroom, but on her good days she knows everything that goes on here at Luxborough, and if today is a good day, she'll be well aware of your presence."

"She's aware that Lord Dunster and I are married?"

Kitty gave a trill of girlish laughter. "I do wish you would not call him Lord Dunster. Here, amongst the family, he is always Jonnie." She paused. "I understand that you have no cause to wish to do so, at present, but Grandmama will find it strange if you keep on calling him by his title." She leaned closer, as if afraid the walls had ears. "And of course, only you and I know the truth about your marriage." She took Verity's hand. "You will love Grandmama, I'm sure. Come along."

Verity sighed, pushing aside the nagging doubt that confiding in Kitty might not have been such a good idea. Although what the old Dowager was going to think about Verity arriving on her own at Luxborough within a day of her marriage, she had no idea. But Kitty had implied the old lady was bordering on senile, so perhaps she wouldn't realize so short a time had passed. Behind her back, she crossed her fingers.

The dowager countess had her rooms in the west wing of the house, opening off a long corridor whose windows overlooked the square inner courtyard. Verity peered out of these windows as she passed, overawed by the size of this house. Never, in all Papa's travels and his ups and downs of finance, had she ever even seen a house as splendid as this one, still less thought to enter it. To live in it, in fact, as the chatelaine. The thought should perhaps have filled her with excitement, but instead, it sent a shiver of foreboding down her back that was impossible to shake off. She was never going to be rid of the sensation of being an intruder, as out of place as a beggar in a palace. Which was exactly how she felt.

Kitty knocked on a large, oak door, and, without waiting to be asked to enter, pushed it open. The dowager inhabited a suite of rooms opening one off the other and the room they found themselves in was furnished as a somewhat old-fashioned drawing room, with a chaise longue by the window and other comfortable but nonmatching seats scattered about. Almost as though someone had gone around the house like a magpie, snatching furniture from whatever room they chose. An unmistakeable air of the previous century hung about it, and the stuffy air was redolent with an overpowering scent of violets, heavy and cloying to Verity's nostrils. The windows, despite the warmth of the day, were firmly closed.

She let her eyes scan the room, searching for its occupant.

She proved difficult to spot. The old lady, a tiny, shrunken figure almost camouflaged amongst all the furniture, occupied a Bath chair which stood near the empty fireplace. She turned her head as Kitty bounded into the room, ever the skittish colt. "Grandmama, it's Kitty come to see you."

A pair of faded-blue eyes fixed her granddaughter with a gimlet stare, sharp with intelligence and curiosity, and not at all with the confusion Verity had been expecting to encounter. "I can perfectly well see it is you, child," she snapped. "I have not gone blind since last you were here, which I believe was only yesterday." Her gaze slid past Kitty to rest on Verity, who bobbed a hurried and not all that elegant curtsy.

"Good afternoon, Lady Dunster."

The dowager looked her up and down, giving Verity the uncomfortable sensation she was being assessed. After a pause that was a fraction too long, she harumphed loudly. "And I suppose you must be the chit my grandson has got himself married to?" She did not sound in the least bit friendly.

How to answer that? Politely. Verity was experiencing a strong urge to make a pert reply. Good sense won over. "You are correct in your assumption, Lady Dunster." She was having trouble keeping from staring at the monumental gray wig the old lady was wearing. It towered above her dwarfing her frail body and looked as though the least gust of wind would send it bowling away across the floor of her parlor. Very much the fashion of the last century, and probably not the most recent decade of it.

The old lady gave a cackle of laughter that shook her tiny frame. "Come closer, child, and let me have a better look at you. I may not be blind, but my century's not far off now, and my sight's not of the best."

Verity approached the Bath chair and halted six feet off, hands demurely clasped behind her back.

The old lady lifted a quizzing glass to one eye, which magnified it to the point of being startling, and further peered at her visitor.

Verity waited.

"What's your name, child? I seem to have let that piece of information slip my mind."

"Verity, Lady Dunster."

The old lady nodded. "A good old-fashioned name. Truth. I like it. My grandson could have done no better than to shackle himself to a girl whose name means truth. Could do with a bit of truth around here, mark my words."

What an odd thing to say. Verity stayed silent.

"Come," the old lady said. "Sit down here and talk to me. Kitty can order us some tea." She paused. "And over there, child, on the sideboard, there's my port. I'll have a glass of that before the tea arrives." She dissolved into a cackle of laughter once again, her small, bird-like body shaking with a mirth Verity didn't understand. When she finally subsided, she slapped her knee, which, by the look of the rest of her, must be very bony. "People have often asked me the recipe for my long life, young Verity. And I tell them a glass of port for breakfast, one at luncheon, one in the middle of the afternoon, one at dinner in the evening, and one before bed. That's how I've reached ninety-nine years old."

"Ninety-seven," Kitty whispered, before heading to pull the bell rope to summon a servant, and fetch the port. She poured a generous measure of the rich red liquid into what looked like a whisky tumbler and brought it back for her grandmother.

No sipping here. Lady Dunster knocked it back in one go and smacked her wrinkled lips in relish. "Nothing like port to preserve the body beautiful."

If she drank that much port five times in any one day then she was probably pickled.

Verity sat down on a seat near the dowager and Kitty joined her.

"Now," the old lady said. "Tell me all about yourself. What was your name before your marriage?"

That bit was easy. It was the next bits she was fearing. Perhaps she could distract the old lady into talking about the Farrington family, at least just the bits of it that were respectable. All hope of this being an interview with someone who was not quite compos mentis had already faded.

"This is a good day," Kitty whispered under her breath, as if she'd heard Verity's thoughts.

"What? What's that you say?" the dowager almost shouted. At least she appeared to be relatively deaf.

"I was saying what a nice day it is," Kitty said, the lie coming smoothly to her. Impressive.

Seeming satisfied, the dowager gave Verity a peremptory nod. "Your family?" It was a querulous prompt.

Verity swallowed and fixed a pleasant smile onto her face. "My uncle is Viscount Somerton."

The dowager nodded as though she knew who Verity was referring to. "That pipsqueak." What would Uncle Adolphus have to say about being described thus? "Knew his father when I was a girl. Danced with him when I had my coming out in Town. Very handsome man." Her expression softened. "Remember the sons when they were little boys in the nursery."

She must mean Papa as well as Uncle Adolphus. Verity quelled the impulse to ask the old lady about Papa as a boy. He'd always seemed so old to her it was impossible to imagine him as a child in the nursery.

The dowager kept going. "Don't live too far off. Wiltshire, ain't it? Been to the house for a few balls in my time." She paused. "Not such a fine house as this one, mind you. Nowhere near as big. Not that I can get about in it any longer. Getting old's not much fun, I can tell you. Make the most of being young, both of you, or you'll regret it later."

Nothing could be such a fine house as this one, but Verity didn't say so. Instead she kept the bland smile fixed on her face. "I was married from my uncle's house in London," she tried. It was hard to think of things she could say without giving away too much, positive as she was that the dowager would be horrified to hear of the circumstances that had led to her marriage.

Kitty bounced on the seat beside her. "She has the most beautiful gowns I've ever seen." She sounded wistful. Did no one here ever provide the poor child with new gowns of her own? The one she was wearing should have been replaced at least a year ago. Not that Verity's clothing had been much different until little more than a week since. She had a lot to thank Aunt Josephine for.

"Gowns don't make a lady," Kitty's grandmother snapped. "As well you know."

"But they do make a lady look nice," Kitty retorted, unabashed.

Her grandmother tapped the closed fan she was holding on the arm of her Bath chair. "Do not try being pert with me, young lady. You're not too old for me to have you spanked and confined to your bedroom for the rest of the day."

Kitty assumed a contrite expression and hung her head. "I'm sorry, Grandmama." Although Verity doubted very much this was true.

With Kitty silenced momentarily, she seized the opportunity to direct the conversation. "You must have seen a lot of change here at Luxborough in your time?"

The old lady sucked her lips in over what appeared to be toothless gums and nodded. "I was married at seventeen and that was over eighty years ago now. There's been a lot of changes here over the years, although before that woman took over the Dower House, I lived there after my Marcus died. A long time ago now." A hint of resentment had entered her voice. "Had to give it up when my daughter-in-law, that infernal French woman, became a widow herself. Had the cheek to demand it of me as though it were her right. Though, if we're being pedantic, she's only merited the title of dowager since your wedding, missy."

So the other dowager, Jonnie's mother, had removed herself from the main house possibly the moment her husband had died. Had that had anything to do with Kitty's arrival, and her beloved brother Jonnie's determination she should be treated as part of the family? She must have been incensed at the idea of housing her late husband's illegitimate child. Could that have made her up and depart for a completely different house?

"I have not as yet had the pleasure of meeting the other Lady Dunster." How odd it was to be one of three living Lady Dunsters. Awkward at the least.

The Dowager, whose sagging, wrinkled cheeks had flared with spots of angry red, hawked and spat into the cold fireplace. "Pah. You'll not find much pleasure in her company, I can assure you. A pox on the woman. The only good thing she ever did in her life was to give me my Jonnie and then take herself off in a huff sixteen years later. We can do without her here."

Well, there was no dissembling with her. Interesting to find the old lady in agreement with her granddaughter. Verity thought of the portrait in the haunted hall and a shiver ran down her spine. The other countess did not look like the sort of woman she could take to. She was inclined herself to agree with the consensus of opinion, even though she'd not met her yet. And forewarned was always forearmed.

It might be a good idea to steer away from subjects that made her hostess angry. "The house is most impressive," Verity tried.

"Were you brought up at Somerton?" the dowager asked. "Beautiful house. Parts of it a sight older than this one." She waved a dismissive hand. "This place was built from scratch towards the end of the sixteenth century, but Somerton goes back a century or more before that. Lovely old place. Always liked it but I don't suppose I'll ever see it again now. Can't get about any longer. Can't even get out of this chair on my own. Old age can be most humiliating."

This was easier to answer. "When I was a child, I lived in the Dower House with my own grandmother. About a mile from the main house, across the park. I had a very happy childhood there. My grandmother was a wonderful woman."

A snort of laughter. "And you think I might not be?" The old lady reached out a liver-spotted and skeletally thin hand and seized Kitty's small plump one. "You tell her, child, whether I'm a wonderful woman or not."

Kitty made no move to escape, but turned her cheerful face to Verity. "Grandmama is the nicest person here at Luxborough, you can be certain."

Was she? So far Verity had only seen an acerbic and dictatorial old lady. That didn't say much for the rest of them.

Kitty must have seen the skepticism on her face, for she nodded with vigor. "When I was born and my mother died,

Grandmama backed up Jonnie against his own mother so that I could be brought up here, which I believe was one of the reasons his mother decided to retire to the Dower House."

Might the old lady have only done this to spite her hated French daughter-in-law and perhaps drive her from the house she considered her own? A distinct possibility.

Kitty beamed at her grandmother. "I may not be legitimate, but Grandmama has always treated me as though I was." She turned her own hand over and threaded her fingers through the old lady's bony ones. "I love her very much."

As for Kitty, she seemed to love everyone. Except Jonnie's mother, of course.

Was that the sparkle of real tears in those rheumy old eyes? The sensation that the love was mutual settled over Verity and made her smile. She spoke from the heart. "You are both very lucky to have each other." If only her own grandmother had not died, how different would her life be now? "Your grandmother has you to brighten her days, and even though you have no mother, in its place you have the love of a grandmother, which I know is a treasure beyond all other things." Both of them had grown up without a mother's care. They had much in common, which might be why she'd felt so confident in revealing her secret to Kitty.

The dowager retrieved her hand and harumphed. "That's as may be, but don't I recall that young whippersnapper viscount uncle of yours having a ne'er-do-well brother? Is that man your father, missy? I assume he must be."

There was nothing for it. "He is indeed my papa."

The sparse eyebrows, that had been painted in with a harsh line of black, rose towards the old lady's impressive wig. "And if my memory serves me right, which it so often don't, didn't your papa leg it to the Continent with yet another French hussy? Seems to me there are all too many French hussies in your combined families."

Determined not to allow herself to be offended and cause a

scene, as, after all, she was dealing with someone very old who probably thought she could say exactly what she thought, Verity had to nod. "Although I have no knowledge of whether my mother was a hussy or not, as I knew her for so short a time before she died. She was not…interested in her child."

The dowager nodded. "If she was French, then she was a hussy. Just like my daughter-in-law. All the Frenchies are either hussies or revolutionaries and not to be tolerated." Those startling brows formed a heavy frown as she glanced at Kitty. "We've had enough of scheming French hussies around here, haven't we, child?"

Kitty nodded with enthusiasm.

This conversation was becoming more and more confusing. Obviously the old lady's dislike of the French was rooted in her dislike of Jonnie's mother. This was a rather sweeping statement as Verity knew well that not all French women were hussies. But it would not be good to provoke an argument in any way on so short an acquaintance and with so elderly a lady. However, from what she knew of her own mother, it was entirely possible the old lady might be correct in her case.

Without warning, the old lady suddenly sank back into her seat with a sigh, her eyes glazing over and staring sightlessly into the distance. Her whole body had deflated, the spark of life she'd been exhibiting doused, as though someone had blown out the candle of her mind.

Kitty leaned towards Verity. "She's having one of her turns. I'll fetch her nurse. She has the room next door. We'll get no sense out of Grandmama again today." She gave a little shrug. "We were lucky she was so receptive and alert, I suppose. She's like this." She waved her hand at her grandmother. "More often than not nowadays. Chatting away to me one moment and the next away with her head all befuddled."

And she departed to find the nurse.

Verity sat back in her seat, regarding the Dowager. Gone was the acuity and intelligence and in its place only the husk of a woman remained. And with it had gone the vitality that had been apparent when she'd first laid eyes on her. She now looked every one of her ninety-seven years. How cruel life was, to rob her like this of herself, to snatch away her memories of those she loved.

Verity had encountered an old man like this, far away now in a villa in Italy, outside Florence. Papa had wanted to steal his money, but seeing the state of their mark, Verity had refused. Papa had not been pleased, but he couldn't have done it alone. She could still see that old man's face as he smiled up at her out of eyes as rheumy and faded as the Dowager's, thinking she was his long-gone wife returned to him. She'd sat and held his hand until he'd slept, then crept away to rejoin Papa, full of guilt at what they'd been planning to do.

She wiped a tear away before Kitty and the nurse returned, not wanting them to see.

✦ ❧ ✦

CHAPTER SEVENTEEN

TWO DAYS AFTER her meeting with Kitty and Jonnie's grandmother, Verity encountered the woman both the older Dowager and Kitty seemed to nurture such an aversion to. As it was a Monday, Kitty was safely ensconced in the schoolroom with Miss Bligh, for whom Verity had formed an immediate liking when they'd been introduced.

Everything about the middle-aged governess shouted spinster sister of a vicar, from her austere and plain gown to her tightly constrained hair and sensible footwear. Had Verity been asked to conjure such a person up, she would undoubtedly have chosen to describe someone of Miss Bligh's upright appearance and briskly capable manner. And it had been obvious straight away that however Kitty liked to complain about her governess, in fact, both of them were very fond of one another. Miss Bligh possessed a pleasing twinkle in her gray eyes and an air of indulgence to her young charge.

So Verity had cherished no worries about abandoning her new young friend to her studies and, as the day was sunny and warm again, setting out to explore more of the rolling parkland. She went with the avowed intent of doing her duty, unpleasant though it might turn out to be, and calling upon the woman who was now her mother-in-law. Having already been at Luxborough long enough for it to be considered rude that she'd not yet done so, and despite an understandable reluctance, she could put it off no longer. Jonnie's mother deserved to meet her son's wife, even if she held that title in name only. She certainly wasn't about to reveal the truth to her. Let Kitty remain the only one she'd confided in.

And besides, she was going to enjoy an excursion into the wider area of the park, where her maid had told her, with obvious trepidation and wariness, she would find the Dower House. Although she'd spent the last fourteen years with Papa traveling from one European city to the next, she had, of course, grown up on an estate not dissimilar to this one, although considerably smaller, and had also experienced the pleasurable vagaries of Europe's countryside. Enough to know that it was the country-side she preferred to the bustle of city life.

Really, Lord Dunster, in dismissing her from his presence, could have done nothing kinder than dispatching her off to his country estate. A little part of her heart, especially as the day was so fine, would have liked to be able to thank him for the present he'd so unwittingly given her. And if she cared to admit it, she felt quite glad she was not at this moment back in heat-drenched France with Papa, on their way to his next victim. The stability of life at Luxborough was already creeping into her heart alongside a liking for not just Kitty and her slightly strange grandmother, but also for the house and gardens. And now the wide expanse of the park as well.

So, with a jaunty spring in her stride, and the least ostenta-tious of her new gowns on, matched with a pert straw bonnet, she set out from the house as soon as Miss Bligh had swept her pupil off to the schoolroom. Kitty's strident complaints could be heard echoing around the house as Verity let herself out of the front door, but she ignored them. Not that Kitty herself wanted to pay a visit to the younger Dowager, of course. No, the naughty girl just wanted to avoid a morning spent in the schoolroom.

In front of the house lay the redundant, and immaculate, circular gravel drive which should have enabled the easy dropping off of visitors. Not a single weed dared to mar its perfection. Not that it was likely any visitors would have the temerity to call. Kitty had informed her that no one had visited in over a year, the last arrival other than a Dr. Collins for her grandmother having been Jonnie himself, for a brief overnight stay. As this meant he hadn't been to his estate in more than a year, did it also mean she might be allowed to live her life here in peace? For some reason Verity wasn't quite as pleased about that as she felt she ought to be. With determination, she pushed that thought aside and set off across the drive's central circle of neatly mown grass. There must be a lot of gardeners here to maintain this perfection.

A low wall encircled the drive and, at the far side, the wrought iron gates through which her carriage had entered just a few days ago stood open. Beyond lay the rolling parkland she'd so far only glimpsed from the confines of the house and garden. Feeling as though she was making an escape, Verity stepped into the outer extremities of Luxborough Park.

Here, the grass had been grazed rather than mown, but was nearly as short and neat as the garden lawns. "Sheep," Kitty had said when Verity had first asked. "We have sheep to keep the parkland grass short. Because deer are browsers and mostly eat the trees. And although in the gardens we have lots of gardeners, at least one of whom keeps the grass everywhere trimmed, it would take hundreds of them to do the same for the acres of the park." She laughed. "And there's a pony who wears slippers on his hooves who pulls any machinery they need. When I was just a little girl, Arthur, the old head gardener, used to sit me up on the pony, whose name was Slipper, of course, because of his footwear, and lead me about the little paths in the rose garden." A pleasing image of a childhood not dissimilar to Verity's own. A childhood which for her had ended at the age of nine.

The estate's many sheep had been busy, with the inevitable result that Verity had to watch where she was putting her feet. However, undaunted, and glad her gown was not long enough to sweep the ground, she set off eastwards across the springy grass.

Her intent was to follow the line of the ha-ha that separated the formal gardens from the park, and take her maid's suggested shortcut towards the lake she could see from her bedroom window. For beyond the lake lay the road which would lead her to the Dower House.

Reflecting the clear blue of the sky in the most attractive fashion, this lake swung in a wide curve a little reminiscent of a giant comma, when viewed from the upper floor of the house. However, from down here, it disappeared out of sight behind the house to her left, and to her right narrowed towards a long, five-arched stone bridge which was where she would have to cross the water. Here she escaped having to dodge around what the sheep had left behind and re-joined the gravel drive.

In the middle, she halted to view the park from this new angle, as the late morning sun beat down on her back and made her glad of her bonnet to protect her face. A countess needed to take care of her complexion rather more than the daughter of a professional gambler did.

Turning a slow circle on her heel, she observed how the park stretched away in every direction into a hazy beyond. To the north lay distant hills, while the boundaries of the other three points of the compass were forested in pleasingly mixed hues of green. Was all of this Lord Dunster's estate? As far as she could see? Bessie had implied it was. "The estate goes on for miles, milady. My ma and pa's farm is up near them hills, a goodly walk off. My ma says if you walk to Oxford from our farm, you do it almost all on Dunster lands."

Surely that wasn't true? No one should own that much unless they were a king or queen. Which made her think of poor Marie Antoinette of France, the news of whose execution she could just remember hearing as a child in the Dower House at Somerton. It had clawed itself a place in her head, for she'd been aware that her own parents, unknown to her as they were at that point in time, were in France, and that her mysterious, absent mother was French and possibly in danger. Fear for them had subsumed her for days, until Grandmama had assured her no one was about to execute some jumped up tavern-keeper's daughter. Which had also been the first she'd heard about her mother's less than noble origins.

Along one side of the lake waterlilies grew, their creamy cups open wide in adoration of the sunlight, their flat leaves green plates covering the water, no doubt harboring a good few frogs and such like. Further along, drooping willows stretched long fingers down to trail in the dark, shadowy depths. A walk around the lake would be a pleasure, perhaps with Kitty for company, but not one she could allow herself to indulge in this morning.

A lime avenue opened up before her, the trees throwing leafy shade to either side of the gravel drive. It headed south away from the house and the road which would lead back to the imposing gatehouse, and it was down here, according to the knowledgeable Bessie, that the Dower House lay. She'd been more than a little unwilling to offer directions, her eyes round with shock that her new mistress had shown a desire to visit "the French Dowager," which must be what the servants called her, and perhaps the tenants too. But Verity had wormed what she needed out of the girl.

The shade cooled her by-now-warm cheeks, for the day was fast becoming hot, and she strolled along, in no hurry, enjoying the sound of sheep bleating in the distance and birdsong in the trees. This lack of haste might also have been because now she was drawing nearer to her destination, she was experiencing a desire to put off what increasingly felt as though it would be a moment of confrontation. The meeting face-to-face with the striking woman from that painting in the haunted hall, who was one and the same with the woman in the portrait in the parlor in Cavendish Square.

The turning to the Dower House lay a bare two hundred yards down the avenue, unfortunately for Verity, who now found she had reached the point where she could no longer put off this encounter. Turning off the main drive, she found herself passing through a small wood which, after a few minutes' walk, led to high walls and a gateway flanked by tall stone pillars.

She stopped, aware of her heart hammering within her ribs at a ridiculous speed. If only Kitty, and Bessie too, had not implied this woman was a dragon. If only the old Dowager had not referred to her as a French hussy in such derogatory terms. If only one didn't have to be polite and introduce oneself to one's new relations but could pretend they didn't exist. But if she left it any longer, or worse, ran away now and didn't bother, Lady Dunster would be sure to know and consider it an insult. And she was not about to be thought rude.

She pushed one half of the gates open just enough to squeeze through, and, with reluctance, let it close behind her. Now she felt truly trapped, as though that click of its shutting had been the springing of a trap. But she was made of stern stuff and she was not about to allow the tales told by others to put her off. The dowager might turn out to be much nicer than she thought. Surreptitiously, she crossed her fingers. She had faced far worse things than a disdainful mother-in-law.

With a bravado that was anything but genuine, she marched up to the door and gave the bell rope a vigorous tug. The sound echoed inside as though the whole house might be empty. That would be the best possible outcome. No one would answer the door, and she could go home and claim she'd tried and failed.

No such luck. After a full minute, just when she was thinking of beating a hasty retreat, the door opened to reveal a liveried footman, his wig slightly lopsided as though he'd had to don it in a hurry. Perhaps the Dower House had as few visitors as the main house and he'd been slacking somewhere in deshabille.

"Good afternoon," Verity said with asperity. "I am here to call on the dowager countess."

By the look on the young man's face, this came as a big surprise. Perhaps her first surmise had been correct, and the French Dowager did indeed have as few visitors as the main house. The footman managed to remember himself enough to bow as he held the door open for her to enter. "Who shall I inform Her Ladyship is calling?" Clearly he had no idea who she might be. Or did he? Was he just checking so he didn't make a mistake?

Verity took off her gloves and risked a quick glance about the hallway she'd just stepped into. "You may tell Her Ladyship that her daughter-in-law has come to visit her."

There'd be no doubt about her identity now.

The young footman fought a losing battle as he struggled to control his expression and maintain a calm front. As surely everyone must know of her presence at the main house by now, the fact she was calling at all must be what was so shocking. Was there more to this than met the eye? Perhaps her mother-in-law hadn't thought she would be so bold as to visit. Which was odd in the extreme.

"If you would care to wait in the drawing room," the young man said and opened a door into a comfortably but flamboyantly furnished room.

To oblige him, Verity went in, and he closed the door behind her with what felt suspiciously like relief.

Determined not to be put off, as, after all, she'd braved worse situations than this in her life with Papa, and met plenty of supercilious European aristocrats in her time. This one was not going to intimidate her.

She stepped further into the room, taking in the opulence of the furnishings, which was extensive, although not quite so impressive as the main house. Perhaps some of the items of furniture had indeed come from there. One never knew.

Above the fireplace hung another portrait of the occupant, easily recognisable even though a good twenty years must have passed since she sat for the likeness Verity had seen of her in the haunted hall. In this new portrait she must have been in her early forties and what had been the allure of youth had matured into full-blown beauty. Her dark eyes, so strangely like Kitty's, seemed to follow Verity as she approached the portrait, gazing out from beneath flaring black brows that in turn resembled Jonnie's. Only a few strands of gray showed on her dark head, although that might have been artistic license on the part of the painter to give light to the mass of black curls. Or the other way around, of course. The painter might have minimized the effects of age out of politeness. So many did.

On the far wall another painting caught Verity's eye. A young boy of perhaps nine or ten years old stood beneath a tree beside a pair of black spaniels. Easily recognizable as Jonnie, older than in the Cavendish Square portrait and with his features more formed and less baby soft. He wore knee breeches, a tan coat, and stockings. Behind him, the parkland she'd just walked through rolled away, the sparkle of the lake recognizable in the distance. His inky hair hung in loose curls to his shoulders and his mother's, and Kitty's, dark eyes stared back at Verity reaching down the years to recreate the awkward way he'd made her feel on the first morning they met. He had his mother's sensuously curving lips, as well as those dark brows and seemed more like his mother than his father. How odd that Kitty was superficially like her as well.

The opening of the door disturbed her contemplation and she swung around. A woman stood framed in the doorway, one hand on the lintel and the other gripping an ebony stick. She was still beautiful, but her black hair had vanished to be replaced with pure white. Only the still smooth skin of her face gave the hint that she was not yet an elderly woman.

Verity sank into a curtsey. "Lady Dunster."

The French Dowager came into the room, her stick, on which she leaned as though in need of support, tapping on the floor with every step. She halted in front of the cold fireplace. "So," she said, with some relish and only the slightest of French accents, "you are the chit upon whom my wayward son has chosen to bestow his choice." She tutted and settled herself, with more than a hint of discomfort, into an upright chair. "Come closer and let me have a good look at you, child."

Verity stepped closer and was immediately struck by the

deformities in both of her mother-in-law's hands. She suffered from advanced rheumatics. Her knuckles were knobbly and reddened, her fingers bent, and, if anything, more claw-like than her own ancient mother-in-law's. And although her gown was beautiful, it couldn't disguise the stoop of her shoulders nor the curvature of her back. This was a woman whose body had grown old before its time, leaving her with joints as stiff and gnarled as those of a much older person, while still possessing the lovely, unblemished face she'd always had. Who could blame someone who must be in constant pain for being fractious?

Verity vowed to approach her with compassion.

Lady Dunster, the younger dowager, looked Verity up and down for a moment or two in silence before giving her a curt nod. "You may be seated."

Verity chose a chair as close to the old lady as she could, out of politeness.

Lady Dunster's sharp brows furrowed in a frown. "Now, you might be surprised to know that I am well aware of who you are." She chuckled to herself. "I have my spies everywhere since my body confined me to this house. I would die of boredom here if I didn't hear all the gossip from both here and Town. And I knew your father when I was a young bride myself, new to this bedeviled, rain-sodden country. So different from where I grew up in the valley of the River Loire. A very charming young man he was. Most amusing. I heard he ran off with a tavern keeper's daughter he met in France. I was not surprised. He had the heart of an adventurer, even then."

Good heavens. Verity had not expected anyone to know so much about Papa.

The old lady chuckled again with more than a hint of satisfaction. "I see I surprise you. I should also tell you that I know you've been brought up since you were nine on the Continent, so you have had a different experience of life to the milksop young ladies here in England. More like a French girl. A good thing, I would say. Insipid is the only word I could use to describe most

English girls. Insipid and featherbrained." She chuckled yet again. "If you are anything like your father, then you must be a girl without a feather in her brain at all, just real intelligence." She paused. "Am I right?" This last came out as a bark.

Taken aback by the ferocity of this question, Verity managed a nod. "No one has ever called me insipid or featherbrained, but I would not like to claim high intelligence. My father taught me to be modest about myself."

Her interlocutor snorted in amusement. "Well spoken. Only a fool would claim intelligence. Those with it have no need to blow their own trumpets."

Verity, who was having a hard time equating this lady, every bit as acerbic as the older Dowager, with the ravishing portraits she'd seen of her, could only nod. "I think perhaps you are correct."

The old lady chortled in appreciation, which made her cough. "I see you looking at me and pitying me trapped as I am in this prison of a body. You've seen my old portraits, no doubt."

She must possess psychic powers.

The dowager nodded. "Yes, I was young and beautiful once, and as I aged and my disease threatened to overtake me and rob me of most of my movement, the portrait painters have had to make adjustments. I do not care to be preserved on canvas as I am now. I give them liberty to make me young again. And beautiful."

Understandable. "You are still a beautiful woman," Verity said, as it was true.

Another snort. "My face, perhaps, but my body betrays me. But I can appreciate beauty in others when I see it. I was going to ask you how it is that my rake of a son has decided to marry, but looking at you, I think I can see why."

"That's very kind of you," Verity said, the impulse to reveal all to this woman, whom she wasn't meant to like but was beginning to feel an admiration for, loomed large. "I think it must be this lovely gown my aunt had made for me."

The old lady chuckled. "Now don't come all modest with me. You know perfectly well you're pretty. What girl doesn't? I certainly did when I was young and used it to best effect. I met Edward, my boy's father, in Paris when I was nineteen. Handsome devil he was, just like his son is now." Her eyes clouded. "I knew I wanted him the moment I laid eyes on him, but he was a rake and my father disapproved. Like father like son, I suppose, as Jonnie seems to have inherited his penchant for women from his father." She frowned. "My Edward was much the same age as Jonnie is now. He had no intention of marrying anyone, but I caught him. Despite indulging in all the excesses of a rake, he fell in love with me." Her eyes took on a faraway expression as though seeing her Edward as he'd been then. Verity wondered if a portrait of him at that age existed. It would be interesting to see how much Jonnie resembled him.

The old lady returned to the present. "And I see you've managed to do the same. Sensible girl. A wife is what Jonnie needs, to settle him down. He's sown his oats." She laughed, but it was a bitter laugh. "Been sowing them since he was a boy of fifteen." A frown marred her brow. "No harm in that, you'd think, but you might well not be right." She didn't sound as though she entirely believed what she was saying. "And now I suppose he needs to get himself a legal heir and turn away from his excesses." Another frown. "Or my sainted brother-in-law will get what he's always wanted. Luxborough. A man less suitable to preach to others I've yet to meet." She shook her head in what looked like anger. "Over my dead body, I swear it. Zut alors!"

"Your brother-in-law?" This presented a line of conversation she might find easier.

The dowager nodded. "Sylvester Wintringham. The man is a priest—an Anglican one so not a true man of God. He holds the living of St Mary-in-the-Vale, which is where my husband's family have always worshipped." She snorted. "Not me. I am of the old faith and have my own priest who comes here to give me communion." She shook her head. "But that is not what I wish to say to you. I will tell you about Sylvester, my husband's snake of a brother. Never would Edward believe me when I told him Sylvester wished for his title and the estate…and the money. Never. He was a fool and he thought nothing but good of the man who wanted to steal everything from him. Zut!" She spat into the cold hearth. "Un salopard."

Good heavens. This was quite an outpouring. So Jonnie possessed an uncle who had nurtured designs upon his father's title and estate, and now presumably upon his. Verity, with her extensive education in foreign cities, had more than once come across such envy from a younger son and was not surprised by this revelation. Did Jonnie know of his uncle's envy? She had a feeling he might be as dismissive of it as his father had been before him.

The old lady shook her head. "I am sorry, child. I have nothing to do here but sit and remember and think. I find myself, more and more, dwelling on what happened in the past and letting it make me fear the future. I must not burden you with my thoughts."

Verity once again experienced the desire for honesty with this clearly hot-headed old lady, but pushed it away, even though she hated having to keep secrets. The fewer people who knew the truth, the better.

"Did your husband abandon his excesses once he married you?" The question was out of her mouth before she realized how inappropriate it was. Really, she'd only wanted a hint at whether Jonnie would do so, not a confession from his mother as to what his father had been like as a husband. Although, children learn from their parents, so Jonnie might well have become a rake because his father had.

However, her mother-in-law appeared unfazed by this question. She made a moue. "At first he was a devoted husband, of course. I think he found it hard to believe I'd chosen him. I was a most popular young lady in Paris, at the Bourbon court and at Versailles, you must understand. Of course, there was a king and queen in France back then, and Queen Marie-Antoinette was young and beautiful, so the court was full of joy and fun and handsome young men. Chevaliers, comtes, ducs. I could have had my pick of any of them and probably would have lost my pretty head in the Terror for my troubles." Her French accent returned. "But it didn't last. I find nothing does. Life will teach you that, child. But I forgave my Edward his peccadilloes. He always returned to me, so what did I care." She gave a shake of her head. "I am French, after all, and we French ladies are used to our husband's amors. I'm sure you'll do the same with Jonnie's."

Emboldened by the Dowager's openness, Verity tried another question. "Is that why you don't like Kitty? Because she's the result of one of his peccadilloes?"

The old lady's eyes narrowed. "Who told you I don't like her?"

"She did."

The old lady shook her head. "It isn't that I don't like her, you understand. But she was the cause of my husband's death, and I couldn't bear that. He may have had his faults, as we all have, but he was the man I loved above all else. I would have died in his place, if I could have. And without Kitty, and her mother, that would never have happened." She shook her head. "My beloved Edward might still be alive now were it not for that child."

What a strange thing to say. How could Kitty, who hadn't been born until after the old earl had died, have had anything to do with his death? Hadn't he fallen down the stairs and broken his neck? Verity would have liked to ask more, but something held her back. Instinct told her that to do so would be to pry into this sick old lady's grief, which she could see was as real to her now as it had been sixteen years ago. However, nothing was going to stop her from asking other people.

SYLVESTER WINTRINGHAM AND Thomas Teesdale had chosen Hyde Park for their next rendezvous and were strolling around the serpentine pretending to be interested in the frivolous young people out on the water in their rowing boats. The cloudiness of the day had not prevented what appeared to be a veritable fleet of young people whose loud voices could be heard from a distance. Nobody was looking in Sylvester and Thomas's direction so this was an excellent spot for a clandestine meeting. They could mingle with the crowds of people just like them so easily.

"You have at last arranged it?" Sylvester asked, as they passed beneath a stand of leafy trees. "I have heard that my nephew has dispatched his new wife down to Luxborough, so now would be an efficacious time to strike. While he is alone and before he has time to join her and put some effort into producing an heir and bringing my plans to nothing."

Thomas glanced over his shoulder as though afraid the trees might be listening.

Sylvester gave an impatient huff. Could the man look any more suspicious if he tried? He was beginning to regret he'd ever drawn Thomas into his plans, but it was too late now. And if he spurned his protégé and chose someone else to carry out his plans, then he would expose himself to Thomas's blackmail. He had no doubt at all that Thomas was capable of such underhand and ungrateful behavior.

Having satisfied himself the birds were not listening, Thomas edged closer to his mentor. "I have arranged it for tomorrow night. He goes regularly to White's with his friend Farrington." His lip curled in a sneer. "Anyone would think he doesn't want to be at his own house. They never leave before three in the morning. It will happen then. I have men lined up to carry this out."

Sylvester nodded. "I trust you haven't skimped. Farrington is a noted swordsman and that walking stick he carries is not just for show. It's a sword stick, as is Dunster's. And my nephew boxed at Eton. You should be certain to send enough men. Strong men. Men who don't fight by any recognized rules."

Thomas's turn to huff. "Of course I haven't skimped. I've waited for this moment for a long time. Am I likely to let it fail for want of a few coins in a ruffian's pocket? I've chosen six of the best, or one might say the worst, and I'll be with them to make is seven. One of them's a giant of a man. They're to disable Farrington first so he can be of no help to Dunster. Then it'll be seven against one. You'll be reading of his demise in Friday's morning papers, and hearing it spoken of with sadness all over Town. By the ladies, that is. Have no worries. We will succeed in this."

Sylvester smiled, a slow and decidedly satisfied smile. Seven men to remove the only obstacle between himself and the earldom he'd long yearned for. At last. And then Teesdale could be silently removed by the same method, and he and his son, who was in his final year at Eton, would be safe from any blackmail. Perfect.

CHAPTER EIGHTEEN

IN THE HOUSE in Cavendish Square, Jonathan woke early after a more than troubled sleep. His dreams had been shot through with dramatic images of Miss Farrington's drunken father laughing in his face, and of himself standing up to fight a duel with the old man. He fired his pistol to miss, and Anthony Farrington threw a handful of cards, all aces, up into the air. As Jonathan followed their floating descent, he found himself transported to the top of the stairs at Luxborough, staring down them as his father tumbled head over heels towards their foot. This last had caused him to waken sweating and tangled in his bedclothes at some ungodly time of the morning. After which it had taken forever to get back to sleep, only to waken what seemed like minutes later to find it was morning, gasping for breath and drenched in sweat again.

Damn that whole family of Farringtons, Walter included. Damn that drunken old man who didn't know when to stop gambling and damn his far-too-pretty and determined daughter. And damn his own father for what he'd tried to do. He was not going to waste another thought on any of them. He'd do just what he wanted and ignore the lot of them.

Dim light was filtering in around the heavily curtained windows, indicating the earliness of the day. Determined to recapture his sleep, he rolled over onto his left side, only to discover he was so fully awake and alert that sleep could not have been further off. So damn them all for that too.

Ten minutes tossing and turning produced no improvement, so he got out of bed and rang for Arnold, who arrived within minutes, immaculate as usual and not looking in the least bit surprised that his tousle-haired master had called for him at such an early hour.

"Water for a bath," Jonathan snapped, not at all in the mood for small talk with his man, and stomped over to the window in just his night rail.

Arnold hurried to draw the curtains back for his master. "I'll have the maids bring up the water, my lord." And he was gone.

His bedroom, being at the front of the house, gave onto the square, which was already filling up with early morning vendors and delivery boys. He didn't very often see it at this end of the day, although he did on occasion stumble home just as a new day was beginning, more than ready for his bed.

Despite the early hour, he supposed food had to reach the square's many large houses in time for breakfast. A couple of disreputable coves had taken up residence on one of the benches in the gardens, near the guano-spattered statue of the old duke. One of them was smoking a pipe and the other had a ferocious looking, battle-scarred dog on a piece of string. Jonathan had always been interested in what went on around him, and these two fascinated him enough for him to watch them the entire time it took for the maids to fill his bath. Clearly they had mischief in mind, even if it was only casing one of his neighbors' houses for their next robbery. If he remembered, he'd send word round to Bow Street after breakfast.

Having spent an unconscionably long time in the bath, letting his night time troubles wash away as the water cooled, and then taken a leisurely breakfast, Jonathan forgot all about reporting the two disreputables to the law and chose instead to walk round to Gentleman Jackson's in Bond Street for some therapeutic sparring which went on far longer than he'd intended. Always a good way to clear one's head.

It was well after noon when he finally wandered his way around to White's, which was where he encountered Walter in the company of his younger brother, Robert, just back from taking the waters in Bath. Since childhood, Robert had suffered from an irritating skin affliction, and Bath was a regular haunt of his. He swore the waters soothed his many itches and sore spots and, to be honest, he was indeed looking better than the last time Jonathan had laid eyes on him.

"Why, Dunster!" Robert exclaimed, his thin face suffused in smiles. "Didn't think to see you here, not after you've married my cousin Verity. Thought you'd be honeymooning somewhere." He chuckled. "I remember her well—a pretty little thing with all that red hair." Due to his malady, his parents had never sent him off to school like Walter and Jonathan, so perhaps he'd had more opportunity to see his cousin. "Shall I call tomorrow? I'd love to see her again and do a spot of reminiscing."

Walter had the grace to redden. Had he not informed his brother of Verity's exile to Luxborough?

"She's at Luxborough," Jonathan said, in a vain attempt not to sound curt. He had a nasty suspicion he'd failed.

"By herself?" Robert's voice rose a notch in surprise. "In Ox-fordshire? Not here in Town with you? I mean, you're not there with her? Going to follow her down, perhaps?" He raised his thin eyebrows.

"Luxborough was still in Oxfordshire last time I was there," Jonathan snapped, ignoring the rest of Robert's words.

Walter swallowed. "Forgot to mention your little tiff."

Jonathan fixed him with a hard stare. "So I gather."

Robert frowned. "But you've only been married a week. How on earth do a bride and groom fall out in so short a time? Especially when the bride's such a lovely girl."

Now wishing he'd stayed away from White's, Jonathan shrugged, hoping this young sprig would take the hint. "I would rather not discuss my private life, if you don't mind." He glanced around at the hallowed interior, aware that several heads had turned in their direction. "Particularly not here."

Robert's turn to blush. "Of course. I understand." But by the look on his face, understanding was far away. And of course, he was probably fond of the memories he must have of Verity.

Damn it. Jonathan really didn't want to have to think about her. She'd been blighting his day since he'd woken up, her determined, no, cross if he was honest, face popping up in the most inappropriate of places. On that punch bag at Gentleman Jackson's for a start. That had quite put him off and he'd elected to head into the ring in which he'd given his opponent quite a pasting. Drat the woman. Was there nowhere he could get away from her?

Perhaps he should return home, but he didn't relish a night alone at the mercy of his dreams. And he couldn't go round to Lady Delamere's because he'd informed her a few days ago that their relationship was at an end. He could, of course, go to a gambling house and win some money. Or lose it. He didn't care which. What did it matter to a man with his enormous income? He turned away from the Farrington brothers.

An arm went around his shoulders from behind and a strong stench of tobacco smoke, sweat and brandy washed over him.

"Dunster!"

He turned his head to find Thomas Teesdale, that infernal fellow who'd not only helped in his downfall, if one could call marriage a downfall, but had also made his life a misery in his first year at Eton. The last person he wanted to see. "Bit of a turn up for the books, eh?" Teesdale was steering him further into the club and unless he physically shook the man off, Jonathan was stuck. He caught a glimpse of Walter and Robert following, matching worried expressions on their faces. None of them cared for Teesdale, Walter for the same reason as Jonathan.

They reached a group of leather-covered easy chairs and Teesdale virtually threw Jonathan down onto a double seater and flopped down beside him, taking up most of the seat. By the looks of him, and the smell, he'd already been here a while. Possibly all day, or at least since he'd risen, which had probably been no earlier than midday.

The fact that he himself was normally in a similar state of inebriation escaped Jonathan as his whole being recoiled in disgust from the man. For himself, he'd drunk only a tankard of beer down a side street near Gentleman Jackson's along with a meal of some tasty bread and cheese, so he felt virtually sober. For once. And this was having the effect of making him feel unusually virtuous. Not that one could feel any other way when compared with Teesdale. The man was a blackguard.

Walter and Robert settled into two further seats, and Walter, his expression wary, waved to one of the waiters. "Four glasses of brandy."

"How's married life?" Teesdale turned his large, florid face to Jonathan's, too close for comfort. A blast of unpleasant breath turned Jonathan's stomach. Yes, he was more than glad that Miss Farrington…his wife…no, Verity, had not been given away in payment of a debt to this fellow, whom he felt certain would have fleeced her drunken father in a far from honest manner. The man was a cheat at cards, but he always avoided playing with Jonathan who'd not been able to catch him at it. Even if he wasn't enjoying being married to the far-too-determined Verity himself, he was not such an oaf as to wish her on someone of Teesdale's ilk.

"As you might imagine," Jonathan replied, willing Walter and Robert to keep silent.

They did.

"Was most amused to discover you decided to marry the chit," Teesdale said, with a knowing leer. "Although I have to admit to also being surprised, as I never took you for the sort to actually marry any of your women. Especially not a chit won in a card game."

Any sort of cutting reply eluded Jonathan for the moment, which in itself was unusual, and probably lucky.

Not so Walter. He leaned forwards, his face screwed up in

anger. "I say, don't you go referring to my cousin as a chit. I won't stand to have her insulted."

"And she's my friend," Robert put in. "Some respect, please."

Teesdale's heavy eyebrows rose and a sly leer slid over his large, ugly face. "Your cousin, is she? And her father was happy to pimp her for his debts? I think I might hazard a guess and suggest he is not a gentleman." His lip curled and he laughed.

Jonathan resisted the impulse to head butt him, a move he'd learned elsewhere than at Gentleman Jackson's, but it was difficult. Who knew but he might be doing the blackguard a favor, as a broken nose might improve his appearance.

Instead he fixed his coldest, hardest, and most haughty stare on Teesdale. "I'll thank you not to talk of my wife in such terms." His voice was an icy blade.

Teesdale, like most bullies, was not a brave man, and here he was outflanked by three to one. Under the collected stares of Jonathan, Walter, and Robert, he wilted. "I see Bunbury over there. I have a matter I need to discuss with him." And he was gone, stalking away across the room to where no doubt Bunbury would be surprised to see him.

Jonathan chuckled.

"Can't abide that fellow," Walter said. "Surprised you didn't call him out."

"I nearly did," Robert put in, glaring after the object of their ire.

Jonathan shook his head. "Not worth it. He's so far below my notice I couldn't care less what he says. A nobody."

"A bloody rude nobody," Walter said. "I'd go for swords if I were you. The fellow was as ham-fisted as a girl when we did fencing at school, but I hear he's a crack shot and rumor has it he's killed a man in a duel before now. Hushed up, of course."

Robert sniggered. "Still ham fisted now, but probably with girls this time."

All three of them laughed, and over on the far side of the room Teesdale glanced over his shoulder at them, unable to miss their mirth. His unpleasant face set in a heavy frown.

Good.

CHAPTER NINETEEN

JONATHAN TOOK HIS hat and swordstick from the club's dark-suited butler who'd been waiting patiently and gave the man a nod in thanks. He pulled on his silk gloves and watched Walter as he donned his own hat. They'd spent a pleasantly convivial evening that had progressed into a large part of the night with a few of their friends at a private game of cards. Betting had been limited but Jonnie was going home slightly richer than when he'd left, unlike Walter. Robert had elected to stay a little longer as he'd encountered an old friend and the two of them were busy plotting some youthful devilry.

Walter pulled out his fob watch from his waistcoat pocket and peered at it in the dimly lit gloom of the foyer. "Nearly four," he said. "Hardly worth going home to bed. Do you fancy popping over to the Lyon's Den for a bit? They have some more unusual opportunities to gamble. It's only round the corner, and their doors'll still be open."

Jonathan paused, considering this suggestion. He'd been to the aforementioned establishment a number of times and had been impressed with the welcoming atmosphere, as well as the aforementioned unusual gambling. He'd bet on such varied things as snail races, whether a friend could get a particular woman into bed, how many times a particular bore might say "actually," and how many members of the Lords would fall asleep in the House on a named day. "Another night, perhaps," he said. "I find myself yawning and think, for once, my own bed might be desirable. Although you're more than welcome to come back for a nightcap if you so care."

"That would be most agreeable," Walter said, hurriedly putting his own hat on. "And not too far from the old man's place."

The butler opened the door for them and the two young men stepped out into the warm darkness of the night. St James's Street was well lit with oil lamps that threw circles of golden light across the paving stones, but in between them darkness took hold again. London was not a city used to having clear nights, and both of them were used to making their way to their respective homes along gloomy streets. It was a hazard of maintaining such nocturnal lifestyles. So late at night, or, rather, so early in the morning, there was no sign of any cabs.

Walter chuckled. "Don't tell me you're getting middle-aged in your outlook, Jonnie, and can't stick the pace any longer. I swear that over the last week since you marched up the aisle with my cousin you've turned soft on me and our friends. I know for a fact you've been nowhere near that actress of yours since before the wedding. And you told me yourself you've broken it off with La Delamere." He narrowed his eyes. "Has my little cousin some sort of a hold over you, even though you'd like me to believe otherwise?"

Jonathan ignored his friend and started off down the street towards Piccadilly, heedless of the threat of darkness and what it might be concealing. London at night had never bothered him, which was just as well as he saw a lot of it.

Walter had to run to catch him up. "No need to take a huff, old chap. I was just remarking."

"Well, kindly desist from remarking," Jonathan snapped, not turning his head to look at his friend.

They reached Piccadilly, crossed it, and started up Albermarle Street, where there were fewer lamps to illuminate their way, and not many people about. Almost none, in fact. Four in the morning was late for gentlemen like them, and early for those who had to begin work before their betters.

Behind them, a group of three roughly appareled men emerged from a side alley. Jonathan, who, despite his air of disconcern, always took care to note who else was about at night and whether they might present a threat, glanced back over his shoulder. The men were walking arm in arm, as though somewhat the worse for wear, but something about them, some alertness that didn't match with being drunk, had him tightening his grip on his sword stick. One of them had a powerfully built dog on a piece of tatty rope. Was it the same dog with the same men, plus a friend, that he'd seen in the garden at the center of Cavendish Square? Unlikely, but you never knew. But there were only three of them, and he and Walter could, if necessary, easily deal with them, dog and all.

Disreputable men were to be found all over London, especially at night, but it was a little odd that these were so bold as to dare to pass through such a fashionable area. But as there were three of them, this had perhaps given them the necessary bravura. No sign of any constables on patrol though. These fellows might not be so cocksure if there were.

At the end of Albermarle Street they turned right into Grafton Street then left into New Bond Street.

The men followed them.

Despite its air of modernity and wealth, and its more numerous lamp posts, Jonathan knew this wouldn't stop footpads, even here, if they decided a pair of swells were worth robbing. And most men dressed as he and Walter were carried readies in their pockets. He had friends who'd been set upon on the very doorsteps of their own homes in some of the best parts of the city. Nowhere was truly safe. Hence the sword sticks.

Best to keep an eye on these three men.

Walter, who had consumed a fair bit more brandy than Jonathan had, seemed not to have noticed them at all.

They passed the narrow lane into Bruton Street, where Verity's father had his lodgings, on their left, opposite Conduit Street, and Jonathan could tell from the sound of the men's footfalls that they'd put on a spurt of speed and were now a good bit closer. Some of the lamps had either not been lit or had gone out, making the street darker than ever. And at this time of night it was empty of anyone but himself and Walter. And the men behind them, of course.

Jonathan took Walter's arm and hurried him along. He'd far rather distance himself from them than partake in a street brawl, even one he knew the two of them could win. Although, from Walter's state it might be less three against two and more three against one. And he didn't want Walter getting hurt.

A little ahead, and from out of one of the narrow entrances on their right, that Jonathan knew from experience led into a couple of yards, which at this time of night would be dark, deserted and unlit, four more men emerged onto the street. Four large men, one of whom could possibly be described as a giant. Instead of heading either in the same direction as he and Walter, or turning towards them, these men merely spread out across the street, hands on hips, blocking the way, the giant in the center. Their bulky shapes made a menacing barrier. It was clear they meant to prevent Jonathan and Walter from passing.

"I say," Walter said, as if noticing their imminent danger for the first time. "What's going on here?" Never a man not to mistake an obvious threat, he raised his sword stick and slid the weapon out of its cover with a little difficulty due to his inebriation. The blade flashed in what little light there was.

Jonathan cast a glance over his shoulder at the men behind them, who were closer still now, cudgels having appeared in their hands as if from nowhere. They, too, had spread themselves across the street with the obvious intention of preventing escape that way. Not that flight had entered his head.

He drew his own sword and shifted his cane into his left hand, gripping both with determination. The arrival of the men in front had just lengthened the odds against him and Walter a little worryingly, but he felt confident they could cope.

To either side of them the houses, silent and dark at this time of night, slept on, no one within them aware of the ambush that was taking place just outside their front doors on this fashionable street. And if they did notice, no one was likely to come rushing out to help them.

"If it ain't the Black Earl," one of the men facing Jonathan said with a sneer. "Well, well, well."

"Back-to-back," Jonathan snapped, and Walter hastened to obey, turning to face the three men behind them while Jonathan faced the four newcomers.

The men, their faces almost invisible in the gloom, drew closer and in so doing, began to edge their prey towards the yawning darkness of a second yard entrance. Their intention was clearly to force Jonathan and Walter into it and out of view of any witnesses who might be disturbed by the fracas to come.

"Weren't expectin' this, were you, mate?" The same man spoke again, shifting the cudgel that had appeared in his grip from hand to hand. The dog growled, a low, threatening sound.

Jonathan was not a man to give up without a fight, and neither was Walter. The possibility that handing over his possessions to these footpads might save them from a fight didn't even occur to him. Neither, it was apparent, did it occur to Walter, who suddenly lunged forward with his blade outstretched, flicking it, with astonishing ease considering his state of inebriation, across the cheek of the nearest footpad. This man uttered an unmanly yelp and jumped backwards, his hand to his face, blood seeping between his fingers and running down his cheek. "Clear off or it'll be the worse for you," he snapped, now not sounding inebriated at all.

The dog barked and strained at its lead.

"Well done," Jonathan said. "Good move."

Perhaps not quite such a good move as he'd thought.

Two of the four men facing him suddenly charge forward, the cudgels they themselves had been concealing beneath voluminous jackets to the fore. But Jonathan was as adept with a sword as his friend, and two wicked swipes cut a wide gash across the nearest man's forehead sending blood pouring into his eyes. A move he'd used before as it effectively blinded a man and put him out of the reckoning. With his left hand, he simultaneously brought his cane down hard on the back of the second man's hand and his cudgel shot from his grasp to roll uselessly across the road. He leapt back, nursing his hand, which should contain a few broken bones now. As he was the man with the dog, this had taken that beast out of the fight as well.

All the men retreated a couple of steps, their language loud and appalling. A light went on in the nearest house and curtains twitched.

The one whose forehead Jonathan had opened was now worse to useless as he couldn't see for the blood, and he was groaning.

"Nice bit of fencing there," Walter said, swinging his sword in an arc towards the three facing him to keep them back. Despite the fact they were still outnumbering their prey, they didn't seem keen to risk the sharp tip of his sword. Cowards at heart, only ready to fight if they grossly outnumbered their prey. Typical of bullies.

Another light came on in a house to their left. Someone else must have heard the cries of their attackers and the loud swearing. Impossible not to hear it. This time the curtain was drawn back, and, as this happened, light spilled out onto the road for a moment, illuminating the scene.

Jonathan caught a brief glimpse of the footpads before the curtain was hurriedly closed again. No doubt the owner of the house, or perhaps its butler, had thought better of interfering. Three of them, including the man now blinded with his own blood and the one nursing a broken hand and the dog, were typical of the sort of rough, uncouth men to be found within the Devil's Acre slums. Heavy, rough-featured, and unshaven, they wore tattered, dirty jackets and hefty boots, with filthy old cocked hats jammed on their heads. The fourth, however, despite being clad in much the same fashion as his companions, was different.

Staring out at Jonathan from under a battered hat was a face he knew all too well. Thomas Teesdale, his mean eyes alight with bloodlust, and his teeth bared over lips drawn back in glee, had a hand reaching inside the dirty jacket he must surely have borrowed from the wardrobe of one his new friends. As he drew it out, Jonathan saw the flash of metal on a pistol. A pistol pointed not at Jonathan, but at Walter.

"Teesdale!" Without thinking, Jonathan lunged towards the man who'd made his first year at Eton a torment and who now seemed to have murderous intentions towards his own best friend. A loud report sounded, a burning sensation caught him high in the left shoulder, but he ignored it and drove his sword at Teesdale's midriff. It hit flesh and went on going, such was the power of the blow. Teesdale's eyes opened wide in shock and he staggered backwards. Jonathan held onto his sword with a vengeance, wrenching it free, but as it came out of Teesdale's body, an unseen cudgel scythed down on Jonathan's forearm just below the elbow.

From somewhere to his left, a shout came, the voice angry and cultured. "Hoy there!" It did not belong to one of their attackers.

He both felt and heard the bones snap. His numbed fingers couldn't keep hold of his sword, which went skittering away across the road, but he still had his cane in his left hand. Careless of his broken right arm and injured shoulder, neither of which seemed to be hurting as yet, he swung back into the fray, wielding the cane like his lost sword. Where was Walter? Had the bullet that had undoubtedly caught him in the shoulder gone on its way and taken his friend? Why had Teesdale been aiming for him? If only it weren't so dark and the movement around him so confusing.

With one man blinded, another with a broken hand, and Teesdale now lying in the road clutching his belly and sobbing incoherently to "get the bastard," only four men remained to be fought off. Fighting left-handed wasn't something he was used to, but Jonathan threw himself into it with gusto. The cane swung, catching the nearest man on the back of the head. He went down and didn't get up again, but another lumbered into the fray. The giant. He was a bigger man than any of the others, topping Jonathan, who was himself over six feet tall, by several inches.

Ordinarily Jonathan would have had no trouble besting him, being quick on his feet thanks to the boxing he'd done at school, but this was not an ordinary moment, and his arm and shoulder, which were now beginning to hurt like hell, hampered him. For some reason, he was finding it hard to stand up straight, his whole body seeming to want to curl up on itself around the pain in his broken arm.

The big bruiser snarled like a rabid dog and swung his cudgel, but his sheer size made him slow. Jonathan ducked and almost fell, but forced himself upright again, the effort suddenly enormous. But he still had his cane. For want of any other possible blow, he jabbed it with as much force as he could into the bruiser's belly and was rewarded by the sound of all the air evacuating that man's lungs at once. He was just congratulating himself on a small victory when something heavy struck him hard in the side. He staggered for a moment, tripping over something, or someone, spreadeagled on the ground, probably Teesdale who was always in the bloody way. Another heavy blow followed, the air shooting out his own lungs this time, and he found himself falling sideways to his right, unable to save himself with his broken arm.

His head struck the road surface with force, somewhat superseding the pain in his forearm, and, for a brief moment, he saw stars. A dark shape loomed over him, he had a momentary vision of a swinging boot, and the stars vanished as his head snapped back. Darkness descended.

━━━━ ⟡ ━━━━

CHAPTER TWENTY

THE FIRST THING that came back to Jonathan was a sensation of being jolted about most uncomfortably. The second thing that came back was sound: the rumbling of heavy carriage wheels and the noise of trotting hooves. And then the pain arrived. With a vengeance.

He groaned.

"Lie still," cautioned a voice he thought he ought to recognize.

But of course, lying still wasn't what he wanted to do at all. He tried turning his head towards the voice, but that only set off a ferocious hammering inside his skull and provoked another groan. What the hell had happened to him?

"Told you to lie still," said the voice, somewhat reproving in tone.

Walter. The voice belonged to his friend. No wonder he recognized it.

But whatever was Walter doing in what, from all the noise, had to be a carriage? A carriage of some size, at that. Come to that, what was he doing in the carriage himself? And in what appeared to be a lying down position. What carriage could cater for someone to lie down in it? None he knew of.

"Best do as my brother says," came another voice. "He knows what he's talking about."

Robert. Walter had his younger brother with him.

Why?

Jonathan lay still for a long minute, just breathing and trying to work out why every bit of him hurt. Badly. Maybe he'd better try opening his eyes. With a near superhuman effort, he managed to get his right eye open, but nothing would get his left to do the same. It seemed to be unresponsive. And it hurt. A little alarming.

His surroundings came slowly into focus. Even though he was undoubtedly inside a traveling carriage, he appeared to be lying on a bed of some kind. Since when did carriages of any sort have beds? And what had led to him being so incapacitated as to need one? He couldn't for the life of him remember. In fact, if he strained, which hurt his head abominably, the last thing he could recall was walking into White's and meeting Walter and Robert.

Which might be why Robert was here with them, of course.

He licked his lips. "Where are we?" It came out as a croak and he realized his mouth was dry and his tongue didn't wish to obey his commands. There was a bitter taste in his mouth.

"Going to Luxborough," Walter said, in the no nonsense, inarguable tones of Jonathan's old nanny. Since when had his friend taken on the persona of Nanny Jarvis and become so bossy?

"What?" His voice now sounded a little stronger, as well as somewhat surprised.

"What he said," Robert put in. "Don't worry. We got the doctor. Or rather, the doctor got us. He said you could travel." A distinct air of someone not quite telling the whole truth clung to Robert's words. And what doctor? Nothing of that held any familiarity for Jonathan.

He digested the information he'd just been given. Luxborough? Wasn't there a reason he didn't want to go there? He groped in his thick and fuzzy head but couldn't find anything useful so gave up and shut his right eye, thereby reducing the throbbing in his head. What he really wanted to do was sleep, but this jolting was never going to let him do that.

"Just let me give you some more laudanum," Walter said. "For the pain. The doctor gave me a bottle."

The bitter taste again as liquid was trickled into his mouth. He wanted to spit it out, but didn't have the energy.

It must have worked, however, because the next time he opened his eyes the internal carriage light had been dimmed. Either that or he was dying. In which case it would be Walter's fault for taking him on a journey when plainly he should be home in bed being looked after by a nurse and probably a doctor too. Yes, he would rather die in his own bed.

Someone was talking in a low voice. Robert. "Are you sure we should have done this, brother?"

Walter's reply came, his voice even lower. The fact that they either didn't want to disturb him or, more likely, didn't want him to hear, seemed evident. "Absolutely. It's the only way to get the two of them together. They're clearly made for one another but are too pig-headed to realize it. I had no chance of it whilst Jonnie was standing on his own two feet. So I took the opportunity when it presented itself. Got to take a risk that sometimes, to get what one wants."

"Risk is the right word. He looks an awful shade of gray."

"So would you do, if you'd been shot and had your arm broken and your head kicked in."

So that was why every part of him was hurting like hell.

Robert sniffed. "That sounds like an awful lot of wounds. Are you sure that doctor said it was safe to take him all this way? Are you sure he was a proper doctor, even?"

Silence for a moment. "Of course I am. He heard the rumpus outside in the street and came out with his butler and a pair of loaded pistols to help us. Without his pluck, you'd be looking at becoming viscount after father dies, because those footpads would have killed both of us. Luckily the fools attacked us right outside the house of such a brave, public-spirited fellow, who just happened to be a doctor. He took us in off the street and helped us even further." He huffed a little. "And when I asked him, he said it would be all right to take Jonnie home. So I sent for you and for Mama's carriage. She won't even have missed it yet."

Robert was clearly not to be deflected from his worries. "But that doctor thought home was Cavendish Square, not Oxfordshire."

"A mere detail."

A long pause ensued, the rumbling of the wheels and the steady sound of trotting hooves pushing their way to the fore. Almost lulled by their rhythm. Jonathan would have begun to nod off once more had not Robert spoken again.

"I can see blood coming through the bandage on his shoulder. It must have started bleeding again."

"Leave it alone. The doctor said to leave it in place. It needs to coagulate or something like that. I'm sure that's what he said. Just like your foot had to when you nearly cut your big toe off with that axe."

"But I hadn't been beaten nearly to death."

"Neither has Jonnie. Only beaten a little bit."

"Who do you think did it?"

"Footpads." Walter sounded definitely cagey at this point.

"You said there were seven of them."

"They all went limping away, I can assure you. No one crosses Jonnie Dunster and Walter Farrington."

"Jonnie doesn't seem to have done too well out of it. He looks pretty 'crossed' to me."

"Nonsense, as I already explained when you first arrived, he killed one and near blinded another. I can tell you they departed in a worse state than they left us in, dragging their tails behind them. The sight of the doctor's pistols finished off any thoughts they had of further battery." Again, Jonathan, even in his half-conscious state, divined that Walter was not quite telling the truth.

"I still don't much like it. Supposing..." His voice was so low now as to be almost impossible to hear. "Supposing he *dies*. It'll be our fault. Your fault, really."

A huff, none too confidently done, emerged from Walter. "He won't do that, or I'll have something to say about it." Only

Walter sounded nowhere near as confident as Jonathan would have liked.

"Let it be noted that I'm not in agreement with this kidnapping."

Another huff from Walter. "Go to sleep. I'll give him some more of this stuff if he wakes up again. Best if he don't feel all the jolting about."

The brothers fell silent for a few minutes.

Time ticked on.

Jonathan was nearly asleep when Robert spoke again, his voice a low hiss. "I'd damned well like to know what it was you were up to while that doctor was treating Jonnie. When you sloped off and left me alone with them. You were gone quite a while."

"I said go to sleep," Walter hissed back.

And silence finally fell.

Jonathan listened for a bit longer but neither spoke again, and pretty soon his attention waned and sleep took over. He dozed some more, drifting in and out of sleep, or possibly consciousness. He had no idea which but everything was very jumbled.

In one of his short waking periods, he tried moving his head. Just a little, this time. Something had improved, because he only managed to set off about three quarters as much pounding as earlier. From the bitter taste in his mouth he had a feeling someone had given him laudanum for the pain while he was dozing. Which might explain the strange feeling he now had of floating on a cloud. Perhaps he should try sleeping while he was feeling like this. Yes, that might be an excellent idea. His eyelids drooped and sleep took him again.

The next time Jonathan awoke, the pain was back with a vengeance. Pale morning light was filtering in around the dropped blinds on the carriage windows showing him Robert asleep in the opposite corner, head back and mouth inelegantly open. Walter's legs poked out from the corner he couldn't move his head to see. From the snoring, it seemed apparent that he too was asleep.

Jonathan lay still for a while trying to work out which bits of him were hurting the most. A difficult task as his body felt as though every square inch was in pain. What was this makeshift bed he lying on? His fingers found several layers of blankets under his body but they didn't do enough to disguise the hardness of the bed. Might it be an old door? It certainly felt as though it could be.

His back hurt somewhere between his shoulder blades and all down his left side, and breathing hurt. Did he have broken ribs? He could now vaguely remember going to Gentleman Jackson's. Had someone beaten him in the ring so badly he was in this much pain? Unlikely as he was considered to be among the best of the gentlemen who came to Jackson's establishment. And surely the proprietor would have stopped a fight heading in that direction?

He tried to ease his position but that only sent pain slicing through him as though someone had stabbed him. Not that he knew what that felt like, but surely it must be something like this. The pain slowly centered on his right arm, his left shoulder, his ribs, his back, and his head. He was quite relieved to discover his legs seemed to be intact and undamaged.

How had he ended up like this? His brain refused to reveal this to him no matter how hard he tried to extract the information. And really, did it matter? He closed his one good eye again. Was the other one was so swollen he couldn't open it? That did seem to fit with being at Gentleman Jack's premises. He yawned. What time was it? Early? Why was he feeling so sleepy this early in the morning?

He dozed, but it was a sleep tormented by dreams, possibly made worse by the laudanum he'd been given. He was playing cards and a white-haired old gentleman was parading a string of girls in front of him in varying states of undress, offering them to him in payment of his debts. And all of them, disturbingly, had Verity's face. Then he was at Luxborough and he and his father were standing at the top of the stairs, shouting at one another. The scene changed and he was standing over a blood-soaked bed.

A woman was sobbing quietly and a baby cried. At last, the dreams faded and, exhausted, he fell into the deeper sleep he needed.

SYLVESTER WINTRINGHAM HAD not woken up to the sort of news he was expecting on the morning after the planned attack. His flustered valet arrived at a ridiculously early hour to inform him of a disturbing turn of events.

Sylvester glared at the man who'd had the temerity to awaken him from his dreams of returning to Luxborough and claiming it as his own property at last. He did not look like the bearer of good news. "What is it, man? This is far too early."

His man appeared to be suffering from some sort of shock, for his face was a nasty shade of gray and his whole body was trembling. "I'm terribly sorry, sir, but something important has…arisen." He was clasping his hands in front of him as though trying to wring out washing. "Mr. Stubbs told me I had to fetch you down to see."

Sylvester groaned inwardly. What could possibly have happened to provoke his butler into sending his valet to wake him up at this unearthly hour? Granted, it was daylight, but he liked to rise after nine and take a leisurely breakfast. If this was seven, he'd eat his hat, and dismiss his butler. "Are you sure he said that?" He really wasn't at his best at this hour of the morning.

"Yes, sir," the valet said, standing his ground. "He said you would want to be wakened on account of such a thing as has happened."

"For God's sake," Sylvester grumbled. "Fetch me my banyan and my slippers, then. If I have to come down, I'll come down. But you and Stubbs are going to regret this."

The valet hurried to do his master's bidding.

Only a few minutes later Sylvester arrived in the front hallway of his house where Stubbs was standing by the front door, which stood slightly ajar.

"What is it then?" Sylvester snapped.

Stubbs, for answer, opened the door wider.

The body of Thomas Teesdale, minus his old cocked hat, fell into the hallway from where it had undoubtedly been propped up against the door. Outside on the pavement a small crowd of early risers—street sellers and tradesmen mostly—had already gathered and all were staring at his front door and his early, but definitely dead, caller.

Sylvester was momentarily without words.

Not for too long though. "What on earth is someone like that doing on my doorstep?" he blustered. "Some ruffian, no doubt." Best not to admit to knowing the corpse's identity. "It's Mr. Teesdale, sir," Stubbs said. "The gentleman who called here a few weeks ago. I'd know him anywhere, even dressed like this." He paused and bent down, detaching a note from where someone had pinned it to the body. There was blood on it. "And even if I hadn't, this note identifies him."

Sylvester snatched the note from Stubbs's hand. No need to unfold it, for whoever had pinned it to the corpse had left it open for all to read. He could only hope none of the crowd had read it. The words on it were written in large black capital letters.

THIS IS WHAT HAPPENS TO WOULD-BE ASSASSINS.

No spelling mistakes.

Sylvester swallowed. That someone knew not only that Teesdale had been involved in the assassination attempt that must have taken place on Jonathan seemed obvious. That the same someone knew he was involved also seemed obvious.

What to do with the body? And all this crowd who could testify to having seen the corpse on his own doorstep?

Too late. A constable stepped forward out of the crowd and up to the front door. "'Ello, 'ello, 'ello," he said in the tones of a cockney born and bred. "What's goin' on 'ere then? Who's this feller?"

Sylvester quaked inside, frantically groping for a way to explain away a member of the ton dressed like a footpad and who'd been dumped on his own doorstep. This was going to take some acrobatic ingenuity.

AT LUXBOROUGH, VERITY was already up and dressed and in the act of eating luncheon with Kitty. It was another school day for her new young friend, and Miss Bligh had joined them both in the dining room, which Verity had belatedly made the decision to have opened up for their use.

"It is rather a walk to and from the vicarage," Miss Bligh said as she sipped her tea. "I do find it quite tiring on a hot day. This is most fortifying."

"You really don't need to put yourself out on hot days just for me," Kitty said with alacrity. "I wouldn't want to think of you suffering from heat exhaustion, you know." She accompanied this last with the sweetest of smiles. Anyone who didn't know her might think she was thinking only of her governess's comfort.

"No need to worry, Kitty," Verity said. "I shall send one of the many vehicles you showed me in the carriage house to take Miss Bligh back and forth from now on. I wouldn't want you to miss out on your education for want of a horse to pull a trap."

Miss Bligh looked most gratified. "That is exceedingly kind of you, Lady Dunster. But please don't send anything too splendid and put the grooms out. A simple pony and trap will suit me well. I have no desire to appear ostentatious to my brother's flock. If something more elaborate was to arrive at the vicarage, they might think I had ideas above my station in life."

"A pony and trap it is then. I think we have one of those in the carriage house, do we not, Kitty?"

Kitty pouted. "We do."

Verity smiled. "And to make sure you are up and ready to start your lessons, why don't you be in charge of taking it to the vicarage to collect Miss Bligh?"

Kitty's face brightened as she was very fond of an outing, and Verity had gathered these were few and far between. As the vicarage was a couple of miles distant in the middle of the village, nestled beside the church, taking the pony and trap there twice a day would be a bit of much needed independence and fun for her. "I can do that," she said, sounding mollified. Of course, someone was going to have to check she'd done it or Miss Bligh could be left waiting transport that was never coming, and that someone would have to be Verity.

Kitty laid her napkin down. "I'll go and take my constitutional now, if you'll both excuse me."

Verity nodded and Kitty took herself off. This constitutional consisted of circumnavigating the house three times every morning and then again after luncheon, which was a lot further than it sounded as the house was so large and the buildings had a wide footprint. Miss Bligh herself had introduced this to Kitty's regime as, she'd informed Verity a few days ago, she was a proponent of plenty of exercise for young ladies. Although of course, she herself would be getting less if Kitty fetched and carried her in the pony and trap.

Once they were alone, Verity put into action the plan she'd been formulating ever since she'd met the French dowager. She wanted to know a lot more about Kitty's birth, as it seemed to have had a lasting effect on the older lady. Not that she was truly old, but, apart from her face, it was impossible to think of her in any other way, so ravaged was she by her rheumatics.

She laid her own napkin down. "I went to see Lord Dunster's mother."

Was she mistaken, or did Miss Bligh's expression change at mention of the Dowager?

She smiled, but the smile didn't reach her eyes. "Most appropriate."

Verity nodded. "I had been here long enough and felt it behooved on me to do my duty and introduce myself. I now quite understand why it would be impossible for Her Ladyship to have called upon me. Her condition precludes such an expedition."

Miss Bligh nodded. "That is so. My brother visits her every week, even though she is not at all grateful, and on occasion can be quite rude as he is not a Catholic priest. He tells me she has much deteriorated in the past few years. The rheumatics is a cruel affliction."

"It is indeed. I don't think I've ever seen anyone so badly affected at what must, I assume by her face, be a relatively young age."

"I believe she is fifty-three."

"Still young by many standards." Verity glanced at the window. If she knew Kitty, which she now did to a certain extent, those three circuits of the house would take a good half hour as she'd be stopping to talk to the gardeners and anyone else she found out there. "I must tell you that she said something I found strange. But as she seemed most affected by it, I didn't press her to find out what she meant."

Miss Bligh assumed a guarded expression. "Oh?"

"Yes. I was wondering if you might be able to shed light on what she said."

Miss Bligh raised an eyebrow, managing to look both keen to be helpful and wary of what might be asked of her at the same time. "I could try." She did *not* sound like she wanted to, though.

Verity ploughed on, determined to discover the secret. "She told me she blames Kitty for her husband's death. Only, Kitty has already told me she was born after that unfortunate accident. How can the two be connected?"

Now Miss Bligh's face paled, telling Verity there was indeed something to be discovered here.

The governess swallowed. "I'm very sorry, Lady Dunster. It is not something I am at liberty to reveal."

So she knew at least some of it. "Oh. But can you at least tell me if it's true, or if the dowager is perhaps suffering under a delusion?"

Miss Bligh opened and closed her mouth a few times in a way reminiscent of the goldfish in one of the ornate ponds at the Parc de Saint-Cloud, just outside Paris, where Verity had once walked.

Verity waited.

Miss Bligh cleared her throat, swallowed, and opened her mouth again, this time looking as though actual words might be about to emerge.

She was interrupted by the dining room door banging open and Kitty hurling herself into the room, eyes wide and wild, a look of horror on her face.

Miss Bligh shut her mouth with a snap as both she and Verity turned to stare at Kitty.

"Whatever's wrong?" Verity asked, her heart leaping into her throat. Had something happened on the child's walk?

"Come quick!" Kitty gasped, as though finding it hard to get enough air to speak. "You have to come quick. There's a carriage outside. Jonnie's in it, and I think he's dying."

Chapter Twenty-One

Verity, with Kitty and Miss Bligh close behind her, ran out of the dining room and into the enormous entrance hall. Through the open front doors of the loggia she could see a carriage drawn up on the gravel drive, its doors open. There appeared to be several people milling about near it, but none of them were Jonathan.

Without pausing, she ran down the wide steps and out onto the drive. Cousin Walter, who'd been standing looking into the carriage, turned towards her. What on earth was he doing here? And who was that with him?

"Verity!" exclaimed the thin young man standing beside Walter. "My God, you've hardly changed."

But she wasn't interested in renewing old acquaintances with the man she recognized as her childhood friend. She gave him a swift nod as he and Walter moved aside and let her look into the carriage.

A rough bed had been constructed from seat to seat out of something that looked uncannily like an old door covered in rugs. Lying on it, his face horribly disfigured by swelling and what was going to be massive bruising, lay Jonathan. Or at least she thought it must be Jonathan. Hard to tell with his face so battered. His eyes were closed and as far as she could tell on this panicked first viewing, he didn't appear to be breathing.

Her heart gave a terrible lurch of fear before she saw the

reassuring rise of his chest. Her heart, however, did not react by slowing down. "What's happened?" she asked, turning accusing eyes on her cousins.

"He's dying," wailed Kitty. "Look at him." Tears streamed down her face.

Walter shook his head. "He's not dying, young Kitty. Be assured." But he didn't sound particularly confident.

Verity grabbed his arm. Someone needed to take charge here. "Tell me what's happened to him. Now."

Lucas and two of the footmen were standing back, expressions of deep shock on their normally imperturbable faces. Unsurprising, considering the state of their master.

Walter stared at Verity. "Jonnie and I were set upon on our way home from White's last night. This morning, I mean. Seven footpads. Seven to two is pretty bad odds. Jonnie managed to kill one and incapacitate two, but that still left four. I took care of one. We'd have won, I'm sure, if one of them hadn't broken his sword arm for him."

She looked past Walter at the splint on Jonathan's right arm where it lay across his body.

"A fellow in one of the nearby houses heard the noise we were all making. Must've woken the entire street but he was the only one who took it into his head to come to our rescue. Looked out of his window and fortunately for us fetched his pistols. Came out shouting the odds and our attackers fled." He paused, a slightly shifty look creeping across his worried face. "They dragged their dead friend off with them." His face cleared. "As luck would have it, the fellow was a doctor. Got him to patch Jonnie up and he said we could go home." He colored. "Took it upon myself to bring him here. He needs a nurse…" His voice trailed off.

"Bring him in." She'd think about the fact there was a dead body somewhere that Jonnie had caused and the implications of this later. She turned to Lucas and the footmen. "Help my cousins bring His Lordship up to his room and send someone to fetch his own physician. He must have one. Do you know who he is?"

Lucas, his face pale, nodded. "Yes, my lady. I'll send one of the grooms on a fast horse immediately to fetch Dr. Collins." And he hurried away to fulfil his commission.

A few footmen later and with Walter and Robert helping, it took no time at all to get the makeshift stretcher up the stairs and into what had to be Jonathan's own room. All the while, Verity noted, he gave no hint of coming to his senses. Was he just deeply asleep or dangerously unconscious? She didn't like the look of his face. Someone had given him a terrible beating.

Once he was lying on his bed, a huge, four poster edifice, larger than the one in her own bedroom, there remained the problem of his clothing. "Scissors," Verity ordered. "Now." Two of the footmen departed with the old door.

The redoubtable Miss Bligh turned to Kitty, who'd come into the bedroom and was standing by the head of the bed, her hands covering her mouth, tears still running freely. "You come along with me, Katherine. Your brother is most certainly not dying, but he needs care and attention you cannot give him, and you do not need to witness that. I'll take you downstairs for a fortifying hot chocolate. Come with me now."

With Kitty gone and the scissors having arrived, Verity, for want of anyone else doing anything, took charge. Walter and Robert stepped back, although she missed their exchange of conspiratorial glances. With swift efficiency she snipped Jonathan's shirt away from his body and with the help of one of the footmen, managed to lift him enough to remove its tattered remains.

He possessed an impressively muscled torso, most of it covered in marks that were already darkening to bruising, and a chest endowed with a fair amount of curling dark hair. Not that Verity had never seen a man's naked chest before. Her life had not been so sheltered. She'd also tended to a fair number of wounds in her time and was not at all squeamish. Luckily.

A bandage had been applied to his left shoulder, the blood on it dried. "Has he been *shot*?" Verity asked. "Since when do London footpads, or footpads in any city, go armed with pistols? Surely their choice of weapon is a knife or cudgel of some sort? Pistols cost money."

"Er, some do," Walter said, sounding abashed. "One of these did, at any rate. He was aiming for me, would you believe it, and Jonnie leapt at him and caught the bullet. Didn't seem to affect him at all, though." His voice held admiration. "Ran the fellow through with his sword stick. That was the one he killed." His eyes darted from left to right as though he didn't want to look her in the eye. There was something here he was keeping to himself.

Verity sighed. Men. In Verity's experience most were quite fond of a bit of violence. Some of them a sight too fond.

Jonathan groaned but his eyes didn't open. One of them couldn't have anyway, as the left side of his face, including his eye, was swollen and reddened. He was going to have an amazing black eye before long.

"Boots and then breeches," Verity said. "You can help, Walter."

Walter hesitated. "Shouldn't you go out of the room?"

She set her hands on her hips. "Why? He's my husband."

"But, er, but…"

Verity fixed him with a hard stare. Did he know she'd refused conjugal rights to Jonathan? And did he think she'd never seen a naked man before? Traveling through a Europe that had been dangerously war torn from time to time had provided her with a far more liberal education than any young English girl would ever get. And wounded men, whom on occasion she'd had to tend to, often had to be undressed to be treated. "I have no qualms about this, I can assure you."

Walter, a little wide-eyed, pulled Jonathan's boots off and set them carefully by the bed as though being neat and tidy were now the most important thing of the day. Verity undid the fall on Jonathan's breeches and, with the help of Walter and the remaining footman, they slid his breeches down. He was now quite naked. She determined not to look, but couldn't help her eyes sliding down his body in curiosity. More maneuvering and they got him under the covers, modesty returned.

Verity, however, was in the process of discovering that removing the clothing of the man she'd married but never seen naked was a quite different experience to tending to some unknown soldier. Of course, she knew exactly what a man's anatomy looked like and had not expected to be affected by seeing Jonathan unclad. But she had been. She still was. For now what she was seeing had implications. If she succeeded in teaching him a well-deserved lesson, the part of his anatomy that was exclusively male was a part she would become intimately acquainted with. And it had drawn her attention far more than she wanted to believe. It was no longer something just randomly attached to a human body she was unacquainted with. Instead, it was a thing with a purpose, on a man she knew, and that purpose was to create an heir for his earldom. With her.

She was very glad to have it covered up.

She turned her attention back to Walter. "Has a doctor seen him?"

Walter nodded. "Yes. He said we could bring him back here."

"And has he been unconscious the whole journey?"

Robert shook his head. "No. He was talking some time ago. He seems to be slipping in and out of consciousness, I'd say."

"He was asleep," Walter put in with unnecessary firmness. "Not unconscious."

Robert glared at him. "I said it was too far to bring him."

Verity held up her hand. "Has he had any sort of medicine?"

Walter nodded again. "That doctor in Town gave us Laudanum for him. We slipped a few drops into his mouth while he was sleeping every so often. I think it helped."

Verity eyed the clearly still-sleeping Jonathan. Had they given him too much? It was possible. One had to be very careful with a drug like laudanum. She'd have expected that ride upstairs and being manhandled into bed to have woken him up, but it hadn't.

However, there was nothing any of them could do about that at the moment.

Lucas returned. "My lady, I've sent one of the stable lads to fetch Dr. Collins. By good fortune he lives nearby in the village, so he should not be long. Unless he's already in attendance elsewhere, of course. I've instructed the lad to find him and fetch him whatever he might be doing."

Dr. Collins, a man of scrawny middle age and a long lugubrious face, was luckily not in attendance elsewhere. He arrived on his horse, a racy beast, less than half an hour later, and came running up the stairs two at a time, his black bag in his hand.

He bowed to Verity. "Lady Dunster." And moved over to the bed.

Verity shooed everyone out of the bedroom, even though Walter was reluctant to leave, and closed the door behind them. She went to stand beside the bed. This was, after all, the man to whom she was married.

For the first time she was able to study her husband without him staring back at her. His eyes were still closed, and one side of his face was unmarked, in stark contrast to the side that had taken the worst of the beating. But if she looked at the undamaged side she found he looked different to when he was awake. Reminiscent of the ten-year-old boy she'd seen in the portrait at his mother's house.

His mother. Should she be informed of his injuries? Best wait and see what the doctor had to say. No point in worrying her unduly.

She sat on the chair someone had pulled nearer to the bed and watched the doctor examining Jonathan's wounds. He removed the bandages holding the splint on his arm in place and felt along it gently. The arm was already turning purple with deep bruising, the better part of it close to his elbow. It looked as though he'd received a heavy blow just above halfway down it.

Dr. Collins cleared his throat and began to reapply the splint. "This forearm has been most adequately set. The bones, as far as I can tell with all this swelling, are nicely realigned and, if all goes well, he should have few problems with it once it is mended. He's going to need to keep the splints on for some weeks and resist all temptation to use that arm. I shall, of course, be available to visit every day if required." Being an earl had a lot of benefits, it seemed. Probably Dr. Collins didn't want to risk losing such a rich patient. He'd be anxious to make sure nothing untoward befell Jonathan. Jonnie. Suddenly, using the abbreviation of his name felt natural. Lying here, wounded and vulnerable, he was no longer the man she'd developed such a strong dislike for, but someone for whom she felt compassion.

She could even feel sorry for him.

She could even accept that she had some sort of feelings for him. She frowned. Pity, most likely.

"And his shoulder?" she asked.

Having secured the splint back in place, Dr. Collins carefully removed the bandage the doctor in London must have applied. It was stiff with dried blood and had to be prised off the wound. Fresh blood trickled where the congealed blood had been dislodged. "A gunshot wound." He managed to lift Jonnie's left side and peer at his back. "Did not go through and I would say did not strike any bones. I shall assume the London man removed the bullet and ensured no fragments of His Lordship's shirt were left in the wound. I don't want to set it bleeding again by prodding at it. I'll apply ointment and a fresh bandage."

Verity watched him do so.

He glanced up. "Might there be someone amongst your staff capable of changing the dressing for him every day, my lady?"

She nodded. "Of course. I'll do it myself. I have experience in tending wounds."

His eyebrows rose but he moved onto Jonnie's face. "I can apply leeches here to reduce the swelling. That would be helpful to his recovery."

Verity nodded. "I've seen it done before many times. Most efficacious."

Again he looked surprised at her experience. "And a poultice of linseed meal or bread and vinegar might also help. Do you need help with that?"

She shook her head. "No. I've used both of those before." She smiled at the man. "I have not always been a countess, doctor, and lived in a house like this."

His eyes crinkled in a return smile, making his long face appear much more friendly. "You have the air about you of a woman of good sense. I feel happy to leave my patient in your hands. If you need anything at all, if you feel he is deteriorating, or in too much pain, don't hesitate to send for me." He paused, looking back down at his patient. "Lord Dunster is very lucky to have found himself so capable a wife as you."

He gently felt Jonnie's chest. "I fear more than a few broken ribs. I think if you could ring for a strong footman, I would like to apply supporting bandages."

"I could help."

He shook his head. "No. Not in this instance. His Lordship is not a small man and seems to be sleeping still. I understand he's been given laudanum so this is not surprising to me. The footman can help me lift him and apply the bandages around his chest while he's still under the influence of the drug. It is possible with broken ribs to puncture a lung, and we don't want that."

He took a small glass bottle from his bag. "I have more laudanum here, but you must not exceed the dose I shall recommend." He returned his gaze to Jonnie. "Or this deep a sleep ensues, and that is not good for the lungs. We do not want His Lordship's lungs becoming congested from long periods lying on his back. He needs to be sitting up rather than lying prone, and although I recommend immobility for his ribs, I would like him to be up and slowly walking withing a few days. But I shall be back before then to check on his progress." He put out a hand and patted Verity's. "Do not fear, my lady, I will not allow your husband to succumb to his injuries. All are possible to overcome."

Verity looked down at Jonnie. It was a relief to know he

wasn't dying, as Kitty had thought, and he was in good hands here. Why this mattered so much to her was a mystery, though. She didn't even like him. Did she?

━━ ⊷✦⊶ ━━

CHAPTER TWENTY-TWO

JONATHAN SLOWLY BECAME aware that he was no longer lying on a badly padded old door and that instead, beneath him was a soft mattress of infinite comfort. It had even succeeded in somewhat lessening the pain in his back and chest. Or at least he thought it had. Trying to move, unfortunately for him, had the pain rushing back.

He opened his eyes. In the plural. Well, he opened his right eye fine, and the left one just a bit, but enough to allow light in.

"Don't try to move." A woman's voice. Walter and Robert—where had they gone? And why did the woman's voice sound familiar? And gentle. For a moment he was back in the nursery after he'd fallen out of that big chestnut tree and Nanny Jarvis was looking after him. But that voice was not hers.

With infinite care, as he didn't want to set off the thumping in his head again, he turned his head a little to the right to peer at where the voice was coming from.

Verity was sitting beside the head of his bed.

A knitted shawl hung about her shoulders and her lovely auburn hair had been confined in a thick braid. Was that a peignoir she was wearing beneath the shawl? Was she in her night attire? For the life of him, he couldn't think why she should be there. Most confusing.

His eyes, without him having to move his head, flicked towards the nearest window. The room was lit only by a lamp standing on the bedside table and it seemed outside it must be pitch dark. Nighttime. Hadn't he already been through a night in that infernally uncomfortable carriage ride to nowhere? Was it still the night? The same night? Might it being nighttime explain why Verity looked ready for bed? But not why she was here, at his bedside, with a worried frown on her shadowy face.

He watched her wring out a flannel then lay it across his forehead. It was so pleasingly cool and refreshing he almost gave a sigh of relief, but just managed to stop himself.

She smiled gently, looking the prettiest he'd ever seen her with those escaping wisps of her lovely auburn hair about her face. "You mustn't strain yourself. You have a slight fever from the bullet wound, but the doctor assures me it will pass by morning if you're lucky. It's only natural after an injury such as that."

The flannel cooled his hot skin.

How he wished his mind didn't feel so jumbled. He couldn't even remember where he was. Instead, he hung onto the one fact that seemed to be circulating repeatedly. Verity was his wife.

"We were a little worried my two cousins had administered too much laudanum to you on your way down here," she said. "You've slept for such a long time, although that might be good for you. Your body needs time to mend."

"Down here?" His voice came out as a croak.

Verity started, probably at the sound of it. "You must be thirsty. Let me give you some water." She got up and fetched a glass of water from somewhere he couldn't see. "Don't move. Let me help you." Before he even had chance to lodge a complaint, she'd slipped her arm under his head and lifted him just enough that he could sip from the glass she held to his lips.

Too thirsty to object, Jonathan drained the glass. That was better. His tongue no longer felt as though it was glued to the roof of his mouth. "Another?"

She helped him to a second glass. Seemingly the water had rejuvenative properties as with it percolating through his body, he began to feel slightly human again. Only slightly, but it was a start. "Help me up."

She removed her arm and he sank back onto his pillows. "I'm not sure I should straight away. You are much battered about, you know. Your own doctor, a very capable man called Dr. Collins, said that in a few days he'd like to see you up and about. Which probably doesn't mean the moment you wake up."

He eyed her as realization began to dawn. "I'm at Luxborough?" Of course he was. Even as he said it, the memory of Walter telling him that was where they were bound returned. But then they'd given him more laudanum and he'd slept again after that. His recollection of the journey down here was minimal. Just a jumble of rattling wheels and creaking carriage springs and flashing images.

She nodded, her eyes serious. "Walter decided to bring you down here after you were attacked by footpads. He told me all about it while you were sleeping." Her gaze slid down to his right arm, and his own gaze followed. His arm appeared to be not only bandaged but also encased in a splint. "It's broken," she said. "Both bones. Luckily for you those footpads chose to attack you right outside the house of a doctor. And even more luckily that doctor was brave enough to come out waving his pistols at them. Otherwise Walter says you would be dead. Him too, probably."

Jonathan lifted his left hand and explored his face with wary fingers. Just touching it sent pain lancing through his head.

"Either someone kicked you in the face," Verity said, as though tending to gentlemen with bashed in faces was something she was called on to do every day of her life, "or they hit you with something big. Several times. You're going to have a terrible black eye. But Dr. Collins applied leeches while you slept and the swelling has reduced considerably. You may not want to look in a mirror for a while, but I can assure you, you look much better than you did when you first arrived here."

He made an attempt to raise an eyebrow, but this didn't work. "Leeches? He did? I feel quite glad to have been sleeping, in that case."

She smiled. "They were quite revolting, especially when pregnant with your blood. Not a thing I would recommend anyone witnessing. Not on their own bodies, anyway."

He tried a return smile and failed at that as well. Far too painful. The fear that he might have lost some teeth arose so he did a quick check with his tongue. A miracle. They were all still there. "Do you know the details of my injuries?"

"Broken arm, gunshot wound that is producing this slight fever, broken ribs, much battered head. If I were you, I wouldn't go touching the back of my head. You have a rather large bump on it, and a scab. You don't want that scab coming off and starting the bleeding again. Be thankful you have soft pillows."

He nodded. "Perhaps we could revisit my request for assistance. I would prefer to sit up, if only a by a small amount." He nodded at his strapped-up arm. "And I fear that with this I won't be much use in pushing myself into a sitting position."

"I'll call one of the footmen. They're nice and strong."

A footman arrived with alacrity.

Jonathan cringed a little inside that any of his staff should see him in such a state of helplessness, but there was no other way of doing this. "William, if you could just get me sitting up, please."

William, a strapping young man who'd begun life in one of the estate farmhouses, turned out to be far more gentle than he looked. He might have grown up used to handling recalcitrant cows and pigs, and even plough horses, but he now proved he could be gentle as a woman with a baby. Although comparing himself to a baby was unattractive to Jonathan. But at least now he was almost upright in bed.

He leant back against his plumped-up pillows, struggling to control his breathing as the pain throbbed from his toes to the top of his head. "Brandy, William. Fetch me my decanter from my study. Quickly." He closed his eyes. That would lessen the pain, surely.

"No," said a voice that had to be Verity's but had taken on the authority of his first governess. "He's not to have brandy nor any other alcohol, William. Off you go. I'll deal with this."

The sound of the bedroom door closing had Jonathan opening his eyes. He glared at Verity. "This is my house and if I ask for brandy I expect to get it."

She glared back at him, determination spilling out of every part of her. "And I am your wife and in charge of your care. If I say you can't have it, then you can't have it. Believe me, it will not speed your recovery."

Damn the woman, but he was weak as a kitten or he'd have thrown the covers off the bed and gone and found the brandy himself. However, he had a suspicion that if he tried to stand up he might collapse in an ignominious heap on the floor. And that would do nothing for his pride, as she wouldn't be able to pick him up herself and would have to call for reinforcements. Possibly two footmen and maybe Dr. Collins himself.

"I need it to dull the pain," he muttered, loath to admit how much every part of him was hurting.

She fetched a small bottle. "For the pain you may have more laudanum. But not the amount Walter and Robert must have given you last night. It's a wonder you didn't expire from its effects. Dr. Collins has indicated to me what a dose for a man your size should be. It will help you sleep as well as dull the pain."

"Damn it, woman, haven't I done enough sleeping?"

She chuckled. "Perhaps you're right about that. And I think if you're amenable, some sustenance might be a good idea before you take your medicine. I'll send for something Mrs. Lovell has been preparing for you, and waiting up for you to wake up and need it. Beef broth. It will do you good." She said that as though she expected a protest.

Jonathan remained silent, however. He wanted to say that he'd prefer a plate of actual roast beef, but it would not have been true. Beef broth, much to his surprise, sounded ideal.

And the beef broth, when it came, turned out to be just that. Although it also turned out to be presented in an invalid cup that didn't require him to be sitting up straight to drink, nor any use of a spoon. Jonathan had the sense not to cavil at this indignity. He was too hungry and the broth smelled delicious.

Verity put it into his left hand but, he noted, kept a very good eye on him unless he was about to spill it. After the broth, she administered the small dose he was allowed of the laudanum and he found he was tired, despite having slept what must have been most of the last twenty-four hours.

Verity straightened his covers for him and took her seat beside the bed again, her expression peaceful. Gone was the somewhat argumentative young lady he'd first encountered. This was a different Verity to the one who'd banned him from her bedroom. A softer, gentler, and more pliant one, yet, as had been proven, every bit as determined.

Jonathan relaxed back on his pillows, allowing the drug to take effect, but still watching her through drooping eyelids. Dressed like this, she was even prettier than he'd first thought. Who'd have guessed she'd been hiding the qualities of a nurse-maid? Hidden depths. Still waters run deep. Several more clichés tumbled through his head. At last, however, his body began to feel light and relaxed and the pain to recede. His eyelids became heavier as his whole body drooped. He could no longer keep them open.

HAVING TURNED THE oil lamp down a bit, Verity watched his eyes close in satisfaction. A couple of times they flickered open again, but he was fighting a losing battle there. Laudanum would not just dull the pain but bring him much needed, healing sleep. His breathing became deeper and the drawn look on his pale face softened as his whole body relaxed. Hopefully this would be a deep, pain-free sleep. He needed it.

She'd poured herself a glass of water earlier, and now she sipped it as she studied Jonathan's face in repose.

When she'd seen him for the first time lying in the coach and for a moment thought him not breathing, her heart had performed a lurch of fear that had nearly made her legs buckle at the knee. Only extreme determination had kept her upright. At the time, she'd not had the opportunity to wonder at her reaction before she'd realized he was not dead. Since then, she'd pushed aside her own feelings as she'd helped both Dr. Collins and her staff with Jonathan's care and comforted the distraught Kitty.

Now, alone in the dark bedroom with the man whom, so short a time ago, she'd decided not to like, she had time to reflect on her own feelings, which were more than puzzling.

She set her jaw. She absolutely didn't like Jonathan. She wanted to teach him a lesson. He was spoiled and over entitled, as well as being actually titled, a rich man from a section of society her own father had fled. He was, in short, everything she'd learned to despise after so many years in revolutionary France, and yet she'd allowed herself to be cajoled into marriage with him. There was no denying she could have avoided that if she'd wanted to, and yet she hadn't. What did that mean? Could he possibly represent the stability she'd so often craved in the last thirteen years?

She frowned, watching him more closely as he slept. She could tell herself a thousand times that she'd done it to save Papa, but was that strictly true? Had not a small part of her been attracted to this man who, in many ways, didn't seem to have passed the stage of being an over-indulged child? Did she perhaps nurture the idea she could change him? For the better? Did she think him worthy of that effort?

She scowled at him. He was sleeping soundly now, his impressively muscled chest, most of it now concealed by bandages and blankets, rising gently. Was that not why she'd decided to teach him a lesson and even considered what it might be like if she succeeded? Was it not why she'd asked his mother whether his father had given up his hedonistic lifestyle once he'd been married? Had she been picturing a life for herself with a Jonathan who was no longer a rake?

She began to realize that not only did she not know Jonathan very well, but also that she didn't know herself at all. Everything she'd thought about herself seemed to be sliding away at an alarming rate.

A sobering thought.

Was she no longer the young woman who'd aided her father to extract considerable sums of money from unsuspecting foreigners all over the continent? The woman who'd jaunted about Europe masquerading as a young French woman? Probably not. In fact, it was entirely possible that she'd never been that young woman at all, and that it had all just been a cloak she'd worn over her old clothes to disguise herself. Her true self, perhaps, was the girl brought up by Grandmama at Somerton in the traditional ways of the landed gentry. Hadn't someone once said, "Give me the child until he is seven and I will give you the man?"

Might she, against her better judgment, like Jonathan a bit too much, despite his many obvious failings? Possibly because of them. A ridiculous thought. What was there to like about him, even? She would ignore his good looks, battered as they were at this particular moment in time, as to include them would be shallow, and she didn't consider herself to be a shallow young woman. Beauty, as Grandmama had said many times, only went skin deep.

She frowned, considering what she knew of him, which wasn't much and in no way justified having any sort of feelings for him at all. Possibly a few of those shallow ones, but not the sort that lasted.

She clenched a fist and lifted her thumb to count off reasons why she might allow herself to like him. One: he clearly loved his sister very much. To the point where he, as just a boy himself, had decreed that she should be brought up in his household. She'd been motherless and fatherless and her brother, who should perhaps have shunned her, had ordered her to be brought up like a lady, even though her mother had been nothing but a house-maid. That was surely something in his favor. And on top of that, so maybe this was number two, he'd done this in the face of what must have been stiff opposition from his own mother. To the extent that she'd taken herself off to the Dower House and stopped living with him.

So, from the age of sixteen himself, he must have been independent. And then there was the fact that not only did he appear to love Kitty, but she clearly loved him in return with a devotion that was touching. So that was point three. Kitty had been desperate to do her part in caring for her beloved brother and had sat for a long time before her bedtime at his sickbed, holding his left hand in a most touching fashion and dabbing at the tears which kept springing to her eyes. Surely Kitty would not love someone who was at heart bad? She was not a foolish girl. At least, no more foolish than other girls her age.

So, the question remained. What else was good about him?

She didn't know. There must be other things, but she'd seen so little of them she couldn't think of them. Then she remembered her drive with him. Four: he loved his horses. He treated them as though they had feelings. A rare accomplishment. Anyone who treated his horses well couldn't be that bad.

But that made only four good points. Not many.

But now, in fairness, she had to consider what was bad about him. Yes, he'd offended her, but had he been, perhaps, just the tiniest bit justified in doubting her like that? After all, Papa had, without compunction and to save himself from ruin, given her away to pay a gambling debt. And, as she'd been willing to do that once, no wonder Jonathan had thought she might have done it before. Hot color rose up her cheeks. Was it not more Papa's fault than his? Was not Papa at the root of all her troubles? Had her ire towards Jonathan been a little misdirected?

His left hand was resting on his stomach. She slid out her own hand and covered it. He felt warm but not too hot. Perhaps the fever was passing. He had strong hands with long, elegant fingers. A few manly dark hairs covered the backs of them. She liked the feel of his skin under her touch. What might it feel like if he were to touch her with those fingers? In love. They were married, after all. This should not be a shameful speculation, but it brought fresh heat to her cheeks. How glad she was he was asleep and couldn't see her embarrassment.

The prospective failure of her scheme to teach him a lesson didn't seem to matter.

His eyelids flickered momentarily. Was he dreaming?

She rubbed her thumb over the back of his hand, feeling the strong bones beneath the skin. She'd never held a man's hand before. Not like this. Not with the surprising feelings that were cascading through her head.

But was she feeling like this just because he was lying here wounded and vulnerable before her? Made more attractive by his lack of threat. Right now, there was about him more of the boy she'd seen in that portrait than the dissipate man who'd reeked of last night's drinking excesses. He looked younger, gentler, and kinder with his angry expression washed from his face. And, of course, he no longer looked as though he could see through her clothing to her nakedness. A bit of a relief, all told, even though he was asleep.

She recovered her hand and leaned back in her chair. Perhaps she would try and snatch a few hours sleep. The thought she could go back to her own bed never crossed her mind. She wanted to be there when he woke up in case he needed anything. Both Mrs. Burke, the housekeeper and kind Mr. Lucas had offered to take a turn sitting with their master, but Verity had insisted she should be the one to do so. She was his wife, after all.

She picked up the pillow Mrs. Burke had brought her from where it had fallen to the floor and settled it behind her head. She would just close her eyes for a while and be there if he woke. She'd hear him when he stirred, she felt sure.

SHE DID INDEED hear him.

A shout rent the still air of the bedroom. "No! Leave her be! Get your hands off her!"

Verity came awake with a start that set her heart hammering in fear. For a moment she couldn't remember where she was. The bedroom was almost dark and outside summer rain was pattering against the windows.

"No, no, no! Father, no!" Jonathan's voice rose louder. "Get away from her! She's mine!"

Despite his injuries, he was thrashing in the bed, his hair plastered to his sweaty forehead. He seemed to have no concern for his broken arm. She had to stop him before he did it damage.

Leaping to her feet, she seized him by his powerful shoulders. "Wake up! You're having a bad dream. Wake up, Jonnie, wake up." Her voice rose in panic.

His tossing almost threw her off but she hung on, terrified he'd do himself some damage. There was nothing for it, she'd have to slap his face to wake him.

She hit him hard. She possessed what her father liked to call "a mean right hook" and had floored one or two over arduous gentlemen with it on occasion, and some who were less than gentlemen. She modified the blow a little as she slapped the undamaged right side of his face with a firm back hander. A good thing she didn't wear any rings.

His head snapped to one side and he went suddenly limp under her grip. After a few moments, his breathing began to settle to a less alarming panting, and he turned his head to look up at her out of eyes like inky pools. She must just be a blur in the gloom to him.

But he recognized her with no trouble. "Verity?" He sounded hoarse and unsure of himself.

"Yes. It's me. You were having a nightmare, I think. I'm sorry I had to hit you." She hadn't released his shoulders which had now slumped back onto the bed. Hopefully she hadn't damaged the bullet wound.

His left hand came up and gripped her elbow. "Thank you."

She relaxed her hold on him. "It was nothing. Do you often have bad dreams?"

He was silent for a long moment before he nodded. "Sometimes."

What did a man like him have to trouble his dreams? She smiled in reassurance, wanting to tell him he was safe with her, but managed to stop herself. Instead she said, "I'm here now." She would have said that to comfort a child. To Kitty, perhaps. And now she was saying it to her husband. That he needed comfort was obvious. His left hand had slipped down her arm and now she took it in hers and held it. The most natural thing in the world to do.

He sighed. "I'm sorry I disturbed you."

She sat on the side of his bed. "I don't mind."

He frowned, a little ruefully. "I don't like anyone to know about my bad dreams. They're not usually this severe. I've never had to have someone slap me to wake me from them. Maybe the fever or the laudanum made them worse this time."

She smiled. "You have no need to worry. I won't tell anyone."

"I know."

A silence ensued, but a curiously companionable one. At last, he broke it. "Will you lie here with me, by my side, until I sleep again?"

Surprised, Verity wasn't sure how to answer this. But they were married. Instinct told her that if she thought about it for too long she'd say no, and that he needed her to be close. So, before she could change her mind, she hitched herself further onto the bed and lay down beside him, facing him.

She saw him smile in the dim lamp light. "Thank you. I'll sleep better now." And he closed his eyes.

But she didn't. She lay awake for a long while watching him sleep and wondering what that nightmare of his had been about.

CHAPTER TWENTY-THREE

VERITY AWOKE TO pale sunlight slanting between the heavy drapes on Jonnie's windows. It was early still, and the night rain must have ceased with the arrival of the sun. For a moment, she couldn't work out where she was, nor why she was lying on a strange bed with a man asleep beside her. Admittedly, he was under the covers and she was lying on top of them, but still. Then she remembered the events of the previous day and her own vigil at Jonnie's bed and agreement to sleep beside him. Her instinct had been that he'd needed her, and she'd barely hesitated.

Looking at him sleeping peacefully now, she decided she'd been right. He certainly seemed to have slept better with her beside him. No more nightmares had disturbed his slumber, and he appeared to be sleeping like the proverbial baby. She propped herself on her elbow and watched him for a few minutes, taking him in. To her surprise, this was a pleasurable occupation.

The dishevelment of his dark hair had allowed stray curls to flop across his forehead and around his ears giving him a distinctly boyish appearance. For the first time, she noticed how long and thick his eyelashes were, resting now on his still pale cheeks. His mouth was slightly open showing even white teeth and his breathing sounded regular and healthy. She had to allow that even with one side of his face darkly bruised, he was every bit as attractive as she'd thought on first impression. More so in this state, perhaps.

She put a tentative hand on his forehead. Nothing. No untoward heat. The fever had gone.

His lashes flickered and his eyes opened at her touch. His turn to be momentarily confused. And then he smiled. A sleepy smile.

Verity's heart lurched. She'd seen him smile before, of course, but never like this. Never in sleepy spontaneity. Before, his smiles had been for a reason, holding more than they should have. This one meant nothing like that. Instead, she was shocked to see it was a smile of pure pleasure at seeing her. He was not out to seduce her. He was not besting her in argument. He was purely pleased to see her, and that was all. And it worked far better than any attempt at seduction could have. Uninjured and whole, he'd been easy to resist. But now...?

Her heartbeat began to quicken.

She smiled back. Could he hear the pounding? They were that close to one another it seemed entirely possible. What would he think?

He licked what must be dry lips, the action only serving to speed her heart up even further. "Verity." His voice was low and husky. Of course, all her life she'd heard her name spoken. But not like this. Damn it. What was there about this man? Did he possess some kind of magic?

She swallowed. "Yes?"

"You stayed."

"Of course I did. You're injured, and you're my husband."

"You stayed all night long."

She could feel her cheeks warming. "I did." Why did she feel so flustered? Anybody would think she'd woken to find herself naked inside his bed with him, not lying pretty much fully dressed on the top of the covers.

"Thank you." His voice was soft with wonder. A thought occurred to her. Had no one ever cared enough for him to offer simple comfort? For that was all she'd done. She'd stayed to make sure his bad dreams couldn't disturb him again.

She needed to think of what he might need now, or she was

going to be lying here staring at him all morning. "Are you thirsty?"

He licked his lips again. "I am. That laudanum dries one out, I fear, and leaves behind a bitter aftertaste."

Glad of the opportunity to escape his unconscious magnetism, she rolled over and slid off the bed and realized with a shock that she was in her nightgown and her peignoir had come loose. She hurriedly retied the sash. "I'll pour you some water."

By the time she'd done that, he'd managed to pull himself up into a sitting position and was able to take the water for himself. "I'm not using that damned invalid cup again. You can throw it out." He must be feeling better, which was encouraging. Yesterday, when he'd been in such a deep, drug-induced sleep, she'd not been entirely convinced by Dr. Collins saying he was going to recover.

However, there was a distinct disadvantage to his upright position. Like this his nakedness from the waist up had become more obvious, despite his many bandages. Her gaze was drawn, against her will, to his bandaged chest. She couldn't help but notice, again, how powerfully built he was, with a musculature that indicated his probable practice of sport of some kind. He possessed wide shoulders and arms that boasted sizeable biceps.

More heat crept up her face and she looked away in a hurry. Undressing him yesterday had posed no problem due to his having been comatose, but now, with him wide awake, she couldn't look, not even at his chest and arms.

He finished the water and handed back the glass, then dropped his own gaze to the bulky splint on his right forearm. "Drat this thing."

She smiled. "I take it the pain isn't so bad this morning."

He grimaced. "Still there enough to remind me I'm not whole at present."

He was probably making little of it on purpose. Men and their pride.

She sat on the chair beside the bed, glad of the new distance between them. Acutely aware that when he was not trying to be seductive, he was, in fact, far more likeable. "Do you remember what happened to you?"

He gave a shrug, which made him wince. Probably the shoulder wound which Dr. Collins had said was not serious, but would be painful while it healed. "Not much. I recall being at Gentleman Jackson's all morning, boxing. At some point yesterday, I wondered if that might be how I received these wounds, although this," he indicated his left shoulder with a slight nod of the head, "cannot have been dealt out at that gentleman's premises. Pistols are not acceptable combat there, I can assure you. Without a doubt, some blackguard has shot me, and I'm damned if I can remember who it was or how it happened." He put a hand to the back of his head. "Although I suspect this notable bump is the reason my memory is so poor."

"Walter told me you were set upon as you walked back to Cavendish Square by a large group of footpads."

"Armed with pistols? They mostly use knives and cudgels, in my experience." Had he been set upon before by their like?

Might he even have killed one before? A question for another time, if ever. She shrugged.

He nodded at his broken arm. "Although this might have been the result of the blow of a cudgel, I'll allow."

"It's going to take some weeks to mend, your doctor informed me."

He frowned. "I know. I suppose it will give me a match pair, as I fell out of a tree as a boy and broke the other one. I was nine and found it an infernal nuisance to have to wear a splint for weeks on end. I sympathize with my nine-year-old self. It's going to be even more of a nuisance now, I fear."

"No more boxing at Gentleman Jackson's," Verity said with a smile. "And you need two hands to drive your curricle. Probably your doctor will also tell you to desist from riding."

"I can see a life of indolence lies ahead of me."

"For a little while."

Silence fell between them. Verity stifled a yawn.

"I bore you?"

She shook her head. "Not at all. I'm just a little tired. Yesterday was quite hectic with you arriving back overdosed on laudanum by my well-meaning cousins, and having to send for the doctor, and cope with Kitty throwing hysterics because she was convinced her beloved brother was dying."

His eyes narrowed. "You have assured her I am well now, I trust? Well and on the way to a speedy recovery. She has no one else but me to care for her."

Verity smiled again. This was a different side to the Jonathan, no, Jonnie, she'd seen in London, and she liked it far better. She liked his genuine concern for his sister. "She will be asleep still, I think. She found yesterday very trying and sat with you for some of the evening until I had to order her to bed with a hot posset. Otherwise, when you awoke, you would have found her here as well, having to prop her eyes open to stay awake. I judged it better that she get some sleep. She's very young."

"Fifteen. Nearly the age I was when I inherited Luxborough."

Was that a hint of bitterness in his voice? That there was some mystery about how his father had died seemed obvious. A mystery that involved Kitty. But now was not the time to pursue it. "She's a lovely girl."

His eyes softened again. "She is indeed."

Had he been about to say more?

He closed his mouth into a thin line and shook his head, changing the subject. "If you would call one of the footmen—I don't imagine Walter took it upon himself to bring my valet along with him yesterday? No? Well, I'll temporarily promote William. He'll do well as a stand in. Trust Walter not to have thought of that when he made his precipitate plan to kidnap me. No wonder he overdosed me with laudanum. I need help to get up and dressed. I'm not lying in this bed a moment longer."

"I can help you."

He gave her a measuring look. "No. Send for William and

take yourself off back to your own bedroom, I think, for some well-earned sleep. Off you go."

Verity hesitated, moved by the fact that for the first time in their acquaintance he was putting her needs before his own. "I won't go until William is here. You shouldn't be alone. You had a very bad blow to your head. Several, in fact, by the look of you. You should perhaps refrain from looking in the mirror for a few days. Even now a blow to the head could still prove dangerous." She paused. "That is why I sat with you." A bit of a lie, but what did that matter? "I'll ring for William."

"You are a strict nurse, I see." But he was smiling and it was still the friendly, likeable Jonnie before her.

"Strictness is what you need."

He gave a burst of laughter and winced, clutching his chest. "I shouldn't have done that."

She rose to her feet. "Then don't. Lie still like a good patient and wait while I call William."

Once William arrived and it had been explained to him that his master wished to get up, get some decent clothes on and go downstairs for breakfast, with strictly no brandy to be imbibed on pain of severe punishment, Verity left and hurried to her own room, which of course was only next door, as befitted the wife of the earl. This time she didn't bar either the door onto the hallway nor the one to Jonnie's room. After all, he was in no fit state to come knocking and demanding his conjugal rights, was he? Something she found to her surprise was slightly disappointing.

However, it did mean she could remove her peignoir and climb into bed. Within minutes, she was fast asleep.

She didn't wake again until after midday. A tug on the bell pull brought Bessie hurrying to wait on her mistress, and within forty minutes she was dressed in a pretty morning dress, courtesy of Aunt Josephine, and was descending the wide staircase.

She met Lucas at the foot of the stairs. "His Lordship is in the library and requested that you should join him as soon as you were up, my lady." He sounded a little disapproving, as though he felt Jonnie should still be lying in bed like a proper invalid.

Luckily she knew where the library was, as Kitty had given her such an informative tour of the house. She asked Lucas to bring a tray of tea and cake and left him in the hall.

The library opened onto the side of the house that looked out over the lake and was a long room with four wide windows giving onto the view. As one would expect of a library, it lived up to its name and all of the walls were covered in shelves of books that looked suspiciously as though they'd been bought in a job lot to make its owner look good.

Jonnie occupied a winged chair in front of the fireplace in which a small fire was burning. He was wearing a silk banyan, one sleeve flapping loose as his splinted arm must be inside it. Someone, Kitty probably, as she was sitting at his feet on a footstool, had spread a plaid rug over his knees, and he rather resembled a grandfather in a Bath chair, but for the youth of his unshaven face. Walter and Robert were sitting on the other side of the fireplace, playing chess, but looked up cheerily as she entered.

Verity chuckled as she approached her cousins and the siblings. It probably wouldn't be a good idea to tell Jonnie her thoughts about what he resembled.

Kitty looked up, her face wreathed in smiles. "Verity! See how much better Jonnie is. You wouldn't think that yesterday he was dying."

Jonnie made an unsuccessful attempt to throw off the rug. "I was not dying. That was your vivid imagination."

Kitty put the rug back and tucked it in. "Dr. Collins said we had to keep you warm."

He raised an exasperated eyebrow at Verity. "Not this warm. You seem to have forgotten it's summer, child. I'll be suffering from heat exhaustion if you have your way."

Kitty pouted. "After you have always looked after me so well, allow me to do the same for you, please." She shot a look of appeal at Verity. "Tell him he must, Verity."

"Better do as you're told," Walter put in, winking at Jonnie. "Now she has reinforcements she'll be unstoppable."

Jonnie chuckled. "If you and Robert could only form a united front with me, we would outnumber these irritating women." But he wasn't angry.

Verity sat down beside Robert on a comfortably upholstered settee. "If you join Jonnie in calling Kitty and me irritating, Walter, I will have to forbid you the sick room."

"The sick room?" Walter spluttered. "Thought this was the library."

"The room Jonnie is in at the moment is perforce the sick room," Verity retorted. "And he needs peace and quiet and, as Kitty so wisely pointed out, he needs to stay warm. So there will be no objections, thank you."

Robert suppressed a snort of laughter. "You always were a bossy girl when we were children together. I see you've not changed a jot."

Verity nodded. "And a good thing too, with cousins like you two. Bringing Jonnie down here in a bumpy carriage in his condition was almost certainly not a good idea. Not to mention pouring laudanum into him the way you did. You're very lucky you didn't kill him yourselves. You do know it's possible to die from an overdose of it, don't you? From now on, everyone is going to do what I say. Or there will be repercussions." She shot Walter a frown. "And you are not to give Jonnie any brandy. Not combined with the laudanum at any rate. Similarly bad for him."

"If I might get a word in," Jonnie said. "I fancy the brandy would do me more good than the laudanum. But I haven't had any because everyone's afraid of disobeying you."

Verity shook her head. "It would not. And combining them is not a good idea."

"I'd like to know how you know all this," Walter muttered. "Sounds to me like you're making it up as you go along and just enjoying lording it over us men. Typical woman. Power's gone to your head."

Verity fixed him with a stern gaze. "You seem to forget I've spent thirteen years traveling around Europe. A Europe that has not always been peaceful. In that time I've had occasion to tend the wounds of soldiers I've encountered, so I can assure you I know what I'm doing."

"That's telling you," Robert said. "Don't cross her, I say. Even as a girl she was determined as hell."

Kitty shifted on her stool. "Well, I think she's wonderful. Just like Jonnie. And I'm glad he's here now, and safe from those awful footpads, so thank you, Mr. Farrington, for bringing him back here to us. He hardly ever visits, and I miss him terribly when he's not here." She beamed at Verity. "And I'm also very glad our earl and countess are together as they're meant to be."

If Verity hadn't known that Kitty knew the circumstances of her and Jonnie's marriage, she would almost have believed this. As it was, she shot a hard stare at the girl, who'd assumed an expression of utmost innocence. Was she attempting to match-make?

This was going to be an interesting few days. Weeks even. Would Jonnie stay now he was on the road to recovering from his injuries, or would he race back to London and assume his other persona? Who knew.

She rather hoped he wouldn't.

CHAPTER TWENTY-FOUR

MUCH TO HIS surprise, Jonathan found sitting up in the winged chair by the fire in the library, the winged chair his father had favored, strangely tiring. It wasn't as if he were doing anything. Not even playing chess, as Walter and Robert were—something Robert far exceeded his brother at in skill, and therefore kept winning, to Walter's annoyance. It might, he had to allow, have been Kitty's almost constant stream of chatter that tired him out, or, more probably, a combination of that and the fact his body needed its energy to heal.

He resisted the impulse to call for William and get the fellow to help him back up the stairs to his bedroom where he could lie down in peace. However, as the day wore on, he found his head beginning to nod.

Kitty didn't appear to find that any barrier to talking about everything she'd been doing at Luxborough over the past year, and everything everyone else had been doing as well, though. He would have leaned back in the chair, had not it been nowhere near as soft as his pillows for his sore head. Instead, he tried leaning to one side and resting his head on the side of the chair. But he refused to allow himself to sleep. Only old men did that.

He was awoken by a gentle hand on his good arm.

Opening bleary eyes he found Verity bending over him, a look of concern on her face. No one else remained in the library and the fire had thankfully been allowed to die down.

She removed her hand. "I think you need to be in your bed."

With some effort, he succeeded in gathering his thoughts, and the one in the forefront of his mind was that he did *not* want to be treated like an invalid any longer. He took a deep breath in order to say this and immediately wished he hadn't. Possibly sitting still in a chair for so many hours had stiffened him but his back and chest hurt like hell. The uncomfortable realization that he was indeed an invalid settled over him.

He grunted in a mixture of pain and frustration. "Nonsense. But I've stiffened up sitting here. If you would be so good as to offer me your arm, I'll get up and walk about for a minute or two, just to loosen up."

Her delicate brows almost met in a frown. "Are you sure? You look quite drained of color to me. Exhausted, if I might venture to suggest."

He gave a shrug, which he then also regretted. Damn it, he couldn't move without some part of him hurting. "I'm absolutely sure."

Thank goodness he'd chosen this chair as it was not low to the ground and with him leaning on his left arm, which hurt his shoulder of course, and Verity taking hold of his upper right arm, he managed to rise to his feet. All of which made his broken ribs hurt even more. He tried to disguise the gasp of pain but from the look on Verity's face, he'd failed at that, too.

"The terrace," he muttered through gritted teeth. He needed some fresh air after all this time in bed or in the stuffy library.

Double doors at the far end of the library opened onto a terrace that was raised above the gardens and gave a good view of the lake. The lake he'd learned to swim in as a boy.

Taking shortened steps so as not to jar his damaged ribs, Jonathan made slow progress to the doors and Verity opened them for him.

Last night's rain had evaporated under the day's sunshine and the terrace was bathed in the warm light of encroaching evening. He took a tentative breath to avoid worsening his rib pain and inhaled the scents of the rose garden wafting up through the warm air. The scents reminded him with a jab of emotional rather than physical pain of carefree summer days here long ago. But he wouldn't think about that.

With Verity by his side, he walked slowly the length of the terrace and halted at the far end, as far away from the rose garden as he could get. He put a hand on the stone balustrade and tried to disguise that he was leaning on it. Verity had probably noticed though. There appeared to be nothing he could hide from her.

"You have a beautiful house," Verity said, looking out at the view, which was unparalleled. "And beautiful gardens."

He nodded. "If you like country estates."

"Who could not, although I must say yours is a little large to be what I would call homely."

He smiled. "I would never call it homely, have no fear. Although when I was a boy, I enjoyed living here. As an only child, I had no companions of my own class until I was sent away to school." He frowned at the thought of his tormentor.

And swayed where he stood as a lost memory resurfaced.

Before his eyes that loathsome face reared up, eyes wide and spiteful and full of open hatred. But Teesdale was wearing the filthy clothes of the London backstreets, and it was fully dark.

He blinked and the image was gone.

"What is it?" Verity's voice came from far away, edged with concern.

He shook his head. "Nothing. Well, something. A flash of memory, that's all. Momentary."

"If you tell me what it was, that might help. What did you see?"

He shook his head again even though doing so made it throb. "I don't know. It was strange." He paused and now turned to rest his posterior against the balustrade. "Just a flash. I saw the face of the man who bullied me when I went away to school."

Somehow, it wasn't difficult to admit to Verity that he'd been bullied. He'd never told anyone before, not even his mother. And his father would have told him to man up and take it on the chin.

"Was that who was in your nightmare last night?"

"No. He's never in my nightmares." She didn't need to know what and who was.

"Why do you think you saw him then, after what must be many years?"

He pressed his lips together. "It isn't after many years. I've seen him all too recently. And it wasn't so much seeing his face that startled me, but what he was wearing and where he seemed to be."

"Go on. Talking could help you remember more."

The sun was warm on his back. "He was dressed like a common footpad, for want of any other way of describing him." He paused again. "I think he was there when I was attacked. In disguise."

Her eyes widened. "Do you think it possible?"

He considered his answer. Did she need to know? Somehow, confiding in her seemed natural. "I think it might be. I think he must have been with them."

Her turn to frown. "But why? It isn't as if you were the one who'd been doing the bullying, and he wanted revenge on you. He was your bully. You should have been the one wanting revenge. So why would he hold some kind of a grudge against you?"

Jonathan tried stretching his stiff back, but that only hurt his ribs more. "My father ruined Teesdale's father, I'm afraid. He did to Teesdale Senior what I did to your father. Won all his money. Only with Teesdale it was a house as well, and a small estate. Everything the man owned. My father didn't want it. Didn't need it. But he liked winning." His voice had become bitter again. "He always insisted on winning. At everything."

"So Teesdale wanted to punish you for what he saw as the sins of your father?"

"Possibly. His father had shot himself, you see, not long after I went to Eton. Perhaps he saw my arrival there as a chance to wreak revenge on the son of the man he thought had caused his father's death." He sighed. "But he was four years my senior and after my first year there, he left. Thank goodness. I had no idea he might be harboring such a grudge."

"It does seem a long time to do so." Verity touched his arm with her fingertips. "Let's get back inside, shall we, and see what your Mrs. Lovell has prepared for your dinner. No doubt it will be something she thinks appropriate for an invalid."

He gave a rueful chuckle. "I have to admit that in matters of food I do feel I might be a genuine invalid. So long as it doesn't arrive in a damned cup with a spout as though I were ninety or so. She probably has a collection of them to use for my grandmother on her bad days."

But he had to admit that he was hungry.

VERITY LOCATED WALTER and Robert back in the library after dinner that evening, smoking and drinking port. Thanks to her persuasion, Jonathan had agreed to go upstairs to bed. He'd been looking more and more drawn as the meal went on, with dark circles under his eyes that were quite worrying. His lack of rebellion over this reinforced her opinion that he must be exhausted.

Walter looked up as she entered the library, a slightly guilty expression on his face. "Good heavens," he said in mock astonishment, "can't a fellow get a bit of peace from the petticoats?"

Robert was more welcoming. "I've been wanting to reminisce about our childhoods with Verity ever since we got here. You can keep drinking your port if she's here, can't you, brother? Nothing to stop you doing that."

Verity sat down in the winged chair Jonathan had occupied that morning. "I'll have a glass myself, thank you. And I didn't come here to reminisce. I came here to obtain some truths."

"Truths?" Walter looked uncomfortable.

She nodded. "Yes. Truths. Neither of you got your head

knocked about by those footpads. So you know what happened. Were you both there?"

"Just Walter," Robert said, as though in a hurry to absolve himself. "I was on my way back to his lodgings, where I've been staying."

Verity fixed Walter with a hard stare. "You'd better tell me about it then."

He shifted under her gaze. "We was set upon by footpads, Coz. That's all there is to say."

She shook her head. "That's not the whole truth, is it?"

"You'll have to tell her," Robert said. "She's his wife. And she's Verity. You can't resist her determination, believe me."

"Well?" Verity said.

Walter glared at his brother. "Perhaps they weren't quite regular footpads."

She nodded. "I suspected as much. Jonnie's memory is coming back, but only in small shreds. You'd better tell me. Knowing the truth will help him."

"I suspect they were after Jonnie. Not me."

Robert nodded. "You know they were."

"All right," Walter said. "They were."

"And one of them was not a footpad," Verity said.

The eyes of both her cousins widened in shock. "How do you know?" Walter muttered.

"That's the bit Jonnie remembered."

Silence. They were both clearly thinking about this.

"Er, does he remember who it was?" Walter asked, at last.

Verity nodded. "A man called Teesdale, whose father his father ruined."

"Oh." This was said in unison.

Verity went in for the kill. "And did you see him too, Walter?"

Walter nodded. "I...er...I did."

"And?"

"Tell her," hissed Robert. "She can take it."

Walter's eyes darted left and right as though seeking a means of escape. "Jonnie killed him."

Verity stared. She had not been expecting this. Her husband, the man she was beginning to like because he'd dropped his veneer of being a rake, had really killed a man. Walter must have witnessed it. "You're sure it was him?"

Walter nodded. "Ran him through with his sword stick."

She'd seen that stick. She'd never guessed it contained a sword. "I think you'd better tell me everything. Leave nothing out."

Walter, more than a little reluctantly, began a recitation of the night's events, beginning with the three of them playing cards at White's and then leaving Robert in order to head back to Cavendish Square together for a nightcap.

He covered the surprise attack, telling it from his own point of view rather than Jonnie's, of course. He'd seen Jonnie run one of the footpads through, but not seen a second one of them break his friend's arm. He'd seen his friend go down and the gigantic footpad kicking him, and then the alarm had been sounded. The man who'd turned out to be a doctor had emerged, waving his pistols and shouting the odds. The injured footpads, deprived of their fallen leader, had fled, leaving behind the body of Thomas Teesdale.

Walter and the doctor, once he'd established he was helping a pair of gentlemen, had got the unconscious Jonnie into the house and the doctor had begun treating him. Walter, meanwhile, had sent one of the doctor's servants, a boy who'd been woken by the noise, round to fetch Robert and the two of them had dragged Teesdale, whom they'd both recognized, off the street before it grew light.

With the doctor still busy with Jonnie, they'd acquired a barrow from somewhere, probably stolen Verity assumed, and wheeled Teesdale's body the conveniently short distance round to Sylvester's house.

She held up her hand. "Who, pray, is Sylvester?"

"Ah," Robert said. "The wicked uncle."

"The wicked uncle?" Was this some melodramatic piece of fiction?

Walter nodded. "He's wanted Jonnie's earldom all his life. His father's younger brother. A vicar, would you believe, but one with a blacker heart than any man of the cloth should possess."

"I thought Jonnie was the one with the black heart. Isn't he known as the Black Earl?"

Walter snorted with laughter. "Oh, that. Well, that's all a bit of a show. He likes to be called that, but he's got a heart of gold, if truth be told."

That was a turn up for the books, or it would have been had not Verity already surmised that he was nowhere near as black as he was painted.

"So his wicked uncle sent this Teesdale to…to assassinate him?" It sounded ridiculous when said out loud. "Why would he have waited until now?"

Walter frowned. "That's escaped me too. I have no idea. But I'm certain he's behind it. Teesdale's an out and out bastard, if you'll pardon me for saying so, but not daring enough to do something like this on his own. Or rich enough. The man lives by being a card sharp, Jonnie says. He's very good at spotting a fellow cheating. That's why Teesdale never plays against him."

Robert interrupted. "I think I know why he's suddenly decided to rid himself of Jonnie." He pointed at Verity. "You. Jonnie's married now. And you know what happens when a fellow gets wed." He blushed. "Babies. An heir. You know." His face went redder still. "Until now Sylvester's just been waiting for Jonnie to die. In a duel perhaps. On a horse. With no heir, Sylvester would have got the earldom. Him and his dreadful son. The moment Jonnie got himself a wife, it must have been like signing his death warrant."

The thought that all Jonnie's injuries might be her fault was a sobering one. Supposing those footpads had succeeded? Her heart gave a frightened lurch as she realized how that would have left an empty hole in her that could never be filled.

She swallowed. "So you put Teesdale's body outside Wintringham's house?" The daring of it amazed her. It could almost have been called funny if it hadn't involved someone being dead. Even if he had wanted Jonnie dead in his place.

"On his doorstep," Robert said, with a grin.

"With a note pinned to his chest."

"A note?" Verity echoed, feeling a little faint, which was most unlike her.

"Of course," Walter said. "A note to warn Sylvester off. And hopefully, before his household rises, that body will have attracted quite a crowd. He'll have some explaining to do, I should think. Especially as before we left to come down here, I sent a note round to the Bow Street Runners. Told them, anonymously of course, that old Sylvester's involved in a plot to assassinate a peer of the realm and that his coconspirator could be found dead on his doorstep. They'll have found that first thing in the morning. At much the same time as Sylvester's servants must have been discovering their visitor."

"Clever, ain't we?" Robert said, fairly preening himself with smugness.

"I hope no one saw you walking through London with a corpse in a barrow," Verity said. "You are my cousins and your mother would be horrified if you were to be hanged, or sent to Botany Bay."

Walter grinned. "We were careful, Coz. No one saw us at all. We know the streets of London well, don't we Robert?"

Robert beamed. "We certainly do."

Chapter Twenty-Five

On the following day, Jonathan was able to come down to breakfast in something other than a much chopped about shirt and a banyan. He'd managed to get himself, with the aid of William who was enjoying his promotion to valet, into a proper shirt over which he'd draped his coat.

His shoulder wound was paining him less, mainly because of the fact that it hadn't damaged any bone and was just a flesh wound, according to Dr. Collins when he came to call that morning and found him sitting out on the terrace in the sunshine at a stone table. The good doctor also insisted that he should be careful with his broken arm, a fact which annoyed Jonathan, who was itching to be back to normal, and not only because the doctor had thought to caution him about it.

Verity had spent some time that morning upstairs with his grandmother, who'd sent several worried messages down via the servants and had had to be reassured by a visit from both Kitty and Verity. The thought of struggling to speak to her himself, didn't appeal, so he'd turned down Kitty's eager offer to accompany him to her rooms. He'd wait a few days for that. His present appearance might not be enough to convince her he was on the mend. Best to wait until his facial bruising lessened and he could have a much-needed shave. If she saw him now, she might think she was having a visitation from a pirate.

"Nevertheless," Verity said, before going up there, "I shall assure the dowager that you are in fine form and improving. I wouldn't want to upset her with the details though, of how you came upon your injuries." She was probably thinking that as his uncle was also his grandmother's younger son, it wouldn't do to go revealing his part in the assassination attempt. For now that he'd spoken with Walter, on Verity's advice, he was very much aware of what had happened and who had orchestrated the attack.

In fact, with Walter's gentle prodding, the entire debacle had begun to return and he was able to recall a fair bit of that night for himself, up until he'd hit the ground and someone had kicked him in the head. He'd laughed uproariously when he'd heard about the deposition of Teesdale's body on Sylvester's doorstep, and the informing of the Bow Street Runners.

And now he was sitting outside with a book in the warm sunshine. A nice respite from Kitty's continuous chatter. She was clearly trying to make up for the past year when he'd not been even once to see her. Playfully, he'd suggested to her that the reason for his long absence had been her overactive tongue, but she'd just laughed and not believed him. Perhaps he was bad at lying. No doubt she was at present talking her grandmother's stockings down instead of his.

But sitting outside with his book did not in any way mean that he was reading. Or, at any rate, that he was digesting the words of his book, a treatise on horsemanship he'd read several times before. He'd been reading the same page over and over again and nothing had so far penetrated further into his brain than the outer barrier of his eyes.

He set the book on his lap and squinted into the sun across the wide, rolling acres of Luxborough towards the hazy horizon. Now he was back, the love he'd always had for the place burgeoned in his heart. It was easy, when living life to the full in Town, to forget how lovely the estate was. He frowned. How close had he come to losing this? He didn't really want to think about it, but now he knew that Walter was convinced Sylvester was behind the attack, that was the only thing in his mind.

Of course, he wasn't stupid and he'd always known his uncle was jealous. Jealous of his father, and also jealous of him. He'd been very young when he'd realized this. And of course, his mother had warned him as he grew older. When his father had been alive and his mother had been in residence, Sylvester had called infrequently, but every time he'd done so he'd given Jonathan the most malevolent of looks. The sort of looks it had been easy to read as a death wish, even as a small child.

Then all the bad things had happened, and his father had died. He didn't want to dwell on that for long. His mother, too, had gone, although not quite so far and to a less hot place, swearing she wouldn't stay under the same roof as... No. He was definitely not going there. Nothing would induce him to conjure up Mary's image again. Nor his mother's. He did, of course, pay his mother his respects in the briefest of possible manners whenever he came down, but that didn't mean he had to think about her now.

But he found he couldn't stop thinking about what had happened all those years ago, no matter how he tried.

After his father's death, he'd refused to return to school. With his mother gone, only his grandmother had needed overcoming, and she'd already commenced her slow decline into senility. "I'm an earl now," he'd said. "And I don't need any more education. I know everything they could teach me, anyway, and none of it's going to be useful to me as an earl."

Grandmama had, with very little resistance, conceded victory to him.

Walter, however, had been incensed at the unfairness that his best friend was not returning to the hallowed walls of Eton, but as he'd been invited over for the holidays with frequency, he'd put up with it. "I don't myself wish my own dear papa ill," he'd said glumly, "but if having a title means one can do without school, then I freely admit to being jealous of you and wishing for a title."

Jonathan smiled to himself. Walter had got over his jealousy and himself left school as soon as he could to join Jonathan in London where the two young bucks that they'd been had commenced living life to the full. Wine, women, and song had been their aim, and with Jonathan's seemingly endless funds behind them, they'd been able to fulfill this aim, Jonathan significantly more than Walter.

And all of that had silenced the dreams for a while. He'd found early on that spending every night in someone else's bed had kept his dreams to a minimum, and at the same time that he had a talent for pleasing women. With his good looks, he'd had no trouble finding bed mates, and the life had suited him. At first. Well, for a long time.

And then Verity had come into his orbit.

Her father first, the old reprobate, and then her. And everything that could have gone wrong had gone wrong.

He sighed.

Verity. Truth. He'd seen a different side to her here at Luxborough. A nurturing side. A less defensive side. She no longer seemed to be the bane of his life, a woman he'd been forced to marry who'd then turned against him. And wasn't that his own fault, anyway? Hadn't he insulted her in a thoughtless manner, the manner of a man who thought he could do and say just what he wanted. Reprehensible behavior he should be ashamed of.

A flock of ducks flew overhead in a *V* shape in the direction of the lake.

The problem was, he found he now wanted her to like him. A lot.

He stopped chewing the nail on his left little finger, a habit he'd had as a child, and set that hand on his knee, out of harm's way.

Well, they were married now so she couldn't escape. Not really. And he could try a lot harder to be nice to her and see how far that got him. He liked her determination.

A swan rose up from the lake near where the ducks had landed, its great wings beating the air in a steady rhythm. He loved the noise made by swan's wings. How much he'd missed that when he'd been in London.

But what about Kitty?

He had to consider her because she was his responsibility. She had no one else but him. And she loved him, despite all his drawbacks. She accepted his long absences and every time he returned treated him as though he'd only been away overnight.

Kitty, with her mother's petite figure and heart-shaped face…

He could see her now, on the first day she arrived at Luxborough. It had been the school summer holidays and he'd been at home, sitting reading in a corner of the library when she'd come in to lay a fire in the hearth, ready to light later on. She'd been shocked to find him sitting there so early.

She bobbed a curtsy and made to hurry away, but he'd stopped her. "Don't leave on my account."

She'd hesitated. "I'm sorry, sir, I didn't think anyone would be about so early." She had a soft, country burr to her voice, and she was very pretty, with curling dark hair and a heart-shaped face…just like Kitty's.

"I like to sit here and read when I can't sleep," he'd said, which had been more than he'd ever told anyone else.

She dimpled at him. "I'd do the same myself if I weren't supposed to do so many chores before the family's up."

He was surprised. "You can read?"

She nodded. "My ma taught me when I was a little girl. She said it'd stand me in good stead later in life. She wants more for me than just being a housemaid." Her voice dropped. "I think she fancies me being a housekeeper one day, and for that you need to be good at your reading and reckoning."

He put his book down as this was much more interesting. The holidays had been long and boring so far, and he was missing the companionship of his friends at school. "A good ambition…so what's your name?"

"Mary…sir." It seemed she was conscious she should be addressing him respectfully.

He grinned at her. "No need to call me sir. My name's Jonnie."

Her eyes widened, presumably as she now realized who he was. She bobbed another curtsy. "I'm really sorry, Master Jonathan. I didn't mean to be rude and disrespectful. I've not been here long, so I didn't know as it was you." So someone had told her his name.

He shook his head. "You're not being disrespectful." He got up from his window seat. "And to show you that, I'll help you lay the fire. I'm very good at that. My nursemaid taught me how when I was just a little boy and I often laid the nursery fire for her."

She backed up a step, clutching her basket of fire materials closer. "I can't let you do that. It's not right you should do it. Not with you being His Lordship's son."

He went to the fire. "Why not? Don't I benefit from the fire when it's lit? It gets quite chilly in here even in the summer, and my mother likes to sit in here after luncheon sometimes. She lets me set light to it. I might as well lay it as well."

And so had begun their friendship.

Mary was two years older than he was, but that mattered nothing. She was a country girl from one of the bigger farms and had tales that made him laugh of misbehaving cows and contrary pigs and chickens. He enjoyed her company and, very soon, on her half day off, they were meeting in secret to go walking in the woods where no one would tell her off for fraternizing with the nobility when she shouldn't be.

And one thing had inevitably led to another.

He'd fallen in love with her, and she with him. They'd discovered one another's bodies in a mossy clearing under dappling sunlight, as two young people should. And he'd been happier than he'd ever been.

Until.

He snatched himself out of his reverie as it was heading to a place of nightmare where he didn't want to go.

In the distance he could just make out the shapes of deer grazing near the wood where he and Mary had… No. Wrong direction again. He must think of something else entirely.

Luckily for him it must have been approaching luncheon, for footsteps sounded on the gravel and Kitty's laughter carried to him. She was not a girl to ever miss a meal. Perhaps she was another, much better, reminder of that time, one he could hold close and allow himself to enjoy.

She ran across the gravel, kissed him on the cheek, and sat down on one of the spare chairs. "You're out here, and I was in there in Grandmama's stuffy old rooms playing draughts with her. You lucky thing. I wish I was already grown up. So much easier if I didn't have to always do as I'm told. Grandmama was on fine form today and understood everything we told her. For now. I daresay she'll have forgotten it all by tomorrow, though and Verity and I will have to go up there and repeat it."

He smiled, glad of the distraction. "And if you do, it won't be a chore, will it? For you love our grandmama."

"I do." Kitty nodded firmly. "Very much, but I do wish she was like she was today every day. So unfair that I didn't know her when she was younger."

"One of the perils of having a grandmother," Jonnie said. "They are almost always old." He indicated one of the spare seats. "Why don't you sit down and let me look at you? You're so like a little whirlwind it's hard to focus on you."

For answer, she laughed and leaned over to throw her arms around him, completely missing his wince. And only then did she sit down. "And I love you, too. I miss you so much when you're in London. I wish…" She hesitated.

"What do you wish?"

"That you and Verity would stay here forever. I already love her dearly. She's been so kind to me. Just like you, but better than you for she is here, and you hardly ever are."

Did he want that? Was it possible?

He smiled. "How about next year, when you're seventeen, you come up to stay in London with me?" Would that even work? Although, no one but Walter knew about Kitty's existence and her illegitimacy. It might be possible to hide her origins and give her a proper season.

Kitty's eyes narrowed. "I'm not at all sure I would like that, you know. Not after living here. Verity says London is all houses and paved streets and hardly any grass and no wide-open spaces like here at all. The best you have is Hyde Park, she says. And I don't think that sounds a very nice place to be. She says it gets crowded and everyone is looking at everyone else and criticizing them. She says that's why people go there. Because they want to be looked at. I shouldn't like that at all."

He shrugged, which didn't hurt quite so much as the last time he'd done so. Still hurt quite a lot though. "She may well be right. But for now, I'm here at Luxborough, and I have no intention of going anywhere else at the moment. You can rest assured of that."

She leaned in for another kiss. "Do you promise?"
He nodded. "I promise."

CHAPTER TWENTY-SIX

SHOUTS WOKE VERITY from her sleep with a hammering heart. They were coming from Jonnie's bedroom. With her drapes closed she was in near total darkness and couldn't hope to find her bedside candle to light in a hurry. Besides which, she might inadvertently set fire to the house if she tried.

She pushed back the covers and scrambled out of bed. Where was her peignoir? She couldn't go in there in just her nightgown. But her peignoir eluded discovery.

Another anguished shout.

Abandoning her search for her peignoir, she ran to their adjoining door and pushed it open. There was slightly more light in here as Jonnie's curtains had at some point been opened. For a moment she looked for him there, thinking to find him looking out of the window, but no one stood there.

She turned back to the bed. He'd thrown back his own covers, and, thankfully, proved to be wearing a nightshirt. But he was tossing back and forth, muttering now rather than shouting, but clearly very disturbed by something.

Another mysterious nightmare?

She approached the bed.

His eyes were wide open, staring sightlessly up at the ceiling as he tossed on the mattress. Her first worried thought was that his fever had returned. He was indeed flushed and hot, but she doubted it was fever. He'd been fine at dinner and even eaten something other than Mrs. Lovell's beef broth. This heat was due to his disturbed sleep.

She caught his left hand. "Jonnie, Jonnie, you need to wake up."

He snatched his hand back. "Leave her alone or I'll kill you." The words came out as an angry hiss.

She caught his hand again. "It's me, Verity. Wake up Jonnie."

His eyes swivelled towards her, but she had the feeling he wasn't seeing her. "Make him stop," he said, his voice pleading. "Don't let him do it."

She took his face in her hands, the stubble rough under her fingers. "Jonnie. Wake up. You're dreaming again. Wake up."

She could slap him again but this time, she feared, he was deeper in the dream than before and she'd read it could be dangerous to waken people suddenly and violently.

He was staring up at her, tears at the corners of his eyes. "Please. Make him stop. You can't let him do it. You can't."

What to do?

On an impulse, and partly because she'd been wanting to do it for at least the last day, she leaned forward and pressed her lips to his in a kiss. Under her mouth she felt his lips part, but she was inexperienced at kissing and had no idea how to respond. His body lost its rigidity as he relaxed. She straightened up.

He was looking up at her out of surprised eyes.

"Verity." He was a little hoarse after all that shouting and had to clear his throat. "What are you doing here?"

Conscious of the gaping neck of her nightgown, she took a step back from the bed and pulled it closed.

"You were shouting again. Another nightmare, I think. I, er, I didn't want to have to slap you again. I thought it might be bad for you."

He put his good hand to his lips. "So you kissed me instead."

"I did." At least he couldn't see the hot blush that seemed to have suffused her entire body in this darkness. "I must apologize."

"Please don't. I believe I liked it, and it was a good way to wake me." He grinned, his teeth flashing white in the faint moonlight that was streaming in his open window. "In fact, I find I might like you to do it again."

Now her body was flushing not with embarrassment but with a sensation Verity hadn't known she could feel. Her mouth had gone dry, she felt weak at the knees just as she had when she'd seen Jonnie's inert body in the carriage, and a molten, alien feeling seemed to have centered itself somewhere below her navel.

She tore herself away and fetched the chair. "I'll sit with you a while so you can go back to sleep."

He grinned again. "I'm not a baby in the nursery, you know."

Her heart must be pounding at two hundred beats a minute. "You have nightmares when you're alone, it seems. I'll sit with you and keep them at bay."

Silence fell and she shivered. Despite the warmth of the day, nights in Luxborough House were cool and she was only in her nightgown.

His hand came out towards her, his fingers brushing her arm. "You're cold. Get in. I'm in no condition to violate you, and we're man and wife, after all. Have no fear. Get in and I'll warm you."

The temptation was enormous. She sat rigid in her chair, his fingers still on her arm like two hot brands. He was right. There was nothing at all wrong in a wife being in bed with her husband, and he was also right in saying he couldn't do anything about it in his condition. And, after all, she'd done it once already. And she now found she wanted to do it with her whole being. So why not?

She rose from the chair and climbed onto the bed.

"Pull up the covers," he whispered, his voice suddenly low and very close to her ear. "Or we'll both be catching a chill. And lie down here, next to me."

She pulled up the covers with trembling hands and lay down beside him, but with a good foot between them. She was still cold, though.

He lifted his left arm, wincing a bit as he did so. "Come here. I promise to do nothing you won't like. Nothing at all but hold you and keep you warm."

She propped herself up on her elbow and looked at his dim form in the gloom. If he had his left arm around her shoulders, he could do nothing with his splinted right one. She would be safe. She moved over and, with wary care, lay down beside him. His arm came around her shoulders, his hand on her left arm, fingers relaxed.

Heat shivered through her body.

How warm he was, all along one side of her, from her head down to her toes. And what a strange sensation it was to lie beside a man, to feel his alien body beside hers, to smell the faint muskiness of him and the scent of his cologne. She liked it.

He turned his head and she felt his lips brush her hair. "Good night, Verity."

She lay awake a long time listening to his breathing deepen until she too slipped into sleep.

JONATHAN WOKE IN the morning to find Verity snuggled next to him and still sleeping. The pleasure of her body so close to his had the normal morning effect on him and, for the first time in his life, he was embarrassed by it. He didn't want her waking up and finding him like this and being frightened off. Sometime in the last forty-eight hours he'd decided that he'd been quite wrong in thinking her lacking in innocence and, now that he'd acknowledged this, he didn't want to upset her by his own natural bodily reaction to being so close to such a lovely creature as she was.

He watched her for a few minutes. Her hair, that had been confined in a long braid, was now much in need of a brush, with little bits having come out of the braid overnight. Her lashes, dark instead of the expected auburn of her hair, fanned out across her pale cheeks where one or two faint freckles just showed. And her lips were slightly parted as she slept, only serving to render her prettier than ever.

He frowned at his own shallow thoughts. Of course he liked the fact that she was pretty, but it was more than that. He liked her determination, her independence, her loyalty to her father, her strong will. And now she was in his bed and he could do nothing about it. How ironic.

Damn those footpads to hell and back. What he really wanted to do was roll over and take her in his arms and awaken in her a passion to match his. An impossibility in his present condition. Not with his broken ribs and arm, at any rate. With just the bullet wound, he would have been more than tempted. But as it was, just breathing normally was hard enough. And besides which, she didn't feel the same way about him, and with all his many conquests, he'd never forced himself on anyone who wasn't willing.

He'd better get out of bed before she woke up and noticed his state of arousal.

Very gently he eased his arm out from under her neck and with a great deal of difficulty tried to slide out of bed without making any noise. An impossible task. Firstly it hurt, and secondly the bed creaked. He fought to suppress a groan of pain.

Verity stirred.

He glanced down at his nightshirt. It possessed a definite tent pole effect. He turned away from the bed and put a quick hand down there and tried to suppress it. Another failure.

Verity yawned and stretched. "Jonnie?"

Damn it. "Yes?" He kept his back to her, willing his arousal to stop being so aroused, which seemed to be having the opposite effect.

"Where are you going? You should be staying in bed and resting."

At least she didn't seem to be horrified to be waking up in his bed.

He spotted the door to the water closet. "Just going to relieve myself." And dashed in there and closed the door. Not that it was much of a dash, more of a hobble with the way his ribs were feeling and how each step jarred them. But at least he and his damned arousal were out of sight.

And now, as if to tease him, everything subsided. Thank goodness.

He waited a couple of minutes then opened the door again.

The bed was empty. She'd gone.

He looked at the door into her room. Could he?

He pulled on his banyan, as though that might afford him protection from further bodily mishaps, and tapped on the door.

"Yes?"

"Can I come in?"

Silence, then, "Yes."

He pushed open the door to the room his mother had once had. Verity was sitting in the window, the drapes drawn back and her peignoir wrapped around her, as if she'd been admiring the view.

He crossed the room to the window and sat down beside her. "You didn't need to run off, you know."

She inclined her head. "I know. I just wanted to." She gazed into his eyes. Hers were the deepest blue he'd ever seen. Like cornflowers or the sea in summer. He could drown in them if he wasn't careful.

He cleared his throat. "Thank you for staying with me."

She smiled. "It seemed the only way for both of us to get a good night's sleep."

"I'm sorry I disturbed you."

She leaned forward and for a moment her nightgown and peignoir gaped, giving him a tantalizing view of her soft white breasts. His arousal threatened to raise its head again and he had to fight to think of something other than caressing those breasts. At least he was sitting down and in a banyan.

She smiled, a compassionate, gentle smile. "Tell me what it is you dream about that disturbs you so much."

He'd been fearing that question. What to say? He could confess. She was his wife and could never be caused to testify against him. Why not tell her? She seemed to have taken his killing of Teesdale in her stride, after all.

"I dream of the day my father died."

Her eyes widened. "Go on."

He swallowed. Where to begin? "The story doesn't start there, however."

"Where does it start?"

"You'll keep my secret?"

"Of course I will. You have no need to ask."

"Then I'll tell you."

VERITY CAUGHT HIS hands in hers. How very sad he looked. "Tell me what it is that makes you cry out in the night like that." She wanted to wrap her arms around him and tell him everything would be all right, but she didn't. He was very much the hurting little boy and nothing like the Black Earl at all.

He began with his meeting and friendship with Mary, and how their relationship had transformed to become that of lovers. She nodded him on, unshocked.

"Unfortunately for me, my father had a penchant for pretty housemaids. Pretty everything, in fact. He wasn't bothered by a woman's status in life, nor whether she was married, widowed, or a maiden. He turned his attentions to Mary." He looked down at his hands, almost as though he couldn't meet her eyes. "He was an enthusiastic exponent of what could be called *droit de seigneur*."

"Oh no." She could see what was coming. A stolen love. A boy who couldn't compete with an adult male, his own father, a girl who wouldn't be able to say no to the master of the house.

"He tried to take her from me."

"I guessed."

His hands gripped hers in a vice. "I had to stop him."

What had he done? The sudden fear that it was something terrible arose, making her heart pound afresh.

"It was early morning but still gloomy in the house. The

servants were at their work but my father was up and on the prowl. I heard cries. I came out of my room and found him at the head of the stairs. He had her by the wrist. He was hurting her. She was terrified." His Adam's apple bobbed as he swallowed. "I had to stop him. He was taking her to his room, and she was mine. Not his." He paused. "And I was hers. She was…she was…" He put his hand on his own stomach. "I couldn't let him. He was going to hurt her."

Suddenly, Verity understood all his secrets. Kitty wasn't his father's bastard at all, she was his own daughter. And his father hadn't died in an accident, Jonnie had pushed him down the stairs in order to save the girl he loved. "Oh my goodness."

Silence again. This time a long one. "You think badly of me for my actions," he said, his voice low. "You have no need. I think badly enough of myself."

"I don't. Jonnie, I don't think badly of you." She squeezed his hands. "You were only a boy yourself. A child, even. Your father was going to hurt someone you loved. I—I would have done the same myself, I think. You're not to blame."

He raised his eyes to meet hers. "I must have done wrong, else why was Mary taken from me when my child was born?"

He thought he'd been punished. His nightmares, when he slept alone, must every night be full of how he came to push his father down the stairs. That was why he'd become a rake. Because he wanted to never sleep alone. He was afraid of doing so. Did the ghostly specter of his father invade his dreams? Did he see the girl he'd loved in them?

"So you refused to let Kitty be given to some foster parent. You kept her here in the house to remind you of Mary."

He nodded. "I did. I loved Mary and I love her daughter. I had to keep her."

"At the expense of losing your own mother."

He nodded. "She blamed me and Mary and through her, Kitty, for causing my father's death. She refused to live under the same roof as the child she claimed had led to my father's death.

She thinks we fought because my father had taken the girl for whom I had a schoolboy's love. She doesn't know the child she thought my father's is mine. I couldn't tell her the truth." He paused. "You're the only one who knows."

And now she did free her hands and stretch out her arms to him and he came into them in relief. She put her arms tight around him and held him close, his head on her shoulder, the bulk of his splint against her breasts. "It wasn't your fault," she whispered in his ear. "It wasn't."

CHAPTER TWENTY-SEVEN

FOUR DAYS HAD passed since Jonathan's confession to Verity. In that time he'd sent Walter and Robert off to Somerton, to which no doubt their father would have returned after the wedding, and resigned himself to a long recovery. He'd also been forced to think deep and hard about what he'd told Verity, because it wasn't quite true. He'd wanted to be totally honest with her about his past, but he'd held back on one thing. Someone else knew full well what had happened that night and had elected to keep his secret. And that someone was his mother. The only thing she didn't know was that Kitty was his child, not his father's.

Having formed the resolve to remain at Luxborough for his recuperation and probably for some time after that, he'd decided he was going to have to go and see her. She was, after all, both his mother and his neighbor.

So on the fourth day, which happened to be a Friday, he sent for the barouche as there and back in one day was still too far for him to walk, and set off on the short journey to the Dower House. He'd left Kitty in lessons with Miss Bligh and Verity perusing fashion sketches for dresses for her new stepdaughter, unbeknownst to Kitty, of course. They were to be a surprise.

On arrival, having sent his coachman and the barouche back to the stables, he was escorted into the parlor by one of his mother's footmen where he found her seated in front of a blazing fire.

He bowed, more than a little stiffly. "Mama."

She regarded him with cold eyes. "Jonathan."

"I shan't wait to be asked to sit," he said, and, sweeping his coat tails out of the way as best he could with one hand, settled in an upright chair opposite her. "I trust I find you well."

Her expression didn't change. "You find me much as you did last time you were here. I believe that was four years since. I am a little more stiff in my joints, a little less mobile, that is all. I doubt you would notice."

He eased his ribs, which were aching, and leaned back in the chair, hoping for a respite which didn't come. "I would have called last year when I was down, but Kitty had a cold and I didn't want to pass it on to you."

"How thoughtful."

Damn the woman. He was her only son and, as a child, he'd always thought she had affection for him. Maybe she had, at first. Until that fateful night, that was, when she'd stood in her nightgown in the shadows and witnessed the fight at the top of the stairs and his father's fall to his death. She'd emerged from her hiding place hysterical, and with only a passing glance for her son and the shaking Mary, she'd raced down the stairs to the crumpled, broken heap at their foot. The sound of her sobbing over his father's body pursued Jonnie as he hurried the terrified Mary back to the servants' quarters, out of his mother's way.

He remembered the venom in her eyes as she'd looked up at him when he returned, and how her lips had stretched back from her teeth in a vicious snarl. He'd never forget her words of accusation. "You've killed him. You've killed my Edward. What did you have to interfere for? She's just another servant girl, you fool. You should have let him have her." They were engraved on his heart. She must have seen it was an accident. That his father had lost his footing and that the shove he, Jonnie had given him had been in retaliation for the blow to the face his father had dealt him. He'd had the bruise to show for it afterwards.

But could he excuse himself like that? Hadn't he wanted his father dead rather than let him violate Mary?

He'd been nothing but a green boy himself, in the throes of a passionate first love. He'd almost tumbled down the stairs after his father in his haste to get to his mother. He'd gone down on his knees beside her, desperate to explain how this had happened and for her not to be looking at him with naked hatred in the way she was. The words, the excuses, had come pouring out, his heart beating a terrified tattoo in his ears as the import of what had happened sunk in.

"He was going to hurt Mary. He was going to take her to his bedroom. You know what he wanted, Mama. He's done it before so many times. He was going to rape her, Mama, I know he was. She didn't want it. I couldn't let him. I love her." This last had come out as if he were begging her to understand, as he looked down at the shattered, sprawled body between them. "I didn't do it on purpose. It was an accident."

It hadn't worked. She'd not cared a jot that her son was beseeching her understanding, terrified by what he'd done, with tears streaming down his face. Because she'd never loved him. The only person she'd ever loved, despite his countless dalliances, or perhaps because of them, was his father. And he was dead, by the hand of a son she now despised. That much was clear.

She'd looked up at him in vicious fury, tears streaming down her cheeks. "Look what you've *done.*" It came out as a hiss. "You saved a worthless, ten-a-penny *servant girl* and killed your own father. Swapped one for the other. I can never forgive you. Never. He was worth twenty of you. Twenty, thirty, forty of you."

He reeled back, unable to understand, knowing he'd played a part in this but also knowing the blame lay at his father's door. Knowing also that it was a mother's job to protect her child. What if it had turned out differently and it had been him lying broken on the hall floor? Would his mother have been this angry with his father? His mother had always been the one he'd thought had loved him. His father had always been distant and uninterested in his only son. More interested in the maids and in other people's wives and his own hedonistic pleasures.

He swallowed. Just the way he now was himself. Like father, like son. He'd turned into his father, a man he'd hated.

He fought these thoughts into the back of his mind. "I came to let you know I'm recovering well after the attack on me."

Her thin brows knit. "The attack? What attack?"

She must have noticed his arm and bruised face, surely?

It had been nearly a week. Had no one told her? His own staff associated with hers at the Dower House, he knew. Any hope that she might retain a modicum of concern for him vanished. He indicated his splinted right arm. "I'm not wearing this for fun, you know."

She pursed her lips. "I assumed you had fallen from your horse."

He sighed. "No, I didn't. I was set upon by seven footpads and one of them has turned out to be in the pay of my Uncle Sylvester."

That did shock her. "Your uncle?"

"Yes. My uncle who has spent all of my life wishing me dead. He nearly got his way last week."

Her frown deepened. "What happened? If you were set upon by seven, how is it you are here in my parlor apparently little harmed?" Her tone was cool and matter of fact, as though it didn't matter to her whether he'd lived or died in that attack. The determination washed over him that if he and Verity were lucky enough to have children one day, he would not emulate either of his parents. He would love his children above all else.

"You will be glad to hear I fought them off," he said, careless of the little lie and the sarcasm.

She bowed her head. "Fortuitous for you."

"I am flattered you think so."

He eyed her knobbly hands. In the four years since he'd last seen her, they'd grown worse. They looked like gnarled tree roots, the fingers twisted and bent. When he'd been a child she'd had hands like his, smaller, of course, but with long, elegant fingers on which she'd worn a variety of beautiful rings that had fascinated him and played the harpsichord with skill. And her hair had now gone completely white. A brief memory of standing in her bedroom while her maid brushed out her waist-length dark hair flashed into his head. How different she was now. How cruel life could be.

She cleared her throat. "I assume there is a point to your visit. It cannot be from feelings for me."

Could it not? Just because she didn't love him, it didn't mean he didn't love her, in some small way. Perhaps he'd loved her properly, once, but she'd killed all but a small vestige of that love. A child's love for the distant parent who occasionally would appear in the nursery in a beautiful gown, reeking of exotic perfume, to pick him up and hold him close, his face in her warm neck. Had he mistaken that longing for her attention for love? Had he been wrong all along?

"I came to tell you that I shall be staying on at Luxborough for the foreseeable future."

"And I need to know that, why?"

"You are my neighbor." He refrained from telling her she was his mother. Surely she knew that. "I need time to recover from my injuries and Verity likes it here better than in Town." He gave a rueful smile. "And I have no intention of returning to London before I'm capable of defending myself from possible assassins."

She fixed him with a hard stare. "If you get yourself an heir, you will automatically be safer." She paused. "Until a son of yours sees you as a barrier to his own progress." Her tone was icy, tinged with long-matured dislike. Hatred, even.

He bristled. Did she really think that of him? "I shall endeavor not to follow in my father's footsteps by pursuing the female servants and so offending a son of mine."

An easy promise to make as, since Mary, he'd never compromised a member of his staff, although more than a few had given him looks that had indicated their inclination to oblige him if he so wished. Would it be as easy to foreswear the London habits he'd formed since he was a boy of sixteen?

"I wish your wife luck," his mother said, with a curl of her lip. "I formed a liking for her when she visited. You can tell her she's going to need it."

His interview with his mother over, Jonathan descended the stairs with care and received his hat and gloves and cane from her butler. The man opened the door for him and he emerged into the summer warmth. A gentle walk back would do him good.

He managed to make it to the avenue more easily than he'd expected and was glad of the shade afforded by the limes. At the junction, he paused to get his breath back. Deep breaths were still difficult with his broken ribs only started on their road to being mended. Up ahead he could just make out the distant sparkle of water through the trees. He would return via the lake rather than taking the longer route along the main driveway.

He walked slowly, pausing every now and then to regain his breath, and was glad of his cane for once for its normal usage. Birds sang in the trees and beyond their shade sheep grazed, fat lambs by their sides.

Idyllic. Why did he not spend more time here?

Because when he was in London, he could put behind him what had happened here. He could put behind him his father's behavior, his death, his mother's hatred of him. He could forget Mary and the way she'd died on a bed drenched in her blood. Of course, that had also meant forgetting Kitty, his biggest regret. For he loved her dearly, as much as she loved him. That she had accepted his infrequent visits still astonished him. He would spend as long here this time as he could, as much time as possible with his daughter.

But, there was someone else he wanted to spend time with too.

Verity.

As a man for whom female companionship had meant blissful oblivion as much as heavy drinking had, he would have been surprised if anyone had suggested he was in love with his wife. He liked her very much, he was ready to accept, but love? What was that? He'd known so little of it in his life. Just Mary, and that had been so fleeting he could barely remember how it had made him feel.

If it meant he was longing to see her face, to hold her in his arms, to feel the warmth of her body beside his in bed, then it might be love. If it meant he was impatient with his infirmities that prevented him from taking their new relationship further, then that might just be lust more than love. And that was something he'd felt many times, with every woman he'd ever seduced. But for none of them had he felt the former. None of them had inspired him to want to spend time with them that wasn't occupied by being in bed and indulging in physical pursuits. Physical pursuits he'd thought had driven his fevered dreams away.

And yet, in the past four days she'd come to his bed at night and slept by his side, her presence comforting and soothing, and no nightmares had troubled him. There'd been no physical side to this arrangement. Not even a kiss after that first one she'd bestowed on him when she'd woken him from his nightmare. He'd lifted his good arm and she'd snuggled up on his left-hand side and sleep had come to him. Healthy, revitalizing sleep not induced by pain-killing drugs nor the aftermath of lust.

What magic did she possess? Or was love itself a kind of magic? Would he ever know?

He'd been walking along the edge of the lake for a while now, having crossed the bridge without even noticing he'd done so, and he was suddenly jerked back into reality by a voice calling his name.

"Jonnie." Verity's voice, as though his thoughts had conjured her. "If you keep going that way you're going to get wet."

He stopped, aware for the first time of his surroundings, and blinked in surprise. He was on the very edge of the lake and in front of him the bank curved to his left. Another two steps and he'd have had a decent ducking.

Verity was sitting under a stand of drooping willows, on a plaid rug, with a parasol, and the leafy branches, giving her shade. She looked utterly charming in a pale-primrose gown embroidered with tiny white flowers. Fresh, friendly, sweetly smiling at him. Welcoming, even.

He said the first thing that came into his head. "I thought you were engaged in studying suitable new gowns for Kitty?"

She laughed, a sound that to him had all the attraction of music to his ears. "I have selected four, as you suggested, and we will send for a dressmaker from your nearest town, or perhaps Oxford itself, to come out and measure her for them forthwith. You will be pleased to hear that, without Kitty's constant interruptions, I have been able to choose gowns that are modest and therefore suitable for a girl her age. She would have had them slightly less proper, I fear."

"I look forward to seeing her in them. I'd quite forgotten that girls of her age are inclined to grow, or I would have had Mrs. Burke see to her apparel sooner."

"I don't think she minded too much, but she's very excited to be receiving new ones." She paused. "A penny for your thoughts? You were walking along the lakeside with the air of someone with his head in the clouds. I could only assume you were miles away. I began to fear for your life if you were to tumble in. I don't believe it's terribly deep, but with only one arm I was afraid I should have to undertake a rescue."

He laughed. "I'm fairly sure it's only a few feet deep here. Your rescue would have amounted to giving me a hand out and perhaps removing my boots for me in order to empty them of water."

She joined in his laughter. "And any damage to you would only be to your pride."

He moved closer. "Might I be so bold as to ask if I may sit

with you?"

She shuffled over. "Of course you may. You need no invitation, but do you need any assistance?"

He'd had enough of being helped, so shook his head. He managed to sit down without showing himself up too badly.

She clapped her hands. "I see being one-armed is becoming second nature to you."

"I would rather it didn't."

She gave a little shuffle that brought her back into her original position, closer to him. "I quite understand. But that was deftly done. I doubt very much I could so the same with such elegance."

"You would be hampered by your skirts."

Another peal of laughter. "Which would be the biggest problem when I tried to rise. Believe me, just sitting down in an elegant fashion with two useful arms when wearing a dress is not an easy task. I myself might need assistance to rise." She looked up at him out of those beautiful, dark-fringed eyes and he felt his insides melt, so much so that he could think of nothing to say.

To be fair, it appeared she was in the same condition.

The silence between them stretched out, with neither of them looking away. Her tongue darted out and licked her lips and he felt himself harden. What he really wanted to do was kiss her, an action that had never been difficult for him before. With the women who'd succumbed to his seduction, they'd been almost panting for his first touch. Verity was not the same. No air of desperation hung about her, and yet, he was certain she wanted him. What was it about her that made her so different from every other woman in his life? Except for Mary.

Yes. She was like Mary. An innocent. The thought that he'd accused her of being the exact opposite arose and he felt his cheeks heat.

She appeared not to notice. Instead, she leaned towards him. "Might you perhaps pretend to be asleep and let me waken you as I did a few days ago? Like Sleeping Beauty in her tower."

An analogy he'd never heard applied to a man, especially not one with the sort of experience he had. Still… "You may." He closed his eyes.

Her hand touched his chest, gentle as a feather. "You must lie down if you are to be a true Sleeping Beauty. Will you be uncomfortable?"

He would suffer any amount of discomfort for her. For a kiss. He shook his head. "I'll be fine." And he let her push him back until he was lying on the blanket, the inside of his eyelids flashing bright and dark as the sunlight filtered through the leaves above his head.

By instinct he knew she was hovering over him. Then her lips met his in the lightest of butterfly kisses. He let his own lips open and his tongue darted out to taste her mouth. A slight hesitation betrayed her, but she didn't retreat. Her lips remained on his, and he let his tongue probe further into her mouth, searching for her tongue to dance with.

She pulled back. "If that is how Sleeping Beauty was awoken, then I'm not surprised it worked."

He chuckled, keeping his eyes shut. "Kiss me again and I'll show you more."

But she sat back on her haunches and he had to open his eyes, squinting against the glare. She shook her head. "I shouldn't be doing this, you know."

"Why not? You like it, don't you?"

She nodded. "It's just that from the moment I met you, I decided you were not a nice man, and then later, after you insulted me so badly, I decided you needed taking down a peg or two and teaching a lesson. This doesn't feel anything like the lesson I intended."

"Do you think I still need it?"

She shrugged, but her eyes were dancing. "To be truthful, I think you probably don't. No one is this good an actor. Since you arrived here, you've shown me you possess a different side. In London I formulated an impression of you as a libertine, a gambler, and a rake, who cared little for others." She paused. "Yet here you seem to have an alternative personality. You're kind and gentle and all things you appear to lack in London." A frown marred her brow. "I have come to think that the you of London is nothing but a mask you wear—a disguise to hide the real Jonnie. In London you are the Black Earl, but here you're just Kitty's father." She paused again as though considering her words. "And I think that here I could accept you as my husband, too."

He tried to push himself up towards her but her hand on his chest held him down with little effort on her part. He was weak as a kitten. She shook her head. "Let me speak. I didn't like the London Black Earl, but I do very much like Kitty's father. But I fear losing that man if we were to return to London."

He reached up and laid his left forefinger on her lips. "I have no intention of returning to London. I'm on my way back from the Dower House. I owed my mother a visit and now I owe you the missing part of my truth. I missed a fact out of my story the other day. My mother witnessed my fight with my father and saw him fall. She thinks I fought with him because I was angry at his behavior, which is partly true. I did tell her I loved Mary, but she barely listened. That explains her dislike of Kitty and her ostracism from me. I told her I was staying here for the foreseeable future. With you. And Kitty, of course."

"You are?" The words came out on a little gasp.

He nodded. "I am. Now, kiss me again, if you don't mind, and I'll try hard not to think how much else I want us to do and that we'll have to wait far too long for."

So Verity kissed him, and nothing mattered anymore but lying there in the sunshine in his arms, with the gentle lapping of the water beside them, and the birds singing in the trees.

Life was good.

THE END

About the Author

After a varied life that's included working with horses where Downton Abbey is filmed, riding racehorses, running her own riding school, owning a sheep farm and running a holiday business in France, Fil now lives on a widebeam canal boat on the Kennet and Avon Canal in Southern England.

She has a long-suffering husband, a rescue dog from Romania called Bella, a cat she found as a kitten abandoned in a gorse bush, five children and six grandchildren.

She once saw a ghost in a churchyard, and when she lived in Wales there was a panther living near her farm that ate some of her sheep. In England there are no indigenous big cats.

She has Asperger's Syndrome and her obsessions include horses and King Arthur. Her historical romantic fiction and children's fantasy adventures centre around Arthurian legends, and her pony stories about her other love. She speaks fluent French after living there for ten years, and in her spare time looks after her allotment, makes clothes and dolls for her granddaughters, embroiders and knits. In between visiting the settings for her books.

Social Media links:
Website – filreid.com
Facebook – facebook.com/Fil-Reid-Author-101905545548054
Twitter – @FJReidauthor